Breaking East

Bob Summer

This story is a work of fiction. Names, characters, events, organisations, and places, other than those in the public domain, are either products of the authors imagination or used fictitiously. Any resemblance to real people living or dead is a coincidence.

This book has been registered at BookCrossing.com so its journey is being tracked.

Please go to

www.BookCrossing.com

and enter

BCID: 904-12825241

Then read and/or pass it on for someone else to enjoy.

Thank you

Bob Summer

CHAPTER ONE

There'd been a steady stream of customers in and out the caff all morning but there was still no sign of Joe. I grabbed a bottle of water from the fridge and slammed the door.

'Woah,' said Gavin. 'What did that ever do to you?'

I gave him the glare.

He stepped back. 'Just asking.'

'Well don't.' Behind him, more customers clattered in and the queue stretched out the door. 'What's going on out there?'

'The Law are bringing in another truck load of cons so everybody's come out to have a nosey.'

I passed him the water and took his cash. 'Bad ones?'

'Yep. Murderers and the like so the rumours say. They've put the checkpoints up at the bridge already.'

'Right, that's it.' Checkpoints meant I'd have to queue to get east and I needed to be there fast. 'Everybody's going to have to leave.'

'Eh?'

'Come on. Out.'

'But I've just got my drink.'

'Take it with you.' I was heading around the counter to usher everybody out the door, when in sauntered Joe like he had all the time in the world. 'Where've you been?'

He frowned and stood a little straighter, annoyed no doubt at my having a pop at him in front of the kids in the queue. Well he should have thought about that before promising to be back in an hour and then staying away for three. Today was my last Matur class and if I missed it I'd have to sit the whole course again. Pulling my toenails out would be less painful.

2 ~BREAKING EAST

'Have you seen the time? Or did you just totally forget what day it is today? I wanted time to go home and shower.'

He checked his watch and then ping! I saw the date hit him behind the eyes. 'You look grand as you are,' he said. 'It's not a fashion parade, you'll be fine. Better get a move on though, the Law—'

'—Have put up checkpoints, I know.' There was no time to argue or chat. I headed out the door and away.

Finishing the course was supposed to be something to celebrate. Other kids had parties with glasses of fizzy stuff and a big, squishy cake, but then again other kids had proper families, whereas I just had Joe, my dad's best mate. And Joe might be many things, but guardian of the year he was not.

I kept in the shade and set off at a jog, dodging the rubbish at my feet and weaving through the people gathering along the pavement. The Reds, dressed in their signature white Tees and red bandanas, kept their hands on their Tasers as they moved kids off the street corners, putting a stop to trouble before it got started. Tomorrow they'd be back in the east letting us get on with things and everything would slip back to normal, but today, of all days, it looked like the Law wanted total control.

Running in the heat took its toll and, by the time I got to the checkpoint, I was huffing like a dog. Not as fit as I thought. Or hoped. And the place teemed with people. Boogah.

Camped alongside the river bank, getting on the Reds' nerves, were the usual protesters — average age of a hundred and two. Okay, slight exaggeration, but they were definitely old with a big fat O.

I joined the back of the queue to cross the bridge into East Basley and plotted what I'd say to Joe if I missed my last class. The only way I'd get my adult papers was by completing the Matur course. And I was so sick of being a kid. I counted the people ahead of me in the queue. Too many. Maybe I could jump a few if I kicked off a little. I shouted down the line, 'What's going on up there? What are we waiting for?'

The crowd fell quiet. Only a crinkly old protester had the guts to join in. He waggled his walking stick at me. 'Way to go, Atty. You tell 'em, girl.'

I grinned and gave him the thumbs up and yelled a little more. 'What's with the delay? Some of us have places to be.'

A Red, one of those skinny, geezer types with a tattooed head and a ring through his nose, walked over and pulled me to one side. Result. He guided me past the queue and stood me near a van with the Law logo splashed across its flank. A scanner had been set up on top of a table. 'Look at the screen,' he said.

I looked into the face recognition box. My reflection appeared to be a long way away and, as always at such times, it didn't look anything like me. Even the colour was off. I might have a tan, but I wasn't cow-pat green. The machine beeped and chunted out a slip of paper. The Red mused at it. 'Bethany, eh?'

'That's what it says.'

He gave an upside down smile and raised his eyebrows. 'Quaint.'

'Ain't it just.'

'Got your papers?'

I handed them over. 'Do you think I stole somebody's face?'

He fingered my ID, running his thumb over the watermark. 'Pretty name is Bethany. Mind telling me why the old-timer over there called you Atty?'

My dad used to love telling the story about how I kicked my way into the world ten weeks early. He swore I screamed so loud the midwife removed her glasses to check for cracks. 'Holy devil on a moped,' she said. 'Just look at the attitude already.'

'Because he's a friend,' I said. 'But you can call me Bethany.'

He grinned. Expensive teeth. 'Well, Bethany.' Sarcastic as hell. 'What's the purpose of your visit to the east of Basley today?'

I studied the tat, a welsh dragon high on his forehead. 'Why would I tell you?'

He inhaled slowly. 'I'll remind you how this works, shall I?' He flapped his hand indicating the van, the barrier, his badge. 'I ask the questions and you answer. That's how it is.'

'Uh uh. I don't have to tell you anything.' I tapped my papers with my fingernail. 'See? West Basley born and bred. Not brought over in a con van. Born. I can come and go as I please.'

'Let me offer you a friendly word of advice.' He put a megaton of emphasis on the word advice. 'As soon as the new laws are passed we'll be powering up the cage again, and it won't matter what your papers say — entry to the east will be at the Reds' discretion.' He folded my papers along the well-worn crease. 'And you, Bethany, will just have to get used to it.'

I spoke slow and clear like he might be an idiot. He probably was. 'I'll remind you how it works, shall I?' He wasn't the only one who could put on a tone. 'I have papers and the right to go east whenever I like. Caging off the paperless cons is one thing, but discriminating against the rest of us is a whole other story. Not to mention breaking international law.' I smiled fruity sweet, but what I really wanted to do was spit up his arrogant, bony nose. 'No new law,' I put heavy emphasis and scorn on the word law, 'can lock up innocent people.'

His eyes were the deep shiny blue of a bluebottle and, for a moment, we stared at each other and I sent up a small prayer that I hadn't over-cooked the bolshiness. The last thing I needed was to get arrested. His eyes narrowed. 'You don't think?'

A fat man in a brown suit stepped out from the passenger seat of the Law van. I grabbed the chance to look away first without losing face. The fat guy's cheeks bulged red and fleshy. Nobody could afford to get that blobby without being on the fiddle. 'Filth,' I scoffed. 'So that's what I could smell.'

The Red turned to see what had drawn my attention and we both watched the journalist wander onto the bridge and lean over the rail to look into the river Bast. The Red called out to him, 'It's supposed to swirl enough toxic waste to kill a donkey in under a minute.' Back at me. 'He's here to report on the riots.'

'What, that lot?' I jerked my thumb behind me. 'You call a bunch of oldies with a few placards a riot?'

'Doesn't matter what I call it. It's what he calls it that matters.' He stepped aside. 'Off you go.' He gestured me on my way. 'Go on. Shoo.' As I walked past him he added, 'Be good,' in the sarkiest, smarmiest voice ever and I so wanted to break his face.

As I strode across the bridge past the journalist and into East Basley, I concentrated on my breathing, calming myself down and cementing each word the Red had said into my memory. The Law would need to justify turning the power on the cage somehow. A few old codgers singing a song does not a riot make, but journalists couldn't be trusted further than I could spit a tractor. If that fat guy did a real good job of distorting the truth, the International Security Services might come down in the Law's favour and send in the troops. And that meant raids, rationing and arrests. Electrifying the cage could be the first step in a process which might end in total lockdown. And last time the west got locked down, the Law killed my mother.

CHAPTER TWO

When I reached the pretty little easty streets, I put my head down and ran along the edge of the kerb, keen to be on time but also hating to be seen lingering. All the happiness and cleanliness of eastern affluence set my teeth on edge. Besides, the Reds were never far away and always more than keen to pick off a stray westy like me, given half a chance. If they had their way, every kid from the west would stay west – locked up and forgotten.

East Basley gym has huge glass doors and a foyer like a hospital waiting room, all shiny tiles and spongy carpets. Other girls mingled around waiting to be called in for the last how-to-be-a-responsible-adult class. 'Personal Responsibility and Action Training' it said on the bumf. Self-defence for idiots would probably be more accurate.

Nobody was around to confuse any idiot Red by calling me Atty and so I scanned in without a problem. We were all summoned into the high-ceilinged, echoey hall and told to get into line. I picked somewhere in the middle, hoping to keep a low profile. A message pinged into my phone. Joe – *Hang around and do a spot of listening while you're over there, will you? Ta.*

Fantastic.

The instructor looked a typical semi-retired Red, bitter and twisted at being taken off the frontline. After he'd panted his way through a demonstration of some basic, not to mention pretty pathetic, moves, he ambled up and down the hall spouting crap and nonsense about effective self-defence being dependent on physique and upper body strength.

'But every case is different,' he said. 'Don't be afraid to use your womanly wiles. Us men know you can be very imaginative when you put the effort in.' He smirked at some girl's chest before giving her a dirty wink. He stopped pacing when he got to me. 'And what about you, my lovely? What skills have you taken from the course?'

I matched his stare. 'Oh I think I'll be okay.'

He adjusted his stance so he stood face on. 'I see.'

'I'm sure you do.'

His eyelid twitched but he kept his voice light and fluffy. 'Why don't you come up front and show us your technique?'

'Sure.' It was the last class, what the hell.

He positioned me so I faced away from him, and spoke to the rest of the group. 'I'm going to play the attacker and my friend here,' he put a sweaty hand on my shoulder, 'will be my victim.' He grabbed me around the neck.

I dropped to a crouch and he let go.

'Woah,' he said. 'I barely touched you.'

I stood, span around thrusting the heel of my hand up under his jaw, caught him with a left to his throat, and stamped the heel of my boot into his right shin.

Gently, of course.

He staggered backwards, slid down the wall onto his hands and knees, gagging — a pussy-cat bringing up a fur ball.

A couple of the girls gasped.

'Oh dear,' I said. 'Are you okay, sir?'

He dropped back onto his heels, wheezing. 'Yes. Of course.'

'Are you sure? Shall I fetch somebody?'

'No, no. I'm okay, thank you.' He pawed at the wall and stood, stooped over. He rubbed his neck. 'Yes, very well done.' He looked over his shoulder at the others. 'Okay, ladies. That's it, you're free to leave. Good luck, everybody.'

The class filed out. I mingled with the others until I was out of the tutor's sight but, rather than leave the building, I strolled through to the members' area. It's huge and plush, and has all the latest digi-devices, including the latest body scanning equipment. A Red walked through an arch and a machine spat out the recommended workout a second later. The scanner analysed and considered every possible factor, from his Granny's medical history to what he'd eaten for breakfast since a week last Tuesday. Naturally, I avoided it. The Law knew more than enough about me already without adding details of how much waste I had lining my bowels.

An area in the corner had been cordoned off with neck high partitions. Coffee machines and snack dispensers lined one wall, glowing under the glare of old-fashioned spotlights. Large soft sofas were scattered across the floor space, mostly full of pretty little things with big hair, waiting for their husbands. I sat on a chair within range of a few of the Reds' wives, plugged my earpins in my phone, and tapped my foot to an imaginary tune. It would be good to hear something worth reporting to Joe. As I'd made the class, I was beginning to regret my earlier hissy fit. As head of the resistance Joe had a certain reputation to keep up: getting popped at by me in front of a caff full of kids wouldn't exactly big him up as the hard man. But I also had my own reasons for listening in. The best way to find out if old bluebottle-eyes had been merely fantasising about caging us all up would be to listen to the women. They couldn't help themselves — they just loved to chatter.

'I'd rather they didn't but what else they gonna do?'

'I dunno.'

'I mean, they must be ready to be released, eh?'

'I dunno.'

'What colour you doing your toes?'

Yawn, yawn. Having to listen to such tedious nonsense is why I couldn't wait to get my adult papers, leave the county and do some proper jobs for Joe.

'Have you tried this new perfume?'

'Oo, I dunno.'

'Have a go. Anyway, I asked him if these psycho-killers — because that's the only cons they've got left to let go — I asked him if they'd be living by us.'

'What did he say?'

'He said he didn't know. Can you believe that?'

'Ah no. You don't say.'

They had to be talking about the new con drop. The government's Early Release Programme was taken to the max in Basley. In fact, the only people who would never get out of the county jail were people like my dad - political activists, resistance soldiers, anybody seeking equality or the upholding of human rights - they were the most dangerous according to the Law. Murderers, rapists and kiddy fiddlers were released to live in the west and do their worst, while my dad objecting to his wife getting her head caved in? Well… I hadn't seen him for years. Some believed he was locked up somewhere. Joe would like to convince me he was off being a hero. Others thought the Law might have shut Dad up for good. Not that they said it out loud, not in front of me anyway.

That's something else about sitting around listening to the posh talk tosh; it gives me too much time to dwell on stuff.

'The thing is, I got a kid to think about.'

'I know, yeah.'

'I don't want no trampy cons living next door to me, do I?'

'No, I know.'

'I mean there's no way of keeping them over in the west, is there?'

'I heard they're making the checkpoints a permanent feature. Or even blocking it all off. They'll be caged in, like they do with mad people.'

'Really?' Pause. 'Okay.'

Yeah, okay dokay pokay. Not only lock us down, but lock us down with the last of the lowest life forms. Nice one. I lounged in my chair and thumbed at my phone like I was changing tracks.

'How about blue? I love blue on toes.'

'Yeah, it's all right.'

'It'll all be fine. They know what they're doing, don't they?'

'Well that's what I said. Or pink, shall I have pink?'

I flicked my phone off, tucked the earpins back in my pocket and walked out through the main entrance - brazen, like I owned the place. Nobody challenged me. The kid on the counter looked like he wouldn't tackle a puppy. In any case, confidence out-smarts doubt every time. Luckily for me, confidence is a bi-product of attitude.

The Law cared little about traffic going west and I jogged over the bridge without so much as looking their way. The streets on our side of the river would never be called pretty. Everything - the buildings, the parks, the people, everything – looked worn out, cracked and bleak. Even Macky-D's had shut shop and gone, the drive-thru a mass of brambles and rubbish. The grimmer it got, the less effort people put in to try and put it right. They'd given up and it showed.

As usual, the sun didn't shine long. It sheeted down all the way back to the caff and I dripped onto the welcome mat.

'Jesus, Atty,' said Joe. 'Why didn't you give us a ring and I'd have come to pick you up on the bike?'

'I wanted to run. I have to get in shape, remember?'

'Well I'm going to have to stick a mop up your jacksie. Look at the mess you're making.'

'I'm touched by your care and charm, Joe.' I stamped my feet and shook my head like a dog. 'There. Happy?'

His mood had darkened since I'd left him and, rather than throwing me a party, he poured two mugs of tea and carried them to the table by the door. 'Got anything for me?'

I told Joe all I'd heard from the wives — the relevant bits, anyway. He'd never been into blue toes as far as I knew. 'It sounds like this last bunch coming out on the Early Release are proper evil gits.'

'Yeah, well. We're going to have to identify them, keep an eye out.'

'I'm more worried about the cage. They're fixing it up to turn the electric back on.'

'Fixing a few holes doesn't mean it's going live.'

'We're heading towards a lockdown.'

'Lockdown? Where did that come from?' He knew how I felt. My mum would have died for nothing if they locked us in again. He looked me in the eye. 'That's never going to happen.'

'This Red told me …'

He sucked air in through his teeth. 'You're not supposed to be drawing attention to yourself, Atty. I told you before, if you want to go pro you need the Reds to *not* see you, know what I mean? You shouldn't gossip to them like they're your mates.'

'I wasn't gossiping. I was gathering information. He told me new laws were coming in.'

'He said there was going to be a lockdown?'

'He didn't use that word, no.'

'So, you took two and four and made twenty-five?'

'No. There was a journo hanging about. Reporting on the riots was the official line.'

Joe chuckled. 'Riots?' He sat back in his chair, relaxed. 'It'll probably come to nothing.'

'Maybe, but that journalist looked too well-fed to be the honest sort. Besides, you said you wanted to know anything I heard of interest so I'm telling you.'

He smiled in that way he always did when he wanted to humour me. 'Of course. You did good, Atty. Thank you. But you can't believe everything you hear. How did the class go?'

'Don't change the subject. And I'm not stupid.'

'Never said you were.' But he looked at me like I might be. Smirking, winding me up. Testing me.

'Can't you stop those oldies waving their stupid banners about? It's not like there isn't enough other stuff to worry about, the cage and loose cons all over the place.'

'Atty,' he said. Oh here we go. A lecture was coming at me for sure. He forever banged on about the good old days before the country went bankrupt, the Great being in Britain, one country, one capital, one set of laws with one police force, the NHS,' blah de blah. 'Those oldies, as you call them, are standing up for what they believe in, the right to a voice, to protest peacefully. It's what the resistance movement is all about and you want me to stop them? If I help suppress the right for people to voice their opinion then we might as well give up now.'

Of course, when he put it like that. 'Even so,' I said, 'things won't stay peaceful if there's a freaking lockdown.

Especially if they lock those scummy cons in with us. We have to do something. Before long there'll be more ex-cons than us native westies. It's like West Basley IS the prison.'

'We need to pick our battles.' He put his massive arms on the table, leaned towards me, and gave me a long look. 'Just because they've been locked up by the Law, doesn't mean they're necessarily the bad guys. You know that as well as I do.'

I sat back in my chair. 'Don't move in on me like that.'

He kept staring.

'Stop it. What're you doing?'

He smiled. 'Just thinking the apple didn't fall far. You were born to be an activist, Atty. Just learn some patience. Your Dad would be proud of you, you know that?'

'Yeah maybe so, but he'd want me to do more. I'm wasted just listening, you know it. And now I've finished that stupid course, how long before I can work on a proper project?'

'Your turn will come, Atty. I promise. Your papers aren't even through yet.'

'But if they do lock us down I'm going to be stuck here forever, aren't I?' I pulled the whine out of my voice and lowered my tone. 'I need to get out of here.'

He blinked slowly before taking a deep breath. 'You can't rush these things. And if you think you can hurry me along by claiming lockdowns are in the offing you can think again.'

'So you don't believe me?'

'I'm saying one passing comment from a jumped up Red means nothing.' He stood and strode away to the backroom. Conversation over.

I stood up and headed out the door without calling goodbye. He cheesed me off when he got all protective.

He put the boys my age out to work on real jobs but because I'm a girl and my dad's kid to boot, he wanted to keep me wrapped up and cosy. Well if he didn't play fair soon I'd find another movement to join. As soon as my adult papers came through I intended to be away, get out of the west, out of Basley and make my mark elsewhere, with or without Joe's blessing. Somehow, maybe, I'd find my dad and we'd both stroll home with money in our pocket and the knowledge and clout to get things done - make proper changes.

On the way home I dropped by Bastion Square to say 'Hi' to Mum. It had been almost six years since the Law had beaten her to death and I wasn't the only one that couldn't forget her. People round our way have long memories. A splash of colour rested at the base of the monument - forget-me-nots. 'Who keeps bringing these to you, Mum?' Crouching down talking to a patch on the ground might seem weird to some, but I've never cared too much about what people think. 'They're extra pretty today, must be the light in the raindrops.'

I chose my words carefully. Mum reckoned that for me to do as well as she hoped, I'd have to learn to talk BBC-speak like an old-fashioned newsreader; definitely no foul language. It's the only thing I recalled her asking of me so I intended to make sure I kept to it. From the day she got killed, I've never dropped an 'F' or 'C' type word, no matter how pushed. I rearranged the flowers, bunching them together to pretty them up, opening the bow a little wider - yellow ribbon, nice touch.

I don't bring anything. I don't stand and pray, kneel, kiss the ground or weep into my sleeve. My dad had reckoned she wouldn't like any of that. All I do is drop by now and then to let her know life's treating me okay.

That, she'd appreciate. And to tell her I'm happy. After all, it's what she'd fought and died for.

CHAPTER THREE

The rain stopped but the purply clouds hung heavy and dark. I looked forward to getting home and curling up with the cats and a decent cup of Hot Blue. Joe's black market tea left an after taste like stale pee. Blue Juice hardly fitted the rock-chick image I liked to go for, but innocent indulgence and all that. I ran down the disused train tracks - fast - three sleepers a stride. I lived in an old train carriage parked in a tunnel under the M4; nobody could call it a palace, but I called it home and it suited me, scruffy but solid: unique but cosy.

Joe had tried to persuade me to move in with him, but facing Joe in his boxers every morning didn't appeal to me in the slightest. He must be at least fifty – no exaggeration. He shaved his head to try and hide the fact he was balding and still tried to carry off a young-buck swagger. All that was embarrassing enough, but there was always a steady stream of middle-aged and desperate women sniffing about. I didn't want to see them either, scurrying the landing in their knickers. Besides, I liked the freedom of living alone.

Fran was waiting for me on the steps. I hadn't seen her in a while and she didn't look great.

'Hey, how're you doing?' I gave her a half hug. 'Ugh, sorry I'm all soggy. Why didn't you go on in and wait in the warm?' The Law paid regular visits, smashed their way in if they had to, so leaving the door open saved me the trouble of building a new one every month or so.

She shrugged. 'Manners I suppose. Knocked into me from birth.'

I studied her face to get a feel of what she might be thinking. She'd had it rough as a kid and been beaten about a fair bit, but it was rare she mentioned it. 'Everything okay, Fransie? It's not like you to be so gloomy. What's happened to all that chirpy optimism? You know, all that cheery joy that irritates the hell out of me?'

'I'm okay.' But her smile was a little too slow in coming and a little too weak when it got there.

'Sit yourself down, I'm just going to get out of this wet stuff and we'll have a girly chat, yeah? Where's the bubs?'

'I've left her with her daddy for the evening. He goes out often enough. It's my turn. I wanted to come and congratulate you on finishing your course.'

'Ah cheers. You're a pal.'

After my shower I got dressed into some dry and comfy clothes. Many a time Fran had been the one who came round and talked all night, laughed and cried with me when I got down about my dad. Too many times she'd picked me out of the gutter, tucked me into bed and hugged me until I slept. Now it looked like she might need me and I was determined to be a good mate. I called to her from the kitchenette, my head in the fridge. 'What are we drinking? Hot Blue? And nibbles? Do you fancy something to eat? Or shall we go out? My treat.'

'Whatever.'

I grabbed a bottle and a bag of snacks. 'We haven't had a night in, just the two of us, since you had Stacey.' Her boyfriend didn't let her out often, a bit of a knob-head as far as I could make out, but she said he was enough. And people like Fran were happy to settle for enough no matter how many times I told her she deserved better. It was her life, her choice. Keeping on might have cost us our friendship so I'd learned to shut up. After all we'd been friends forever. Fran used to come around my house when we were little kids and we'd play warriors and princesses. Calling us close friends didn't quite cut it. We still played and fought with the confidence of sisters. Not something to be chucked away lightly.

She smiled at me. 'How's Gavin?'

'It's not happening, Fran. I told you. He's a player and I'm not up for getting messed about by the likes of him.'

'You could always play him. He's fit, right?'

Just thinking about Gavin made me squirm in my seat. 'Yeah, he's fit.' One whole night we'd had together - one. I thought I'd found my man for life. He'd treated me kind and didn't push for more than I wanted to give, but the next day he went back to his easty girlfriend like I hadn't happened. Then he came sniffing around again.

Fran chewed her lip. 'But it's definitely all over with him and that easty girl for good this time, right?'

'So he says.' I flapped my hand in a dismissive gesture and lowered my voice to mock Gavin's husky tones. 'Ah, Atty hunny. She meant nothing. It's only ever been you I want.' I snorted and finished the Blue out of my glass.

'Well?' she said. 'It's probably true. How many cross-river relationships do you know that last longer than five minutes?'

'I don't care.' I sounded proper sulky. 'It's rubbish, Fran. Jeesh. No way am I letting him near me again. He'd say anything to try and get me into bed. No more guys for me – especially, no more Gavin.'

She shrugged. 'Shame. You'd look so good together. You deserve to be happy.'

'Please let's not get all Aunt Agony about it. I know, let's not talk about it at all, eh?'

So we didn't, we chatted about all other sorts of nonsense but not Gavin. I told her about the class and my putting the self-defence instructor on his backside. She laughed until she cried.

Later, when we'd drank and ate a little too much junk, and we lay stretched out, belching, she looked at me real hard. 'Thanks for being such a good mate. I love you, you know?'

'Shush now, Fran. You're getting carried away with the moment. A full belly always did turn you all soft and emotional.' I grinned. 'And the tunnel trance of course.'

There's this atmosphere in the tunnel at night. The blackness is dense, total, and it feels like nothing else exists. Many a secret has been exchanged in the sort of surrealistic vacuum. It brings out the weirdness and rawness of people more effectively than any drug of choice, even the local ubiquitous lemondrop.

She shook her head. 'It's not just that. I've always wished I could be more like you, do you know that?'

There is a skill to taking compliments and I don't have it. They make me fidget and blush. 'Well I've always wished I could be more like you. You with your long blonde hair, cute little bum.' I looked down and slapped at my thunder thighs. 'You wouldn't want to be me.'

She shook her head and turned to look out of a window at the dense blue-black beyond her reflection. Her eyes filled with tears. 'Oh I would. I so would.'

'What's up, Fran? Tell me.'

A single fat tear ran down her face, she wiped it off her jaw and sniffed. 'Life's just pretty grim sometimes, that's all.'

I curled up next to her, my head on her shoulder. 'Nothing is ever so bad.' I reached to steal her last crisp thinking she'd shove me away and we'd laugh.

She watched me eat it and said, 'I'm not so sure.'

CHAPTER FOUR

Dreams of Gav kept me awake and angry. Fran had lifted the lid at the memory of that night. The guy had left a stain deep inside, and it throbbed, niggling away at my resolve. He was fit all right. And sometimes even I needed a bit of company.

The dead-of-night-silence made my thoughts difficult to switch off and the rats had stopped scurrying under the carriage long before I finally went to sleep.

A text from Joe woke me: *I have a job for you.* My head felt thick with too many unsaid words and my mood refused to lift. If Joe wanted to put me on another poxy listening-to-wives-prattle job I'd have to tell him to stick it. I loved Joe but he needed to accept I was a big girl now and give me some big girl jobs.

When I arrived at the caff, I felt well fired up for putting him straight. 'What's up?'

'You wanted a job? I've got just the thing. It's perfect for you.'

'By perfect I suppose you mean it's safe and cushy.'

He pursed his lips and tilted his head. 'Mm. Might be safe, might even be cushy, but it comes with enormous responsibility.' There were a few kids sitting drinking tea at a table in the window, wasting away the morning. Joe gestured for me to go through to the backroom where all his serious deals went down. 'It's also a way for you to earn a good reputation for yourself,' he said and closed the door behind us.

That's what I needed. Nobody ever saw me as Atty, just my parent's kid. 'What do I have to do? I hope it gets me out.'

'Not right out of Basley, but it's based over east. There's a couple of kids that need keeping an eye on.'

'Babysitting?'

'Not exactly. The boy, Stuart, he's a year older than you.'

'So what does he need me for?'

'He's a regular east-side kid,' said Joe as if it explained everything. It kind of did in a way. Easty kids tended to be a lot less street savvy. If they had a problem, they threw money at it. If that didn't work they were pretty much snooked. Joe checked the water in the kettle he kept on a tray in the corner. 'Their mum isn't around at the moment and he and his little sister have been left home alone. People up high are worried the Law might get twitchy. You know how quick they are to move in on under-occupied houses at the best of times. Two easty kids alone would be really soft targets.'

'What about the dad?' I asked. 'And what people up high?'

'The dad's around but remarried.'

'But he can still look out for them. Besides, what's so special about these kids to get you involved?' My imagination was already running ideas around. Either the mum must be taking part in something dodgy somewhere or Joe was on a wind-up and trying to make me feel important.

Joe sighed. 'Atty. How many times have I told you? It's this constant questioning and wanting to know every damn detail which is holding you back. You're given a task so just go and do it. It's not your place to question why. And this is a request from very high, directly from the top — M. Gee, no less. Nobody questions her orders. Ever.'

He wasn't wrong there. M. Gee had enough money to run the resistance for many years to come. Not only did she keep the finances in the black but she ran some major projects. A big player. Ruthless but fair according to her reputation. If I wanted promotion, she was the right woman to impress.

I looked at Joe hard. 'You'd better not be lying to me.'

'No. I'm not but it's probably best you don't know any more than I've already told you. Stop you reading too much into nothing.' He kept a straight face and looked fatally serious. 'If you get this right you will definitely be on the fast track to some major jobs. Outside.' He handed me a thin file. Inside were two photos and an address. Both kids looked smelly rich but cute. 'Get it wrong and you're in deep, deep shit.'

I looked into Joe's eyes, he meant business. He'd listened to me and he'd found me something worth doing. I just needed to get the job done right. 'Okay, but I need to know what I'm looking out for.'

'You need to make sure Stuart looks after his kid sister and doesn't get himself into any trouble. Without him knowing you're there of course. It should be a doddle - yes, safe and cushy, but like I said, if all goes well and the mum gets back to happy kids, M Gee might pick you for all sorts of jobs in the future.' Joe picked two mugs out of the cupboard to put next to the kettle.

I put one of the cups away again. 'Not for me. In a rush.' I smiled to soften the blow. Joe was ridiculously proud of that urinary tea. 'But yes, okay. I'll take the job. Starting right now.'

'You can do this, Atty. Any doubts just come and speak to me, yeah? I want a daily report. And I do want you to do well, you know.'

Yeah, I knew. I grinned, almost gave him a hug, almost. But we didn't do hugs.

I took a casual stroll around the border separating the west from the east. Parts of the cage shone brighter and sharper - newer - from where the Reds had stitched up the holes. I picked up a stick and reached to touch the barbs. No buzz, whine or flash. The camera on top of a post whirred. I dropped the stick and turned away.

Crossing through the checkpoint at the bridge took me almost twenty minutes because I queued quietly and waited my turn. I saw no bluebottle-eyed Red and no journalist, and nobody asked where I was going or why. Perhaps Joe had been right and all that chat about new laws would amount to nothing. The address I needed lay deep on the east side, so far east it was almost outside Basley towards the edge of the county border. I didn't mind the run, it helped me think. I'd been given my chance to shine and I was determined to focus and do a good job.

The house turned out to be easy to find, nestled at the end of one of the poshest streets. It might as well have been called Stinky-rich Avenue off Tax-exempt Close. The majority of residents were old and carried tell-tale signs of loyalty to the Law - posters in windows, little badges on their lapels. They must have been right peeved to have two left-alone kids in their midst. Talk about lowering the tone. Not to mention the house prices.

I watched Stuart drop his kid sister Gemma at the small local school near where they lived. It had that nice cosy east-side community feel to it, what with the mumsies and kiddy-winks all in pretty flouncy dresses and bows in their hair. Stuart and Gemma looked a little out of place, mainly because of Gemma. If I'd been asked to guess, I'd have said she'd ran out of clean clothes and resorted to dragging out the dressing-up box to make up the shortfall.

As for Stuart, well, the photo didn't do him justice. He stood at least six-two in his bare feet and had massive shoulders, square and solid. The sun-bleached hair ruffed into a precise tousle and his clothes hung a trend-setting sleek. He must have spent time and serious money to get that look. If he hadn't been a soft easty I might have even called him hot.

But it didn't take me long to suspect Stuart felt edgy. He walked quickly, scanning the streets the whole while, and spent a great deal of time ducking behind cars and darting around corners dodging the Reds. The Law were having a massive recruitment drive and loved to approach guys like Stuart. They liked nothing more than coaxing a good, rich, easty kid onto the dark side. Perhaps M Gee thought he might need a little help fending them off. If so, and that's all the job entailed, then I was in for a very easy ride.

The first couple of days passed as smooth and cushy as Joe would have hoped. I fell into a neat routine where I watched the kids go to school, slept for a few hours and followed them home again. Only the privileged got to go to school and take exams. Qualifications had little to do with brains and more to do with bank balances. Naturally, one led to the other, and so the cycle continued.

Each night I reported to Joe and each night he warned me against getting complacent, but the truth was, I wanted something to happen. I wanted to prove I could do more than hang about watching others live their lives.

On day three I turned up outside their house for the school-run as usual. Stuart and Gemma bundled their way out through their front door, Stuart dressed in a tee with *I'll show you mine …* across the front and looking ball-dropping knackered, Gemma in some sort of pink, frilly fairy dress and purple wellies. I've never been one for kids, but she was pretty in a quirky kind of way, and funny. She chatted constantly and looked up at Stuart like he was her very own superman. He answered her as if she was a mini adult with long, complex sentences which would bore the pants off a professor. 'I have a Mandarin exam this morning, Gemma, three hours long. It's crucial for international relations as well as business …' Yawn, yawn. But Gemma listened and nodded. 'Yes, Stuart. Absolutely, Stuart.' Sweet.

As they crossed the road, Gemma dragging her bag and cardi in the grit and dirt, an old man with a walking stick hobbled to meet them. Gemma crouched down to stroke his dog. Stuart nodded, smiled and fielded the old geezer's questions like a pro. I removed my earpins. It looked like another day when he wouldn't be needing any help from me. I waited until they were several metres ahead and followed them down the street. Gemma paused to stare at a limo parked outside an old newsagents and Stuart grabbed her hand to encourage her along. Even the east didn't have such fancy cars hanging around at random, perhaps funerals and the odd wedding but it definitely wasn't the norm, so I filed away the details, just in case. Driver – big, beefy, mid-forties. Passenger – suit, black hair, greasy looking, same age-ish. They appeared enthralled by something on a sheet of paper the passenger held between them.

Stuart waved Gemma into school and upped his pace, checking his watch as he headed off to the old comp. Easy jobs equalled dull, but as I followed several meters behind, I amused myself fantasising about M Gee calling me up, thanking me personally, offering me a promotion, right-hand girl … a tad delusional maybe, but fun.

CHAPTER FIVE

To get to the comp, Stuart cut through a large open park with an area fenced off to house kiddy swings and slides. I tended to jog around the outside, shielded from sight by the trees ringing the border. Most days, only a few other straggling school-kids cluttered my view, but today about half a dozen girls were congregated in the play area. I didn't need to plug my earpins in to recognise what was going on. East or west, when one girl is sitting on a bench, looking at her feet and a bunch of others surround her laughing and chanting, it's clear to an idiot that somebody's having a hard time. Neither is it tough picking out the main instigator. She's usually the noisiest – loud laugh, loud hair, loud clothes, loud make-up, loud everything, and almost always surrounded by a set of wannabe clones, tittering and smirking, giving out the idea she's all that.

Stuart slowed his pace and took a mini diversion which put him within shouting distance of the group. He stopped and looked around, perhaps hoping somebody else might step up and intervene. When nobody else showed any interest, he shuffled his feet and fiddled with the strap on his backpack.

I stepped behind a tree and fished for my earpins which had slipped deep into my hip pocket. The snugness of my combats caused me to make a mental note – less junk nights with Fran.

Stuart turned away and upped his stride to head out of the park leaving the girl to whatever damage the others saw fit. He might look the hot, heroic type but an easty is an easty - spineless. But then I saw a suited man stepping out towards the girls. He waved his arm at the bitch with the loud face. Her cronies backed away but she did at least throw a comment in the suit's direction, probably something inane and pointless. I missed it, only getting my earpins plugged in in time to catch the suit speak to the girl on the bench.

'Are you okay?'

'Of course. Why wouldn't I be?'

He sat down next to her. 'They've gone now, you don't have to pretend with me.'

'They were only joking.'

'I know.'

The girl started to cry. She tried to hide it at first. The tears were in her voice long before they reached her face but once the game was up she gave way and shouted her misery. 'It's not fair. I don't do anything wrong to anybody. I don't know why they're so mean to me all the time.' She did a noisy, gloopy sniff which stuck in my throat and I turned the volume down. 'I hate it here,' she whined, 'I wish I'd never had to come.'

'Are you new to the area?' He spoke slow and precise. Carefully might be a good word.

'I used to live in London,' she said. The pride in her voice stopped her crying for a second. 'My parents were very important people but since they were killed I've had to come and live in this cesspit.'

My sympathy for her took a knock. She really should take a look at the west, it might improve her perception skills somewhat. I mean, the east? A cesspit? Ha.

The suit rubbed her arm. 'It's not as bad as all that. Are you living with grandparents? Aunty and uncle?'

'My uncle. But he doesn't want me. Just the money I came with. My parents were bankers.'

The suit slid along the bench and put his arm around her shoulder.

Us westy girls are warned from the time we can walk how to spot a paedo. And the suit, even from across the park, reeked of a class A groomer. It wasn't my place to interfere, but neither could I not. The whole exchange had taken less than two minutes. Stuart was still walking towards the park exit. The odds of anything happening to him right then were slim. If I put a rattle on, I could distract the greaseball and still catch Stuart up before he got to school. It was an easy decision to make - the girl needed me more. I pocketed my earpins and made my way over, keeping a sharp lookout for any Reds. I waltzed up to the bench smiling and chirruping like an idiot.

'Hey,' I said to the girl and totally blanked the suit. 'How're you doing?'

She swiped at her nose with the back of her wrist then ground the sleeve into her trousers, it looked like a herd of slugs had crawled over her lap. Nice look. The suit offered me a tight smile. His eyes were coal-black, empty and small, like in a dead snake. And he had the blackest, greasiest hair; I couldn't help but gawp at it.

'Friend of yours?' he asked.

He might have been talking to the girl but I answered. 'Yeah, best of friends. And you are?'

He grinned, a gold tooth smack in the middle of his mug. 'Can I see your papers?'

I put on my best stunned face. 'Eh?'

'Papers.'

'Why?'

He removed his arm from the girl's shoulders and flashed a badge from his inside pocket – ISS approved.

'I see,' I said, playing for time. Bad decision, Atty. Only then did I recognise him as the guy from the limo. Suits in limos might be sore news, but give them ISS approval and I was in deep, proper doo-doo. Why oh why didn't I ever learn to mind my own business? As soon as he spotted the west logo on my ID he'd call the Law and they'd cart me home in a nanosecond. Probably with all sorts of conditions stamped across my papers. In red. And that's if they were in a good mood.

He had his hand out, waiting.

I spoke to the girl. 'What have you done?'

'Nothing.'

'Then why are you being questioned by the ISS? If you haven't done anything?'

'I'm not. I haven't.' She wasn't having her best day. First the 'it' girls, then the suit, now me.

'Well, ISS agents don't happen along looking to pass the day in kiddy parks for no reason. They're busy people.'

'Not too busy to take a look at your papers.'

I ignored him. 'So.' My voice must surely be shaking. Hopefully it would pass as fury. I glared at the girl, big sister style. 'What have you been up to?'

She stood up and screamed into my face. 'I haven't done anything!' She grabbed her school bag. 'Why is everybody giving me such a hard time? I just want everybody to leave me alone.' And she walked away.

'Wait up.' I jogged after her. 'We can walk together. I've got an exam this morning.'

She glanced back, wide-eyed scared. 'Who are … '

'Chinese.' I raised my voice and hooked my arm through hers, propelling her the hell out of there. 'Three hours it is. THREE.' The back of my neck tingled and every muscle tensed, waiting for a tap on the shoulder. No way would Greasy-haired Goldtooth let me simply walk away. The girl tried to push me off but I kept tight hold and whispered, 'Just walk. Don't look back.'

She finally began to grasp what I'd been trying to do. 'Stop it, he's okay, he's been talking to me, that's all.'

'Trust me, he's bad news.'

'But if he's ISS approved he's got to be okay.'

Oh the innocence. 'We'll be late for school,'

A tap on my shoulder had been optimistic thinking: he came up behind and gripped my arm so hard I felt the tips of his fingers bruise my bones. 'I asked to see your papers.' He leaned so close I flinched away from his breath, but it smelt clean, like peppermint.

'Okay, take it easy.' I said and smiled at the girl. 'You go on ahead, I'll catch you up, no point in us both being late.' My voice sounded normal enough but my papers felt bulky in my back pocket. Surely he'd spotted them already. I held my hands up, 'Okay. I admit it. I left my ID at home.' I rolled my eyes. 'Come on, it's not like I've done anything wrong. It was her you wanted, not me.' I stopped and tilted my head, feigning quizzical interest. 'Why were you questioning her?' The girl loitered around like a fart, shuffling her bag from one shoulder to the other. 'Go on,' I said. 'You go ahead or you'll be late.'

A familiar voice spoke from behind me. 'Is there a problem?'

'Just checking this young lady's ID.'

'Let me save you the trouble.' Bluebottle-eyes smiled. 'I know exactly who she is. We've met before, haven't we, Bethany?'

CHAPTER SIX

Bluebottle led me to a van parked at the gates. People stopped and stared as he guided me into the back and locked me in what looked like a dog cage. 'Sit tight. Back in a tick.'

In the fraction of a second before the door slammed shut I locked eyes with Stuart, who stood leaning against the gatepost at the entrance to the park. Boogah. Plop went my low profile, right down the flusher.

The air inside the van was cool and stank of stale pee and testosterone. A screen made from chicken wire separated me from a grumpy driver who gazed at me with dull eyes via the rear-view mirror.

'Good morning,' I said.

Each time he inhaled, the folds on the back of his neck rippled causing the bristles of his number one to shimmer in the sunlight. Fat people always made such a meal of everything, even breathing seemed an effort.

'Lovely day for it,' I said. The relief of getting away from the ISS guy sent me giddy and a babbling danger to myself. The safest thing to do would be to shut the hell up.

The driver looked out of the passenger window towards Bluebottle talking to Goldtooth and the girl.

'Do those two know each other already?' I asked.

Fatty's eyes returned to the mirror then looked away.

'Friendly, aren't we?'

Shut up. Shut UP! I shut up.

I watched as the girl wandered away alone in one direction and Stuart in another. Bluebottle and Goldtooth chatted a little more before shaking hands and parting company. Bluebottle climbed into the passenger seat and swivelled to talk to me.

'I told you to behave yourself. What are you doing over here at this time of day anyway? Thought you lot didn't get out of bed until at least midday.'

'Early run. Just making my way back.'

He scowled and spoke to the driver. 'Let's take her home and this time …' turning to snarl at me - again, '… stay there. I'm going to be keeping my eye on you, do you hear?'

The driver started the engine. 'Aren't we going to take her in? Caution her or something?'

'We haven't got time. Not if we want to go to the party.'

The driver gave a filthy laugh and snorted. If he'd rubbed his crotch it wouldn't have been more obvious what sort of party they had planned.

Bluebottle sniggered. 'It's your lucky day, Bethany.'

They dropped me off over the river, back in the grot of the west. Bluebottle gave me one final warning to stay out of trouble. 'Next time, I'll bring you in.'

I went home intending to try and relax a little, listen to some tunes, drink some blue and wait for the adrenalin rush to slow. I felt confident Stuart would be safely tucked up in the exam hall at school. I wasn't so confident he'd forget seeing me in the van. But if I took a little extra care, dropped back an extra meter or two, be a tad more subtle, I could still swing it. I flicked on the kettle and then the radio, just to hear the sound of a human voice. The radio, like all media, was strictly controlled by the Law. Of course that meant it was mostly rubbish, but now and again they did play a little summer cheer to try and up the community morale. Nobody got fooled by it, but we all liked to pretend, if only for a short time, that life smelt rosy.

I caught the tail end of the news. A politician rabbited on why the ERP and letting all those cons out had proved such a good idea. He used phrases like, 'community control' and 'real people at grass roots,' … 'the Law's course of correction has cut petty crime to zero.' It was all about control. I pictured him waving his arms around in genuine excitement. The presenter joined in. They sounded like a pair of ignorant children trying to brainwash the nation. Morons. I turned them off, set my alarm, and waited for sleep, pondering whether I should report the morning's events to Joe. I decided not.

Things I learned over the next few days. Stuart hated his dad. Stuart's dad hated Stuart, despite handing over wads of cash every five minutes. I could love pretty much anybody if they gave me dosh like that to play with. Stuart didn't shy away from spending it either. He wore the best gear and, when not in school, treated his mates to food and drink at home and away. I spent hours loitering outside cafes and arcades. He didn't half have an easy life. Born lucky.

I also saw how fond he was of Gemma. He listened to all her babbling and called her silly names like Hiccup and Fudgkins. He made her giggle and squirm and he stood behind her and scowled at the bigger kids when they teased her for her bizarre dress sense. Lucky little Gemma.

I'd been following Stuart for almost a week and, apart from the one incident at the park, he hadn't spotted me at all. Neither Bluebottle, the limo, nor the gold-toothed greasy guy appeared again and I put them out of my head. Stuart dealt with any approach from the recruiters like a pro. The boy was doing well enough without me. I deserved a break. Not to say I left him to get on with it but one night, after his bedroom light went out, I decided to give Fran a shout and see if she wanted another night in the trance. A more chirpy one this time.

Fran and Carl lived on the Shanks estate in a typical west-side hovel. The Law tend not to patrol or care about such places so the people on Shanks run the streets themselves and that meant mob-rule. Fortunately, Joe runs the mob. But he can only do so much and he tends to focus on sorting the violent stuff. Everything else is left to take its natural course and, left to their own devices, things always run downhill. I trotted down alleys strewn with rubbish, broken bottles and lemondrop needles. Many houses had boarded up windows and patchwork doors. Life on the estate looked grim but nobody ever died from being grubby.

I knocked at Fran's door for ages before the old woman next door poked her head out of an upstairs window. 'Stop making that racket. I'm trying to watch Corrie in here.' She paused and must have thought again when she saw just me, a girl, and her voice softened. 'Nobody there any more, love. Gone.'

'Gone where?'

'Kid went a week or so ago. Haven't seen anybody go in nor out since.' She shrugged. 'It's all I know.' And she slammed the window shut.

Fran wouldn't go away without saying goodbye. I went around the back and found an old pipe amongst the debris in the alley and jimmied it under the bars that covered the kitchen window. It took every ounce I had and blistered my fingers, but after ten minutes of heaving I'd made a big enough gap to squeeze through. I wrapped my fist in my jacket and punched the window in.

The first thing that struck me was the smell. I didn't have to climb inside before it stuck in my throat and I heaved. I pulled the neck of my tee shirt up over my nose and breathed in the heat of my body. No wonder they'd moved out, the whole place reeked. I almost changed my mind and went home but I needed a clue as to where they might have gone. I clambered in and turned the kitchen light on. Everything shone bright and clean. A baby's bottle stood soaking on the draining board and the breadbin lid lay propped against the fridge. Other than that, everything looked as spotless and uncluttered as Fran liked it. I checked the bin but it was empty. Perhaps the fridge. But that too had nothing in it to cause such a rancid stench.

The door from the kitchen led into a passage from which the back door and the living room turned off. And the stairs. It looked like it might be a big coat, or overalls, dangling from the upstairs bannister. I hoped someone might have thrown it willy-nilly and it had tumbled over and got stuck, left hanging by a sleeve.

But really I knew straight away. Probably knew from the minute I smelt the smell. Or from when nobody answered the door. Maybe even from when she told me she loved me.

I rang Joe and, as he always did, he came because I needed him. He took down Fran's body and called the right people to take her away. He carried me back to his house, fed me hot soup, tucked me in, and sat with me all night wiping my snot and tears, letting me cry. Not once did he tell me to shush.

CHAPTER SEVEN

Joe sent somebody else to watch Stuart and Gemma get to school and, by the time I got to the caff, he had news for me about Fran. 'Some guy with a suit, ISS Approved, came and took the baby away. All legit, Carl and Fran signed the paperwork.'

The second ISS approved in a week. 'Gold tooth?'

Joe second-glanced me. 'Never mentioned it, why? Do you know something?'

'No. Just that I happened across an ISS approved last week. What exactly does it mean? ISS Approved?'

'It means he might have come from anywhere in the country, or even out of the country. He can travel around and do pretty much what he likes with International Security's approval. There's a few of them around, could be the same one I suppose.' He gave a shrug and made a helpless gesture with his hands. 'But the baby could be anywhere by now.'

I shook my head. 'Fran wouldn't have signed anything, no matter who had approved what. She loved that baby.'

Joe puffed out his cheeks as he released a slow breath. 'She probably didn't have a choice. Or maybe she couldn't cope any more. People do things you don't expect them to do all the time.'

'She'd have told me.'

'Maybe she wanted to protect you.'

'From what?'

'From how unhappy she was.'

'But I could have helped her.'

'Not necessarily. Life is tough for a lot of people. We can't save everybody, Atty.'

'But if it was the same guy from last week …'

'What?' He looked at me with his mouth open. 'What could you have done?'

I studied the ceiling to avoid his eyes.

'*Nothing* is what, Atty. What happened last week that you didn't tell me about, anyway? I'm guessing it wasn't important.'

Oh Lordy. Way too late to mention it now. 'No. Nothing important.'

'I hope not. I need to know everything, do you hear me? If an ISS agent is giving you grief then I'll have to pull you off the job.'

'It's fine. I saw one flash his badge at some girl in the park, that's all. But if they're out there nicking kids, maybe the park is somewhere we should be watching.'

'Nobody nicked the baby, Atty. Fran signed her over. There's nothing we can do.' Joe turned away and fiddled with something on a shelf. 'Why don't you go away for a few days? I've got contacts up in the hills that'll welcome having you stay.'

'I'm not going to do anything stupid.'

'I never said that. But maybe you need a break.' He'd given all the tenderness he had to offer. It was time I manned up or shipped out.

'I can't. If I blow this, job M Gee might not trust me with another. And besides, what would be the point? I'm better off here, keeping busy.'

Joe studied me hard. 'Don't go doing anything without my say-so. Stay focused on the job.'

'I can handle it.'

I avoided Bastion Square and mum's spot on the way east. I'm not so stupid as to think Mum could have known, but I felt embarrassed at being so angry at the world. Not to mention bone-deep ashamed at the way I wanted to lie down and wallow in self-pity. Yet another person had left me. Me, me, me. Besides, I wasn't in the mood to watch my language, far from it. I wanted to scream and curse and work the anger out of my system.

I watched Stuart wait for Gemma outside her school. He stood right up close tò the door so, when it opened, all the kids came streaming past him like water round a pebble. He kept his hands in his pockets and stood square. The teachers hung back and whispered behind their hands, giving him wary looks. When Gemma didn't appear, Stuart yelled at the teachers and paced about looking agitated.

I plugged in my earpins and tuned in.

'You must know!'

'You need to leave the premises, Stuart.'

'Not until you tell me where she is.'

'Leave now or we'll call The Law.'

I toyed with the idea of wandering over, nipping out any potential trouble before it took root. But Stuart strode away and took his mobile from his pocket.

'Dad? Why didn't you tell me you were getting her?'

He stopped walking and sat on a low wall.

'Boarding school? When? Where?'

My spine turned icy cold. Something was wrong. M Gee would have told Joe if one of the kids was going away. Or maybe she had and he'd forgotten to tell me. Unlikely. A horror shiver ran right from my toes up. Oh God, I'd lost Gemma.

Stuart jogged all the way to his dad's house and hammered on the door. If his mum's street rated posh, then his dad's road, which I didn't even know existed, must rank palatial. They might easily have got away with calling it Greedy Gits Close. There were lawns and cutesy little flower borders, ponds with little stone boys weeing into the breeze - even little summerhouses sitting pretty in quaint designer gardens - all tucked away behind a row of trees and a high spec security fence. Just one of those trinkets might have helped Fran out of whatever hole she'd found herself in.

I stood out of sight of the cameras under a big old oak. Some woman, Stuart's stepmother I presumed, opened the door. I tuned in.

Her voice twanged tinny and cold. 'I'll get him for you.'

She left Stuart stood on the doorstep like a Jehovah.

His dad appeared, in a well-ironed tracksuit, and stood with his hands in his pockets. 'What can I do for you, Stuart? We've got people coming over.'

Stuart sounded angry enough to spit. 'Oh really? Am I being a bit of an inconvenience, Dad? Care to have me shipped off somewhere, like you have Gemma?'

'She's a little girl, Stuart. She needs stability, looking after properly.'

'Does Mam know?'

Good question, Stuart. I couldn't have done better if I'd been in there asking the questions myself.

His dad sighed but stood straight to his full height and folded his arms across his chest. 'Of course she knows.'

'You're lying.'

'Now don't go getting chopsy.'

'You want chopsy? I'll give you chopsy. What the hell do you think you're doing?' Stuart spoke through his teeth, it sounded like he was the strict father and struggling to keep his fists to himself. He turned in a small circle, his hands on his head before stepping back up into his dad's face. 'And I don't just mean Gemma, I mean about you being a sad old git who thinks he's pulled a young, horny little thing.' The words poured out in one big rush. 'Hell, I wouldn't touch her with a dyno rod, and you've picked her, that bony, ugly cow, over your own kids, over Gemma! She's six years old – you selfish, selfish… bastard!'

Holy moly. Breathe, Stuart, breathe. I thought rich people were all "pass the decanter" and horses and cricket. Stuart and his dad stood nose to nose despite his dad having the doorstep advantage. Stuart – tense with clenched fists. His old man – relaxed and controlled.

'Get away from my house.'

'Where's Gemma?'

'She's safe. I'm not going to tell you again. Leave. Now.'

The neighbours came wandering out of their houses, one by one, to have a good nose. They didn't whoop and cheer like they did on Shanks estate, they were worse. They pretended to wash their cars, look down drains, empty buckets in the gutter - all the time creeping towards Stuart and his Dad, hoping to listen in on the drama.

Stuart looked over his shoulder. 'Neighbours friendly around here, are they?'

His dad took a roll of money out of his pocket. 'Take this and concentrate on your exams. Gemma's safe.'

In classic spoilt rich-kid style, Stuart ignored the wad of cash – the great, *fistful* of cash. 'I need to see Gemma.'

'You'll see her soon, when she comes back for a break. Meanwhile, go and finish your exams and have a night out with the lads.'

Stuart nodded his head towards a bloke weeding a border twenty feet away from where they stood. 'He wants to witness a nice little scene … tell the whole neighbourhood how the sad old geezer with the tart for a wife is spoiling the local ambience.'

His dad smirked. 'He'd also like to call The Law to have you removed.'

'Let him. Your wife would love that, eh?'

Stand off.

Somebody tapped me on the shoulder. I nearly jumped out of my boots.

'Shoosh. I didn't hear you coming.' I waved the earpins in the air. 'Music.'

Bluebottle frowned. 'What are you doing here?'

I shook my head and put on my best wide-eyed innocent look. 'Just looking how the other half live.' I pulled a whatever-face. 'You know. Dreaming.'

'I see.' He nodded towards Stuart. 'Friend of yours, is he?'

I laughed. 'Naaa. East – west. Rose – crap. One feeds off the other, know what I mean?'

'Not really, no.'

'Oh dear.' I smiled to show my sympathy, crinkled my nose. 'Never mind.'

He looked at Stuart. 'He's a handsome lad. At least I've heard of uglier blokes attracting stalkers.' He looked around at all the glass and shiny steel on the houses. 'Family money to consider too, by the looks of it.' Back to me. 'Maybe you're smarter than you look.'

'Money isn't everything.'

'No. It ain't.' He studied my face and left a lengthy interview pause.

Stuart walked past behind him but I didn't stop looking straight up into those blue eyes. And no way would I fill the silence, we could stand there all day. I smiled and waited – a look of obedient patience. Leaves rustled in the breeze, bees buzzed and the seconds ticked by.

'I tell you what,' he said, 'why don't I give you another lift back to the west side?'

I grinned. 'Another free ride? In your nice shiny van? Why, yes please, sir. That would be fabulous.'

I sat in the back of the van, Bluebottle up front alongside the driver. We pulled away and cruised down the street slower than I ran. Stuart walked just up ahead.

Bluebottle turned to the driver. 'Let's stop and have a chat.' He put one elbow out the window and chewed on a toothpick. 'Need a lift, mate?'

Stuart didn't look round simply spat out, 'Piss off.'

The driver pursed his lips. 'Oooh not very polite, is he?'

Only an easty kid would get away with telling a Red to piss anywhere, let alone off. Stuart stopped and glanced into the back of the van, straight at me. He caught and held my eye, just a fraction longer than necessary. He swallowed, looked back to Bluebottle. 'I'm sorry. I thought you were somebody else. And well,' he shrugged, 'it's been a tough day.' A small smile. 'Exams, you know.' Another shrug.

'I see. I understand.' Bluebottle turned back to me. 'And you do, don't you? It seems it's a funny old day all round today. Perhaps we'll all start afresh tomorrow, eh?' Stuart looked at me and chewed the inside of his mouth. Neither of us said anything. 'See you later, mate.' Bluebottle eased up the window and the van moved on.

The driver dropped me at the edge of Shanks estate. Whatever game they were playing they'd clearly got bored with it, but Joe was going to be vein-popping mad at me. My cover had been blown. Three run-ins with the same Red couldn't be ignored, I'd have to report it. But the worst and most terrifying thing of all, Gemma had been removed from range and I had no idea where she'd been taken. If her dad wouldn't tell Stuart where she was, no way would he tell me. I paced in circles, my nails digging into my palms. Think. The sensible thing would be to tell Joe, now, or better still yesterday, but the thought of it made me feel sick. I'd messed up. My first job and I'd fracked it so far up it'd soared clean beyond the stratosphere and I could see no way of bringing it back.

Joe's words about the consequences if I fouled up rang in my head all the way home. I needed to shower and grab fresh clothes before doing anything hasty. Think. Perhaps an idea for a salvage operation might drop out the sky but if not, I needn't go and get the rollicking of a lifetime smelling quite so ripe.

The last person I wanted to see after a night of crying, a day of disasters, and stinking in stale clothes, was Gavin. But that was who I found sitting on my step when I got home. I didn't offer the friendliest welcome. 'Why doesn't anybody let themselves in anymore?'

He followed me through the door. 'I just heard about Fran. Jesus, Atty. I can't believe it. Are you okay?'

'You always were the master of stupid questions.'

'You found her, didn't you?'

'I don't want to talk about it.'

He put his hands up in surrender. 'Okay. What do you want to do?'

'Shower.'

'I'll cook for you while you're in there.' He lifted a bag to eye level and smiled. 'Pasta and cheese. Your favourite.'

My eyes followed his arm and wandered down to his waist. His tee shirt had risen when he'd lifted the bag; his tight olive skin stretched across his belly, his warmth, his smell … the list went on.

'Atty?'

Eyeing up talent while my career in the resistance was over before it had even started. Committed, uh? And while Fran lay cold on a slab. Not the greatest friend, me. But I didn't want to be alone. And he looked like he might be a pleasant distraction.

'Yeah, okay,' I said.

Sometimes it's better to step back from a problem and then the answer will slam upside the head from nowhere. Well, it was a theory of sorts and I chose to run with it. I lingered in the shower, listened to Fran's voice replay through my mind, hoping to justify my weak, selfish behaviour. She wanted me to do this. *Thanks for being my mate… He's fit … you could play him … I love you.* But really, it was all about creating delays so I could avoid Joe. I was nothing but a coward.

After my shower I sat and watched Gavin working. His upper body formed a perfect triangle and his movements were smooth and easy, like he slow-danced around the tiny kitchenette in the corner of the carriage. He'd tucked a tea towel in the top of his jeans which dangled from one hip and looked sexy as hell. A tea towel. How did he do that?

'You okay?' he asked. 'Nearly done.' He took the tea towel and wiped his hands before throwing it across his shoulder.

We ate sitting opposite each other. Gavin with slow deliberation, his long fingers holding the fork, gentle but firm.

His eyes held a permanent twinkle of naughtiness. 'Taste good?'

'It sure does,' I said.

Afterwards he cleared the plates.

I smirked. 'Don't tell me you're even going to wash up.'

He feigned pain in his chest. 'Your tone wounds me. Of course I'm going to clear up.' Then he looked at me real hard. 'You will be okay, Atty. I promise you. I'm going to make sure of it.'

'Yeah right, course I will.' He didn't know the half. I fidgeted under his gaze. 'Stop looking at me all sad.'

'Got it.' He turned back to the sink. 'No looking sad. Right. I can do that.'

When he finished and sat next to me I felt the heat of his body down my arm, my thigh and it seeped through my hip, deep into my belly. *Play him.*

Joe's love was the paternal kind - unconditional; he couldn't help himself because it was instinctive and had nothing to do with me being me. He'd have loved me even if he didn't like me. Maybe even if he hated me. But Gavin chose to be with me and he chose to like me. We might not be much as couples go and certainly no fairy-tale love with rainbows and fireworks, but it would be enough… for now. I wanted to be wanted, at least for a while, before I had to face the look of anger and disappointment in Joe's eyes.

Gavin smiled. 'Do you want to go for a walk or something?'

'No thanks.'

'Or there's some kids getting together at the station. It's one of those east meets west things the Shanks mob organise, you know, try to unite the youth of the future as one and all that slop.'

'I just want to stay in, I think.'

He clasped his hands between his thighs and sighed. 'Okay. Shall we do something here?'

I waited until he turned to look at me, stared right to the back of his eyes and said, 'Yes.'

He shook his head. 'I promised myself I wouldn't take advantage of you. You're upset. You've been saying no for so long. I just wanted to help. I don't want the first night of the rest of our lives to be …'

I stopped him saying any more by kissing him, full on. When I pulled away he followed. His rapid shallow breaths tasted like he smelt, hot and musky.

'Oh, Atts. It's only ever been you I want. I swear.'

CHAPTER EIGHT

Of course, when I woke the next morning all that remained of Gav was his scent on my spare pillow. So predictable. Despite my decision to go for it I'd changed my mind as his hands crept down my belly. It would've been at the wrong time for all the wrong reasons. He'd said he'd understood, but creeping away before dawn kind of told me different. Well, whatever, it was another night down and at least I'd had some sleep. I had much bigger worries in that the sky hadn't dropped a miracle into my lap, and I couldn't put off fessing up to Joe any longer. I'd lost Gemma and blown my cover, things couldn't get any worse. Joe would never trust me again.

I stripped the bed and showered before dressing in my best gear to try and boost my confidence. I needed all I could get to keep my nerve intact. I'm not a girly-girl shape, never wore make-up and keep my hair short and spiky. It suits me; gives me a hard edge and stops people trying to get cuddly with me. A rollicking I can cope with - give it to me on my head, mate. Sympathy is a different and slippery ball to get to grips with and I've never quite got the hang of it. I'd give Joe attitude so he could shout louder and we'd both walk away intact. If he looked sad or disappointed, chances were I'd crumple. And crumpling was not in my plan. Before I left, I put plenty of food down for the cats and left a window open. Joe might send me up the hills to lie low somewhere. At least until he managed to find Gemma.

I took a two sleeper jog along the tracks, not feeling any great urge to rush. Whenever I got caught in sticky spots my thoughts turned to my dad. What would he think of me getting into such a mess? What would he want me to do? Stuff like that. It's odd, his face hadn't been too clear in my mind for a while, but I heard his voice, deep and friendly, like a warm cuddle - clear and definite, as if he was standing right next to me, advising and loving me, even giving me the occasional telling off. I missed it all. One of his favourite mantras was, *Trust your instincts, Atty. They are older and wiser than you are.* And as I trotted along the track, my instinct screamed that somebody else was trotting along behind me.

The station was where I usually got off, but I followed the track west towards the blocked off tunnel. There were no corners to duck behind and the bends were all long and meandering. Any trees lining the track were behind a high security fence. No way would I have the time to climb over any fences without getting spotted, so the tunnel was my best hope at dodging whoever followed me. I trotted inside. It was gloopy dark and goose-bumping cold. At intervals there were ledges, high up the arched walls, about head height, and I clambered onto the third one along, and lay flat. So much for dressing to impress, the dirt and grit, inches thick, coated my gear like oil. Not happy. I wriggled into position to have a clear view of the entrance. Whoever followed me wouldn't make it past without me getting a good look. I held my breath and listened so hard I swear I heard the walls creak.

The tail stumbled to a stop and I recognised Stuart's tall and awkward silhouette against the sunlight. He stood still and looked down the tunnel. He glanced over his shoulder and back again. His school bag, packed tight and heavy, hung over one arm, and he fiddled with the strap using both hands. He turned to walk away, changed his mind and took a step inside the tunnel, putting one hand out to hold the wall. He inched in and stopped.

I swung my legs around and jumped down. 'What do you want, Stuart?'

'Ah, bloody hell.' His hand flew to his chest. 'You scared all fifty shades out of me.'

I stepped towards him brushing my clothes down. 'Why were you following me?'

'I want to talk to you.'

If my life hadn't been free-falling into such a serious shambles I might have laughed. I'd thought things couldn't get worse, ha, talk about fouling up. Joe was going to go ballistic when he heard my target tailed me into a dead-end tunnel. But rather than collapse into manic hysterics, I got bolshie, like it was Stuart's fault. 'What the hell do you want with me?'

He got snappy back. 'That guy, the Approved, with the suit and gold tooth. You spoke to him in the park the other day. Who is he?'

'How should I know?' I walked away, annoyed at the state of my clothes on top of everything else.

'But you spoke to him. Him and that girl.'

'Yeah, so?'

'What did you talk about? Where's he from? What's he doing here?' He skipped alongside me, inches away.

'I don't know.' I said. 'I wasn't exactly interested in hearing his life story.'

'He's taken my little sister.'

That stopped me.

Stuart's eyes were rimmed red and he looked scared. 'He took her,' he said again. 'Do you know where to?'

'How do you know it was him?'

Stuart took a huge breath which stuttered when he released it. He swiped at the sweat oozing on his upper lip. 'Do you know anything about him?' He scanned the trees.

This boy looked more than scared. He looked like he might brick himself. 'Take it easy,' I said. A tiny bubble of an idea popped into the back of my head. Perhaps if I got Gemma back right away, Joe need never know I'd lost her. Stuart didn't look like a miracle and he hadn't dropped out of the sky, but messages and strange guises, etcetera. I put my hand out to touch his arm. 'It's okay.'

He shook me off. 'Who are you? Who is he? Where's Gemma?'

'I don't know but I'll help you find her, if you like.' Joe need never know any of the crappy stuff had even happened. He needn't know she'd ever been missing. 'I'll help you find her,' I said again, warming to the idea, 'we can bring her home.'

Stuart stood, hands on hips, looking around. 'What makes you think you can help? You just said you didn't know anything about him.' He stepped away from me, shaking his head. 'I can't trust you.'

'Yes you can. I don't know him, I swear. The only reason I talked to him in the park was because he was acting all creepy towards that girl, remember? You saw him too. He's some weirdo with an ISS Approval is all I know. We can find Gemma. Together. You and me.'

If that weirdo took Gemma, he might have taken Fran's baby. He might even have taken that girl in the park if I hadn't stepped in. Stuart paced about and rubbed at his face with both hands before looking at me real hard. I grinned my friendliest, helpful grin when what I really wanted to do was shake him, beg him, fall at his feet and hug his ankles.

'That Red with the dragon on his head.' Stuart pointed between his eyes. 'Why were you with him and why did he stop me? I mean … you keep popping up all over the place. Why?'

'Coincidence.'

'Yeah right.'

'Alright, it's not. But believe me when I say I want to find Gemma every bit as much as you do. Let's go somewhere and talk.' He looked like he might be thinking about it. I kept up the pressure. 'You choose where. Anywhere you like.' Despite us being safely away from prying ears and any CCTV, he'd surely want to go someplace else. Somewhere neutral where he knew I didn't have any friends around the corner waiting for the chance to jump him. It's what I'd do. As for me, I'd pretty much go anywhere with anybody rather than go to the caff.

'Okay. But if you're messing with me …'

'I'm not. Honest.' I put up my hands like I wouldn't dare do such a thing. But Stuart? Scary? Not ever.

He led me around the edge of West Basley to the beach. Basley beach is long and sandy and, at one time, it used to attract tourists from all over the world, but that was before the sea took on its fluorescent green tinge at the mouth of the Bast. By the time they built the toxi-plant to filter the gunk out, the cage had been put up and nobody, or at least anybody who doesn't have to, crosses west of the Bast.

The toxi-plant did a better job some days than others. Sometimes the sea is reported to be as clear as vodka and giving off a gentle pungent scent, like salty nappies. Sometimes it's so shiny it burns the eyes and stinks somewhere between engine oil and disinfectant. But other days, the in between days, it looks and smells pretty good. The coastline is a natural blockade on one side of West Basley, the river and cage makes up the rest, the plan being to stop the cons breaking back east.

I'd not been down to the shore for a long while and forgotten how good it felt. The sense of space - miles and miles of sand and sea with no one to hassle me – think freedom.

I needed to put Stuart at ease. So I talked. The polite chit and chat has always been a struggle for me, but I put in my best effort, smiled a lot, and tried to change the subject – relax him. 'Apparently, before the boundary between east and west went up, this place was teeming with people from all over.' I glanced at him to see if he was listening. Possibly. I kept going. 'That Red gave me a lift back to the west in his van yesterday. He knew I didn't belong over east. I think they thought I might be casing the joint.' Stuart kicked at the sand. His teeth were clamped shut, his jaw square. His look reminded me of a cartoon superhero. I had to get him to open up. 'That's some house your dad's got.'

'Why were you over by my dad's house?'

'I just happened to be in the area, saw you, recognised you from the park, and thought I might say hi.' I stopped, not wanting to dig the hole any deeper.

'Do you know where my mother is?'

I tried to look affronted. 'No. Why would I? Don't you?'

'I don't know anything. Nobody ever tells me anything and I'm supposed to fend off the Law with their stupid under-occupancy laws and now my dad has allowed Gemma to be taken away by some odd-ball and I don't know where or why. There's only me left. And …'

'If your dad sent her, signed her over …' I trailed off thinking about Stacey. Two weeks, two kids missing, equalled too much of a coincidence.

He didn't notice my distraction and scoffed. 'Means nothing. He doesn't care about anybody but himself.'

'How do you know it was the guy with the gold tooth who took her?'

He looked at the horizon and chewed his lip. 'Because I stole something.'

In the west, people steal stuff all the time and get away with it; it's the violence Joe cracks down heavy on. But in the east, the material stuff is cherished and stealing is taken much more seriously. If Stuart had been on the rob, then chances were he was on the run which explained the clambering around fields and the bag of worldly goods over his shoulder.

'Okay,' I said trying to exude calm, 'what? What have you stolen and where from?'

It might have been my incredible people skills but Stuart's sweating and jittering stopped, or at least eased off. 'A security DVD from Gemma's school. And it shows the guy in the suit taking Gemma away. By the hand. Out the gate.' He gestured a holding hand motion in case I didn't quite get it.

'And you're sure it was definitely the same guy from the park?'

'Definitely,' he said. 'And when I went back to the school, after watching the footage, he was there again talking to the teachers. And a whole bunch of Reds in their full riot gear to back him up.'

'Because of a DVD? Bit picky, even for easty standards.'

'That's my point,' he said like I was some sort of dullard just keeping up. 'And Gemma's got none of her stuff with her. No toys, teddies, no clothes, nothing.' We'd reached the end of the beach and sat on the rocks at the foot of a cliff.

I didn't want to freak him out so asked real gentle, 'Do you think it's anything to do with your mum?'

'Maybe, yes,' the same are-you-stupid tone, 'but Gemma's six. I'm eighteen. If they were going to try and get info out of anybody it would be me. But even I know nothing. What good is a little kid like Gemma to them?' He started to get agitated again.

Softly, softly. 'Right,' I said. Let's go hang around at the school and see if we can catch him again. Maybe we can follow him home or something.'

'I already know where he lives.'

Wow, full of surprises. 'Great work. Where?'

'I'll show you.'

The walk back through the fields was silent and tense. I tried to lighten the mood by mentioning the trees and the weather and all sorts of happy-chatter nonsense but Stuart wasn't having any of it so I gave up.

The house Stuart showed me looked too big for its garden. There were huge windows on all three floors, each blacked out with wooden slatted blinds. Half a dozen steps led up to the shiny, black front door and the whole house looked like it might stand up and walk away any minute. Spooky.

'Let's come back in the morning, early,' I said. 'We can wait until he's gone out and then break in. There's bound to be some clues hanging around in there somewhere.'

'Why would you do that?'

I shrugged and shook my head, wide-eyed innocence. 'What do you mean?'

'Why would you do that for me? For Gemma? Why do you care?'

Good question, Stuart. 'Just because.' I clapped my hands. 'Meanwhile, fancy a drink?'

'Don't do that.'

'Look. I've got nothing better to do.' He didn't look convinced. 'Besides,' I tried to look cute, 'I like you.' He looked even less convinced so I went as close to the truth as I dare. 'That bloke is a prize nob and he's been chatting up young girls in parks. He might have taken others, babies, maybe even a baby I know. Not to mention he tried to put the frighteners on me. I want to cause him trouble any way I can. And I'm a westy. Causing trouble for the authorities is what we do.' Better. His face relaxed and he looked away. I asked again. 'Drink?'

He shook his head. 'Nah. I need to keep my head down. Find somewhere to bunk down for the night. I daren't go home.'

'Stay at mine if you like.'

He opened his mouth as if to speak but no words came.

I remembered the wad of notes his dad had handed over. 'Though there's hotels up east you could likely stay at. Probably more your thing.'

'No, it's not that,' he said. It's just. Well. You don't know me.'

'You don't look like a serial killer. I can tell these things. I've got good instincts.'

By late afternoon we made it home and I cooked an early dinner while Stuart got acquainted with the cats. He picked up the runt of the latest litter, a little girl called Fluff. She looked teeny in his huge hands. His fingers were thicker than Gav's, shorter, and looked too large and clumsy to be gentle, but the kitten snuggled into his palm like she knew him already.

'She likes you,' I said. 'Do you have cats at home?'

'No. No pets.' He turned Fluff over and looked at her belly. 'She's got something stuck in her fur. It's tugging at her leg.'

Fluff's mother sat watching him pull her little one about but never moved to intervene. When he pulled the thorny twig from the matted fur he spoke to her. 'There, that's better, isn't it?'

I saw Stuart looking at the photo over dinner, the one of me with Mum and Dad, but he never mentioned it. He ate with impeccable table manners and for the first time I saw the carriage for what it was - a dump on wheels. When he stood to clear the plates I leapt up. 'No. I'll do it.'

'I don't mind.'

'I do.' I threw the dishes in the sink and, desperate to get him out of there, said, 'Let's go for a walk.'

'Wouldn't it be best to lie low?'

'No.' I didn't mean to snap. 'Sorry. But, no. Come on, it's stuffy in here.'

We walked the tracks in silence and the steady beat of blast funking soul from the station felt warm and welcoming.

'It's okay,' I said when Stuart hesitated at the entrance. 'There're no cameras and the kids are cool.'

'But, it's not safe. For me, I mean. I'm not from round here.'

'It's safe, trust me.'

The station was one of the few places that kids went to relax. The Law came by now and then but for the most part they left us alone and, being tucked away behind an old shoe factory, the rest of the adult world stayed away too. Only a few crumbling walls remained and grass grew through the concrete floor. When it rained it was miserable, but on such a fine midsummer night it was the place to be.

There were loads of kids already clumped into groups and I led Stuart past them all to a table with a selection of drinks. A few of the guys said, 'Hi' and looked Stuart up and down but wandered away to do their thing.

I plucked out a bottle. 'Let's have a drink.'

We sat track-side so we could watch in case any Reds showed up and we needed to make a quick get-a-way. We passed the bottle between us. In my line of work, it's best to keep a clear head at all times. My decision making hadn't been great of late anyway, I wasn't about to make it worse by adding alcohol to the mix, so sipped very little and watched Stuart relax into a happy, easy slouch. The music pounded from mega speakers hooked up to an old butcher's van. The jockey stood on top of the roof and yelled at the girls sitting on the slab near the middle of the grass patch. 'Let's see you shake those toots!'

And they did. They stood and shook and Stuart's eyes nearly leapt out of his head.

'Bloody hell,' he said. I laughed. He looked at me and laughed back. 'What the hell?'

'Don't you recognise any of them?'

He squinted. 'Holy moly. The one in the red used to be in my geography class.'

'We get a lot of easty girls over here,' I said. 'Come looking for their bit of rough.' I nodded to the slab. 'Tarts table, the lads call that.'

He shook his head. 'Bloody hell. Her mum would go nuclear if she knew – she's a right snooty cow.'

Stuart had clearly led a sheltered life. It must have been all that looking after his little sister. The alcohol went straight to his brain. Everybody watched him dance. He moved with an easy rhythm, like the tunes camped out in his bones. He grabbed my hands, 'Come on.' The beat travelled from his fingers to mine and when it slowed he pulled me in, his hand warm on the small of my back, and he sang hot breathy words about love and lust into my hair. A message dinged into my phone and I stood to one side. Stuart grabbed one of the girls queuing to get a turn writhing up close to him. He attracted a lot of attention and he wasn't being choosy who he snuggled up to. So much for lying low. But he didn't appear to be trying to impress any of them, he just wanted to move.

My message was from Joe, - *Why have you not checked in? Don't make me come over there.* – Lying to Joe made me feel queasy but I texted back – *All good, getting early night.* - An immediate response - *Stay safe x.* There was no going back now. At least, not without Gemma.

Later, Stuart vomited behind a stone stack. 'Oh Lordy, I'm sorry, Atty.'

'No probs, mate.'

There was a shift in the atmosphere and the girls on tart's table stood as if one. They messed with their hair and tugged to straighten their skirts. At the entrance, the lads from Shanks estate strutted in, Gav at the front, looking tall and skunky-hot like he'd just stepped out of a magazine. Leaning into him, all eyelashes and lipstick, the easty girl he claimed he'd elbowed for good. I slipped behind the stack. 'Take it easy, Stuey. Everything's going to be fine.' I plugged in my earpins and tuned in. There were lots of slapping on backs and general buddy-buddy man-hugs.

'Hey, Gav, how're you doing, mate?'

'We're all good,' said Gavin, dragging the doe-eyed blonde by her waist, tight to his chest. He leaned into her neck. 'Sheesh, honey, it's only ever been you I want.'

I pulled the pins and grabbed Stuart's arm, heaved him upright. 'Come on. Let's get you home. We've an early start in the morning.'

CHAPTER NINE

Stuart still looked a little green and grubby when I woke him just before dawn.

'I'm so sorry.' He held his head in his hands. 'I don't usually drink.'

'Forget it.'

'I hope I didn't make you feel uncomfortable, you know, all that dragging you up to dance and stuff.'

'Stuart, shut the ducking hell up. It's fine. I said forget it, didn't I?' I got real mad at myself for letting Gav do it to me. I knew he'd go back to her, so why the hell did I feel so pissed off about it? I was supposed to be playing him and still he left me feeling like a top star dumbster. But Gav being a cheating twonk wasn't the only reason for my being so tense. I'd lied to Joe. Knowing I was no better than Gavin irked me something chronic.

Stuart stayed shut up until we got to Goldy's house. We sat behind a wall in the grounds of a derelict looking office block, opposite his gate, with full view of his front door. No way could he leave without us spotting him.

Stuart looked me in the eye for the first time that morning. 'What if he leaves out the back?'

'He won't.'

'Oh. Okay. If you say so.' He looked away but I caught the eye roll.

Ten minutes later, Goldy trotted down the steps and sauntered up the road. The limo pulled up at the corner, he climbed in the back, and it rolled away. The relief settled my nerves just a tad.

'Right.' I said. 'I'll go in through the back garden. You wait here and if he comes back – make sure you stall him.'

The back of the house led onto an alleyway lined with cameras. I lingered at the entrance and wiped the sweat off my face. This was a major tipping point. If I went ahead and broke into an ISS agent's house, the Law would surely find out and then I'd be no use to Joe as a listener ever again. I'd be forever dodging and ducking and, if it proved unjustified and Gemma was with her mum, or even M Gee, and the whole thing was a massive misunderstanding after some minor communicative hiccup, I might even have to leave the county for good.

But if I didn't do it, I'd have to go and tell Joe how big I'd messed up. And I'd lied to him already. He wouldn't trust me again, even as a listener, and probably send me to start again elsewhere. So the same result, whatever my action. And Gemma might be in trouble and I could save her and be a hero and jump the queue for promotion - my heart thumped with the possibilities. Might as well go for it.

I took a few big breaths and walked up the alley, hands in my pockets, whistling. If I looked any more chilled my eyeballs would freeze.

Goldy lived five doors up. The wall around his back yard stood four meters tall with razor wire around the top. His back gate used to be blue but the cracked paint was spider-webbed from years of harsh Welsh wind and rain. Decay had settled along the base. I kicked at it with my boot until two slats gave way, just enough for me to get my fingers behind and yank them out. One winter of ice is all it takes to weaken a gate that old. I dropped to my belly and wriggled under like a snake. If anybody happened to be monitoring the alleys' cameras at that moment, then I reckoned it gave me three clean minutes to do the job and get the hell out. One second over and I had every intention of dissolving into a major, frenzy-riddled panic.

The garden looked rough with neglect. A fake wishing-well stood lopsided and abandoned near the steps leading up to the door. I waded, knee deep, through spiky-sharp grass to the house. I felt the sun branding the back of my neck bubbly pink. I jumped down into the pit by the basement window, hopefully putting myself beyond range of the camera perched high on the wall under the edge of the pitch roof.

The window frame looked solid white plastic, ugly and impenetrable. The panes were at least triple glazed. They'd make out like an explosion if I hammered them in. I cupped my hands to peer through and almost whooped when I spotted the latch hanging askew and useless. Somebody had beaten me to it.

The brief image of a hooded, knife-wielding lemondropper lurking in the shadows ahead of me, flashed through my head and I swear my heart paused. But I breathed deep and forced my grit to pull itself together. Even I wouldn't be that unlucky; I'd had my fair share of the stuff already, surely to God. I eased my fingers under the rim and prised and heaved. It gave like a dream and I scrambled through, dropping into a dusty cellar. I made straight for the inner door, noting nothing but dirt and spiders along the way. I took the stairs three at a time and came out in the passage with the kitchen to my left, front door to my right and living room opposite.

In the living room there was a massive desk parked in the bay window at the front of the house. There were papers everywhere. I scavenged through looking for anything that looked vaguely to do with children and/or boarding schools. The get-ready-to-panic clock ticked way too fast in the back of my head, synchronising with the thumpthumpthump of my pulse, loud in my ears. I tugged at the drawers, one stuck fast, guaranteed to be *the* one. I yanked and rattled so hard the desk jumped out of position but the drawer refused to give. Holy frickety frogging fridges. My head screamed at me to forget it, that it was a crappy bad idea, and to get the batting hell out of there. I raced to the kitchen, rifled the drawers, found a knife and ran back to poke and prod it at the lock. I screeched in frustration before the drawer slid open. Yowzy – always knew I was wasted as a listener. Something panged as I wondered if I'd ever be able to brag about this natural talent at lock-breaking to Joe.

Inside the drawer lay a folder. I opened it for a quick scout and paper-clipped to the top page, thank you all the gods everywhere, was a picture of Gemma. I didn't stop a second longer than necessary but ran for the front door. A complicated double-slip-lock type system almost had me peeing my pants, but once I tucked the file under my armpit to free up both hands, I managed to unclick the latch and was away. Outside, I leapt the steps and legged it across the road like my bum was alight. 'Quick, run!'

And we did. Up the street, onto the tracks, off into a field, along its edge and down into the old quarry. I heard dad whisper in my ear, *Don't look back, Atty. Run.* I scrabbled down the bank towards the water, gravel rolling beneath my feet, dust clouding and sticking to my damp skin.

'Stop!'

I stopped and sat down with a bump that rattled my teeth, panting like a dog at the races. I must have held my breath the whole way out of there. I looked back at Stuart leaning over, his hands on his knees.

'Bloody hell, Atty. You can't half run.'

I grinned and waved the file. 'But I got it.'

He skidded his way down and sat so close our thighs touched. 'Quick, let's see.'

The file shook in my hands. 'Is that you trembling or me?'

He laughed. 'Bit of both I think.' And he moved away, just a little.

I handed him the sheet with Gemma's photo and looked at the next in the pile. I examined the picture of the girl, the same one I'd seen Goldy talking to in the park. It listed her details as twelve years old, her address somewhere over the east side. So he'd got her after all. The next page put my nerves right on edge. The podgy, smiley baby in the snapshot looked the spit of Fran's. The address confirmed it. I read on as Stuart's arm tensed beside mine. There were minutes of a meeting and numbers. It didn't make sense. 'What does it all mean?'

Stuart's jaw twitched. His warm, clean, twinkly, blue eyes turned an icy grey. 'The git. The dirty, selfish, scheming git.'

'What?'

'My dad sold her. Sold Gemma. Look.' He pointed to a signature next to a number big enough to buy the whole of Shanks estate.

I looked back at the paper in my hands. Carl's signature, next to a sum of £300,000. Under that another signature, supposed to be Fran's. But I knew Fran's writing and that wasn't it. It was her name, but in somebody else's hand, maybe - no, probably - it was Carl's.

I'd been mad angry before, of course I had, everybody knows what it's like, but the anger that I felt towards Carl exploded bigger than anything I'd ever experienced before. It slammed huge and uncontrollable into every nerve and muscle of my very being. Tunnel vision, red haze, black hole, whatever. I knew, without doubt, Carl would pay, my head cleared and my mind focused into one stripped-clean thought – kill Carl. I scrambled back up the side of the quarry and strode west towards the toxi-plant.

Stuart followed, prattling away. 'Where are you going? You can't go back there. We have all we need now, look, we know where Gemma is. You said you'd help.'

But nothing and nobody was going to stop me.

Carl had worked at the toxi-plant since baby Stacey had been born. He didn't get the job because he was smart, but because fathers took priority whenever a position came free. The chance to earn money was probably why he stuck with Fran and Stacey in the first place.

The bloke on the gate answered pleasant enough, if abrupt. 'Carl James? Not turned up for a couple of weeks. Lost it now, plenty of others needing work …'

I walked away.

There are only two pubs left in the west, both are twenty-four-hour fleapits. The first I headed for not only sold alcohol, but the local addicts their lemondrops.

Stuart held my arm. 'Atty please, stop. You can't go in there. Jesus no. Please, Atty.'

I shrugged him off. 'Keep back, Stuart. I swear I'll rip your face off if you get in my way again.'

He let go and stopped at the entrance.

I stood inside the door and waited for my eyes to adjust to the gloom. There were several lads sitting at a table in the corner, an old man at the bar, and a couple of creepy guys in old threadbare suits at a table by the back door. None were Carl. I searched the ceiling for the inevitable camera.

A barman with a beer barrel belly came through a door to stand behind the bar. He looked me up and down, slack-mouthed and dull-eyed. 'What can I do for you, love?'

One of the lads in the corner said something which made the others laugh.

'I'm looking for Carl James, worked down the plant, blonde, ugly like a pug.'

The old man snorted, 'Ain't what he claimed, is she?' He chortled until he coughed - a phlegmy smoker's hack. 'You Fran? He told us you were hot.'

I kept my eyes on the barman. 'Has he been in lately?'

He shrugged. 'Maybe, maybe not.'

'Seen a poncy guy in a suit about? Gold tooth?'

He put his hands flat on the bar and gave me the look all blokes did when they didn't want to answer a straight question. 'And what's it to you?'

I smiled. 'Cause he's got ISS Approval.'

He stood straighter, his face greyed out, and he twisted a tea towel between his hands. I looked at the lads in the corner who had fallen quiet and were listening good and hard.

'Yep, an Approved ISS agent. Hope you were all on your best behaviour.'

One of them glanced, he didn't move his head just his eyes, towards the bottom corner of the bar. I walked down the length and there, crouched in the corner, sitting on his heels, looking like some little kid who'd just shat his pants, was Carl. He stood and smiled, *smiled.* The group behind me jeered, one said, 'Oops, caught red-handed, mate.'

Carl squirmed a little and smiled again. 'Hi, Atty. How're –'

'Did you forge Fran's signature? Sign the baby away?'

He shot a look at his mates and shrugged. 'Seemed for the best.'

My fist connected with his face, clean and sharp. His eye socket popped, my second knuckle squelched into the soft tissue behind his cheek bone, his head jerked back, cracking his neck and he got sent onto his scrawny arse.

'Get up. Get up!' I yanked at his hair, trying to drag him to his feet. 'Call yourself a man, a father? You useless heap of freaking crap. Get up!'

He grasped at my wrist trying to support his weight. I raised my knee and slammed it into his face, putting all the force of my grief for Fran behind it and blood and snot spattered in all directions. I flung him sideways. He crashed into the table, glasses flying, blokes stepping back, 'Jesus Christ she's gone mental.'

I looked at them. My teeth ached with mad fury. 'Too fannicking right I have.'

And that's when Gavin walked in the door. He stood staring at me, mouth open. 'What the hell are you doing?'

The barman grabbed me from behind. 'Out.' I dropped to a crouch. He let go. I leapt to my feet, span around thrusting the heel of my hand into his jaw, his teeth slammed shut. I threw my left fist into his throat and ground my heel into his right shin. Hard.

Hands grabbed from all directions, pinned my arms to my side and dragged me kicking and screaming to the door. I spat at them all, the barman on his knees, Carl on all fours bleeding into the broken glass, and Gavin watching from the corner with his mouth drooping open.

When the men got me outside they dragged me down the alley alongside the pub, behind the crates and threw me to the ground. I leapt up and they knocked me down. I tried again and again but each time they knocked me back a little harder. My lips grew tight, my nose turned numb, and my eyes transmitted everything through a tunnel of red.

Then it stopped. Stuart stood square in front of me, legs spread, fists clenched. Calm and solid. 'Leave her alone.'

'You need to rein her in, mate.'

'And you need to take yourself off, mate.'

They laughed, 'Oh do we? Take ourselves orff, eh?' But the laughter became fainter as they turned and wandered away.

Well, who'd have thought?

Stuart knelt next to me. Those huge hands, so gentle, picked the dirt out of my face. 'Bloody hell, Atty. What have they done to you?'

CHAPTER TEN

When I woke the skin on my face felt like it had been stretched tight like a drum and every inch of me flamed red hot. And oh sheesh did everywhere ache, deep into the marrow of my bones. I flinched and squawked when I tried to sit up.

'It's okay, Atty. You're okay.' Stuart eased me back into a lying position. 'You need to rest for a while. Wait there, I'll get you a drink.'

My thick tongue and lips wouldn't work properly and I dribbled the water down my chin. It tasted nasty anyway, like warm rusty iron. 'Where are we?'

'In a beach hut. I didn't know where else to go.'

A torch hung from the ceiling and beamed a weak ring of light onto the dry sand. 'What time is it?'

'About ten.'

I needed to check in with Joe. 'Where's my phone?' It hurt to talk and my voice came out nasal. My nose must be broken. I reached up to touch it.

'Don't.' Stuart held my hand and pulled it away from my face. 'Try not to fiddle. I fixed it while you were out cold. Must hurt like hell though.'

He could say that as many times as he liked. I groped in my pockets and found my phone. No signal, but three voice messages. All from Joe. Then I remembered why I didn't really want to speak to him. I'd spotted a groomer and chosen not to report him. And now it was too late because the creep had taken Gemma and Stacey and God knows how many others. I flung the phone to one side not having the stomach to listen to what Joe had to say. Not yet.

Next time I woke, the sun shone shards of light through the cracks in the hut. I tested each limb and pulled a few faces - frowned, smiled and ran my tongue over my teeth. I wrinkled my nose and instantly regretted it when a sharp pain sliced into my brain. But, all in all not too bad, other than the nose, nothing appeared to be broken. I picked up my phone, checked the battery - still plenty - switched it off, and put it in my pocket. Coward.

I crawled out of the hut and sat in the sunshine. The warmth seeped through my clothes onto my skin, nursing the bruises. Cliffs towered over three sides and only several feet of sand lay smooth and damp between the hut and the sea. A lone swimmer headed from the east, parallel to the shore, in a slow crawl. I recognised Stuart's sun-striped hair. He arrived opposite the hut and waved. I waved back. It felt like we'd slipped into some weird twilight holiday movie. Maybe I'd died.

He called from several feet out. 'Um. Would you like to avert your eyes for a minute or pass me the towel?' He grinned. 'I'd hate to embarrass you.'

I needed a tree or a rock anyhow, so definitely not dead. 'Give us five.' I inched away to the bottom of a cliff edge. My knee throbbed - from smashing Carl's teeth, no doubt. I hoped they'd popped clean out and he'd choked on them. As I ducked behind a suitable rock, I sneaked a peek towards the hut. What they say about the ratio to a man's hands? All true.

I lingered long enough to listen to the messages from Joe. As predicted he sounded manic mental. - *I've had bunches of Reds banging on my caff door looking for you. Do you know how much trouble you've caused? Getting into pub brawls, breaking into Approved houses … what were you thinking? I hope Stuart isn't with you. He'll be better off on his own.* - The last message began with a long silence. When he did speak

Joe's voice sounded thick with disappointment. - *Sometimes, Att, it's better to sacrifice idiots like you for the sake of the movement. You're a liability.*

I wanted to cry.

I turned the phone off to save the battery and wandered back to the hut. Everything had spun clean out of control. And so fast. I sat next to Stuart. 'Without Joe on my side I've got nobody.' I hadn't intended to say it aloud.

'You're not alone,' said Stuart. 'You've got me.'

'No offence, but I'm not sure that's going to help me much.'

'Well, offence taken. You could at least try me?'

And so I told him. I told him how I was supposed to be looking out for him. How I'd been such a crummy best friend Fran had hung herself and that's why I'd taken my eye off the ball and Gemma got taken away. How I'd been such a numbsky to not report Gold-tooth while I had the chance – before he took Gemma. How mad Joe was at me, even let him listen to the messages, I left nothing out and told him all of it. He sat with his legs bent, elbows on his knees looking out to sea. He didn't interrupt and waited until I finished before he said, 'You were sent by the resistance to spy on me?'

'Look out for you,' I said. 'It's different.'

'Course it is. I wondered why you were being so *helpful*.'

I had no defence and I put my head in my hands. It all made me want to curl up and switch the world off.

'And,' he said, 'you knew that guy was looking for kids.'

'Not Gemma. And not exactly. I just knew there was something dodgy about him. I got instincts.'

'Yeah, you said.'

'She's *your* sister.' I wanted to bite the words back.

'Yeah, she is.' He looked beyond furious. 'And what about that Red you keep riding around with, what's that about?'

'He's got this idea I'm up to no good. He seems to be keeping an extra close eye on me for some reason.'

'So let's just clarify the situation here,' Stuart tilted his head, faking a polite interested look. 'Right now we're under the special interest of a Red, the head of Basley resistance would like a word, and we've robbed the office of an ISS approved agent. Anything else I should know about?'

I thought it safest to say nothing.

'And,' he said again – there were an awful lot of ands - 'You lied to me.'

'No. I just didn't tell you everything.'

'Same thing. All that crap about trust and instincts.' He stood up. 'I'm going for another swim.' And he strode towards the water flinging his tee shirt into the sand but, this time, left his shorts on.

I considered leaving. Letting him come out of the water and finding me gone. But the beach was unfamiliar, we could have been anywhere and, well, where and who would I go to? The only advice came from within - Dad, *'Think positive, Atty.'* Yeah, right.

When Stuart came out of the sea he sat next to me, knees bent, relaxed and easy. 'This,' he said nodding at the sea, 'is my favourite place in the world. Whenever anything gets too much, this is where I come.' He looked into my eyes. 'Nothing is ever as bad as all that when you're sat right here.' He pointed at the sand between his feet.

'Ah okay,' I said. It was only a pile of sand - sand, sea and sky. Whoopy doo.

'I hope when I die, not only for it to be in my sleep, but here, with sand between my toes and salt in my eyelashes.'

He looked deep into my head. 'It's not working for you, is it?'

I shrugged. 'Mm. I'm not against the idea.' The cold coming off his skin cooled my arm and I smelt the sea in his hair. It made me feel grubby as a bin bag.

'I've been thinking,' he said. 'If everybody is cheesed off at us at least we know where we stand, right? It means that we know the only people we can rely on is us. Nobody else. Now, I know we might not be a lot, but I reckon we're enough. Between us, we can find Gemma and Fran's baby and bring them home. Joe will be so impressed he'll forgive you for everything. In fact, he'll promote you. He'll groom you to take over when he retires.' He smiled at me. The salt patched in little circles around the stubble on his chin. 'See?'

Talk about delusional. Extreme positive thinking at its best, Dad would love him. 'Well,' I said, 'it was always my plan to get promoted as soon as possible, even be the boss one day. Blowing my cover and getting twelve shades kicked out of me is all a part of that process, of course.'

He nodded and pursed his lips. 'Mm, yes. Well, it's good to know everything's going so well, to plan as it were.'

We both studied the sea. I still couldn't see the fascination. It didn't look like it might be about to do anything spectacular, it just sat there, splashing about.

I took a deep breath. 'I do understand why you might be a teeny bit cheesed off with me too though.'

He pulled a stern face. 'Yes, I bloody am.'

I laughed.

'No. I bloody am. Why are you laughing?'

I put on a mock voice. 'You bloody are, are you? Bloody hell. Are you bloody, bloody?'

'What's wrong with bloody?'

'Bloody cricket and horses ... pass the bloody decanter.'

'Have you suffered a knock on the head or something?' He shook his head. 'Man, you batty-crazy woman.'

We spent some time studying the file and came to the conclusion Gold-tooth must have been the main signatory. 'His name has to be Crawlsfeld,' I said.

'It kind of suits him.' Stuart had drip dried but his hair looked like he'd spent an hour preening. He screwed his nose up. 'Creepy Crawly Crawlsfeld.'

The children had been sent to a place in North Wales called Sapton Manor. There were glossy photos of what looked like a holiday park with ponies and go-karts. Your child is our future read the tagline.

'It all looks so ... well, nice.' I said.

'Yeah.' Stuart didn't sound convinced. 'It doesn't make sense though, does it? If it is all so nice, surely it would cost the parents to send kids there, not the other way around.'

'We need to go and check it out,' I said.

'Mm.'

'We'll get the money off Carl and your dad, and buy them back.'

He gawped at me like I'd suggested we hurdle the moon. 'We can't go back into Basley. We'll get crucified. Or worse, we'll be arrested.'

'Well then we'll get them back some other way. If we have to leave Basley anyway, we might as well go north and suss the place out. What else are we going to do?'

'Given all the people looking for us, we can hardly hail a taxi, can we?'

So much for positivity. 'Well, there are other modes of transport,' I said. 'If we can get to Craffid, we could jump a cargo train. When it slowed at a junction or something.'

Stuart scoffed. 'Um, you've been watching too many movies. And in any case, how far are you going to leap with that gammy knee, uh?'

I stretched my leg and winced. 'It is a little sore, granted.'

Stuart gave me a told-you-so look. 'Let's get a decent night's sleep in so we're fresh for tomorrow.' He reached into the hut and unpacked the last of the food from his backpack. 'The only way I know to get on any transport is to pay top dollar so you're right, we need money. We're going to have to hope one of us dreams up an idea to get some.'

Everything, everything, came down to money in the end.

CHAPTER ELEVEN

I woke early and lay listening to gulls screech and the ocean slap and shrush on the wet sand. Stuart didn't emit so much as a heavy breath let alone a snore - a silent sleeper and another box ticked on the look-at-me-I'm-such-a-perfect-specimen form. I bet I'd snorted and dribbled half the night. I crept out of the hut leaving him curled under a towel and hobbled to the edge of the sea. Its vastness was emphasised in the early light, and it lay so still, as if it might be preparing to pounce. The waves lapped no bigger than puppy licks onto my toes and the water felt dense like cool milk, but looked clear and refreshing. I stooped to scoop and bathe the stickiness off my face. My nose had bled again during the night and black crusts pulled at my lip. I must have looked like walking road-kill.

We'd squabbled a little the night before and failed to agree on what we should do next. Stuart wanted to speak to his dad about money, but I didn't think it was such a good idea. We'd thrown the pros and cons around until we'd agreed to sleep on it. Back to back.

'Yeeeeehahhh!!!' Stuart sent me leaping out of my skin as he ran past me into the water. I stumbled backwards, falling to a sit in the wet, and caught a flash of Stuart's white bum disappearing into the water.

'Argh. Now look.' I only had the one set of clothes and they were already grubby enough. I stood and swiped at the wet sand stuck to my rear.

Stuart's head broke the surface. 'Come on in. The salt water will do you good.'

Yeah, right, like I was about to strip and flop my fleshy bits around in front of anybody, least of all him with his six-packed gut and tight bum cheeks. 'We haven't got time.' I stomped off to my rock and stayed behind it until he'd got out of the water and got dressed. Me, shy. I would never have credited it. We needed to get away from the place, before it turned me soft.

As Stuart pushed the last of his gear into the bag, I tried to convince him that Carl would be a better source of funds. I struggled to stop short of pulling rank and tried to tell him gently. 'I'm experienced at this sort of stuff. I know how people in the resistance and Reds from the Law think.' Stuart, for all his money and education, struck me as being pretty thick. 'Think about it.' I pressed on. 'Nobody will expect us to go back to Carl again. Whereas everybody's going to think you'll turn to your dad, right?'

'Everybody probably will, yes. Then, after they've thought we'll go to my dad, because that would be the obvious thing to do, they'll think there's no way we'll do the obvious.' Stuart used the tone that jangled my nerves, the one that people like him reserved for idiots. 'Which is why they won't bother watching him,' he said. 'And the one person who won't be expecting me to go to my dad is Dad himself. He knows how much I hate him and how I hate going to him for help.' He raised a finger. 'Usually. Trust me, he will be totally relaxed thinking he's finally got shot of me. See? I've thought it all through.' He stood, slung his bag over his shoulder and tapped his temple with his finger. 'Genius.' He walked away.

I limped after him. 'But they'd be even less likely to think I'd go back to Carl. I mean he's got to be mad at me, only an utter plum-head would go and ask for payback, right?'

'So,' he said in a sing-songy, take-the-mick voice, 'you admit, you'd be a bloody plum-head to go and see Carl, right?'

'So,' I sang right back, 'you're just going to waltz up and knock on your dad's door, right?'

'Nooo.' He drew the word out like he spoke to a child. 'I shall arrange for him to drop it somewhere. The quarry strikes me as a good potential spot. We can see people coming for miles from up there.'

I had to admit, the quarry was isolated and barren so not too bad a location for a secret meet. And I didn't really want to risk another pasting. It hurt. 'How do you know your dad will do it? You don't want to make contact if all he's going to do is squeal to the Law.'

'Easy,' he said. 'I'll threaten to tell the Law I've got something stashed at the house, lemondrops or something, and there'll be a bunch of Reds escorting me, in shackles, to his front door before dark. With a warrant.' He gave me a smug grin. 'He won't risk that. All that shame and embarrassment on his doorstep? His tart would throw a right wobbler. Trust me, once she goes off on one there's no shutting her up. Especially if they get thrown out of the neighbourhood – they do that, you know, chuck people out of the community if they show disloyalty to the Law. Dad'll do all he can to keep me and the whole mess out of his wife and the neighbours' way. I know it.'

I decided to let things brew a little in both our heads. Maybe, just maybe, he was right.

At one end of the bay, tucked behind a huge rock the shape of a dragon's head, was a path of rugged steps. On the climb, Stuart stopped to look at the view at frequent intervals giving me chance to rest my knee. How the hell he got me down there I daren't ask. The undignified image of being carried or dragged with my mouth hanging open, shirt up, belly out. It made my head hot. 'Couldn't you find anywhere more difficult to get in and out of? Like the bottomless well on planet Zog?'

'You're very welcome, Atty. Think nothing of it.' Sarky git, when he wanted to be. At the top of the steps Stuart nodded towards something behind a bush just out of my eyesight. 'Do you want a ride?'

I caught him up and looked to see what he was talking about. A rusty wheelbarrow rested upside down in the long, fawny grass. It had a single fat tyre, bald and shiny, it looked comically pathetic and utterly useless. 'Uh. No.'

'No need to look quite so appalled. How do you think I got you here? Carried you over my shoulder like Superman? It's fifteen miles.'

The mental picture of me slumped in the barrow, arms dangling either side, head lolling … it really couldn't get any better. So much for the hard-core, rock-chick look I'd worked so hard on.

'Come on. Sit in it for some of the way at least.'

'No chance.' I strode ahead, stiff-legged and wobbly. 'I'll walk.'

It took hours to get back. Not once did Stuart complain. I saw his understanding silence as yet another example of how darn perfect he was. No way could I have been so reasonable had it been the other way around, and knowing it annoyed the hell out of me.

The quarry was enormous and round with a lake at its base, like an enormous post-squeezed zit on an otherwise flat landscape. They called it a lake, but it was deeper than it was wide and, no matter how hot the day, the water always looked dark and bitter cold. My dad used to reckon that, from outer space, it must look like a neat little septic boil on the arse of the world. Basley being the arse - totally believable.

There used to be security patrolling the boundaries to stop kids wandering in and drowning - electrified fences and armed guards, the full works. But nowadays, local kids stayed away through choice as their parents' recited tales of trolls and goblins living in the water waiting to grab little ankles and drag them down, down, down.

We clambered, me painfully, to the top of the quarry lip. The heat distorted the air above the white gravel, shimmering like gas, the only other movement being the odd fly. I swear I heard the dust settle when we stopped to consider our next move.

'This will do nicely,' Stuart said. 'Can I borrow your phone? I ditched mine.'

'Why?'

'It had a trace on it.'

I wanted to ask who would do that and why but it felt pointless. If it was gone, it was gone. Stuart's earlier chirpiness had vanished and he'd turned back into the scared boy I found at the edge of the blocked tunnel. His nerves unsettled me. 'Are you sure about this?' I asked.

He laughed. 'No.' He looked at the phone. 'This is chipped, yeah?'

I nodded. 'Only Joe will know how to trace it. He has the code.'

'He wouldn't give it to anybody, would he? No matter what. No matter how angry he might be at you, right?'

'He'd die rather than turn me in to the Law if that's what you mean. But be quick. According to the movies you've only got a couple of minutes once he answers.' I waved my hands around. 'You know, in case there are Reds tuned into the airwaves or something.' I didn't like relying on information from old movies, but it was all I had for a base point. Stuart was supposed to be the educated one. Perhaps he should have read more. In science maybe.

'And if Joe turns up?'

'He won't. He just wants me to stay away, remember?' That was an out and out lie. Of course he'd come looking, or at least send somebody else, but hey, it slipped out by accident. 'Just be quick. In case of anything, okay?'

We stood on the ridge at the top of the quarry, nobody else around, no movement, no anything.

'When you're ready,' I said.

Stuart cleared his throat, fidgeted and scanned one last time before thumbing in the number. He put the phone to his ear and drew a swift deep breath, blowing it back out hard, like at a candle on a birthday cake. 'Dad? … Don't tell anybody I rang … bring five grand cash - now. To the quarry. Else the Law will be round your house. I mean it. Place it down by the water, behind the biggest rock and then leave. Oh and have a happy life.' He stabbed at the phone and handed it back. 'Woah, phew.' He panted and sweated as he paced about. 'I feel like I'm in an old spy thriller of some sort.' He rubbed his face with the hem of his tee shirt. The muscles on his stomach were tight and pronounced. Tick.

'Mm.' I turned away. Must concentrate. 'Was that enough of a threat, do you think?' I screwed up my face and adopted Stuart's deep tone. 'I mean it?'

'He'll know I mean it.'

'Okay.' Even their threats sniffed of super snobby politeness.

'All this drama is a bit embarrassing, really,' he said. 'We're probably over-reacting, right?'

'No.' I looked at the time on my phone. 'How long should we give him?'

'Don't know. What do you think? Half hour?'

'Where will he get that sort of cash from in half an hour?'

He frowned and answered like I'd asked the stupidest question ever. 'In his safe.'

'Five grand?'

He nodded, hands on hips. 'Yeah.'

'Well if it's so easy to hand, perhaps we should only give him ten minutes.' The unfairness and bitterness of how some people had it so easy sharpened my words and I could see they poked at him.

He squared his jaw. 'Okay. Ten it is. You're the one who does this sort of thing all the time, after all. What with all this experience you've got.'

'Ha de ha. Five grand? I wish.' I scoffed, deliberately misunderstanding him. 'I've never even seen that much dosh.'

'Well you will today. Let's see how quickly it changes your life.'

It sounded like he had a chip of his own to lug around. Our team of two didn't seem to be gelling quite as we'd hoped.

Ten minutes is a long time.

Stuart yo-yoed between embarrassed and pooping his pants in panic. And he started to sweat. 'He's not coming.'

I checked the time again. 'It's only been two minutes.'

'What if he's gone straight to the Law and dobbed me in? Or to Crawlsfeld? He'll know it was us who broke into his house by now, won't he? Or even Joe…'

'Your dad doesn't know Joe.'

'No. Okay. Hurray for that. He won't go to Joe.' He jigged his knees and his feet shifted in the gravel. 'Out of all the options,' he said. 'I'd have kind of preferred Joe.'

'If you kept still and shut the hell up we'd hear him coming sooner.' I said.

The silence felt palpable. It clogged thick inside my ears like earplugs, as if the air itself tried to stop us from hearing anything. Talk about paranoid.

We heard the high whine and saw the dust clouding above the road long before we spotted the moped bounce its way along the track. Stuart kept his eyes focused on it and started that irritating jig again. 'Shall we try and get the bike off him too?'

His dad looked ridiculous, like he'd never ridden the thing before. He wore a suit, the jacket open and flapping about, his tie stuck out over one shoulder.

'Is it his?'

'Of course. Well, mine. We used to go over the old motocross track when I was a kid. Used to be good fun, back in the day.'

'Then, yes. We need to get to Craffid somehow and that looks like as good a way as any. And we can stay off the main roads.'

'Right.'

Neither of us moved. My knee hurt like buggery, I didn't feel up to a sprint across the open gravel.

Stuart took a deep breath. 'It's going to have to be me who collects the bag and rides the bike.'

'Oh, yes, you got there eventually. Just took a little time.'

He shot me a look. Ha, not so perfect after all.

Stuart's dad careered through the broken gate, the bike's back wheel skidded in the dry dirt, and the engine squealed loud like the whole world would hear it. When he turned it off and stuck the bike up on its stand, my ears continued to ring. Nothing else came up the track behind him. To get to the water he had to climb over the quarry's lip and down into the pit. He adjusted a backpack and looked up and around the rim. Stuart and I ducked, my face squashed painfully against the sharp gravel.

Stuart wide-eyed, mouthed, 'I'm going to hide behind the rock to wait for him.' The sweat bubbled on his top lip and even more ran down the side of his face from his hairline.

I nodded and played dead, didn't so much as breathe while Stuart skidded away.

Stuart's dad stood on the edge of the pit and looked down towards the lake, hands gripping the straps of the backpack, his chest heaving. Thank God he didn't look my way. As he dropped to his haunches to scurry down towards the water I eased over the edge and did the same towards the bike. I'd meet Stuart there. If I couldn't help collect the money, at least I wouldn't be a pain in the backside and delay our getaway. The last thing I wanted was for him to think he might be better off without my tagging along. When Gemma came back to Basley I wanted her to be holding my hand.

The bike stood propped on a stick thing and was much bigger than it looked from up above. And tattier. I gripped the handlebar to test its weight. Definitely heavier than it looked too. I sat astride and kicked at the stand, like I'd seen it done in those movies I'd been banging on about, and almost toppled over when the stand sprung up into its underbelly. I was leaning over looking to see how to pick it back out again when the thrum of another vehicle came up the road behind me. Something big, like a lorry. I looked up to the quarry rim, no sign of Stuart. Through the gate came a van, complete with The Law logo. Holy sheeshing claptrap.

I don't know which bit of which movie I'd seen it in, but I turned the key and stamped on the pedal sticking out by my good leg. When the bike started I assumed the rest would be easy. All I had to do was steer, right? Wrong. Mopeds don't just move - things need to be squeezed, twisted and manipulated. I did it all. Somebody shouted and I did it all again, only with a bit more desperate pleading, and the bike's back wheel span, the front reared, and I was away. Slowly. The brainless Reds ran after me so I twisted and tweaked until my knuckles turned white. Stuart scrambled down the side of the quarry yelling at me to wait for him, but that would have meant, not only figuring out how to stop, but risking getting caught by the gorillas in the bandanas. Instead I veered towards the gate with the intention of leading the Reds in a circle to give Stuart time to get to the bottom. The Reds, not having a brain cell between them, were too daft to consider splitting up. Dumbskies of the first degree. I relaxed my hands to slow the bike as much as I dare, without falling over, and Stuart leapt onto the bike behind me.

He yelled into my ear. 'Change gear!'

'What? How?'

He reached both arms around me and shuffled my hands off the handlebars.

'I need to hold on! '

He squeezed me between his arms, the engine roared, the front wheel reared, and I slid back into his crotch and squeaked.

Stuart's breath warmed my ear. 'Let's get out of here.'

CHAPTER TWELVE

'You squeaked.'

We were sitting eating some bread and cheese bought from a farm. 'My knee hurt, okay?'

'Oh, right, okay.' Stuart smiled. 'I've been thinking.'

'There's nice.'

'We could skip the Craffid and train plan, and steal some fuel from somewhere. Ride the bike the whole way. What do you think?'

'They'll be looking for the bike. I bet they've already got in touch with other counties telling them to watch out for us. And fuel stations have high security.' Without the right paperwork even five grand couldn't buy us fuel.

'I meant steal from a farm or somewhere not a fuel station. I'm not a complete pancake.'

'Still too risky. Besides, that bike makes my arse sore.' My backside was about the only bit of me that didn't ache after my beating and I planned to keep it ache-free. 'I vote we stick with plan A.'

'Fair enough. I suppose risking another theft charge would be a dumb move in any case.'

When Stuart rolled over so easily I got the impression he'd only suggested the idea so he could let me have my own way. I'd seen Joe use the same trick on his lady-friends, as he liked to call them. He'd let the little lady of the moment make a few minor decisions so when something major cropped up he played at being all super reasonable, But honey, you've had your way all the time lately. Now it's my turn. He'd go gooey eyed, bat his lashes in mock flirtation and simper. Just this one teeny thing. Trying to make them laugh. I swallowed. Well, I wasn't going to let Stuart do it with me. Not that he simpered and his face looked pretty much expressionless.

But I didn't want him to start playing games with my head — we needed to focus. We had to find those kids and get them home, not only for their sakes, or Stuart's, but for mine. Call me selfish, but I had to get back into Joe's good books. I needed the resistance group like I needed my blood. I knew nothing else and had nowhere else to go. What started out as a way of keeping my hopes alive for promotion had now escalated to my keeping my home and Joe, the only family I had left.

I broke little bits of bread off a loaf and eased them to the back of my mouth past my split lips and aching teeth. 'I wish you'd got soup,' I said.

'Do you want me to go back and ask? They might have some. Or ice-cream might be good.' He looked at me, straight-faced.

'No. Stuart. I don't think it would be a good idea to draw any more attention to ourselves, do you?'

He shrugged. 'Suit yourself. Stop moaning if you don't want me to fix it.'

Fair point. Annoying though.

We counted the money. Stuart handed two big bundles over to me. 'In case we get separated.'

I held them in my lap. 'I need to shop for some new gear. I've worn these clothes for days and they've got blood all over them.'

'You girls and your shopping.'

He wore all the latest trends. He used shops where people like me couldn't even get through the door and he had the cheek to roll his eyes at me. 'You think I look fit to travel, do you? Blend in? With all this blood and crap all over me?'

'It suits you. The urban fantasy look.'

'Don't be a dick.'

He scoffed and stood up. 'You are so touchy sometimes, do you know that? I was having a laugh. You do know what one of those is, don't you, Atty? It's where people try and look for the bright side in life.'

I stood too. 'Not all of us have a bright side. You and your let's give Daddy a ring for Five. Frecking. Grand.'

'I'm scared too, Atty.'

'Yeah, you would be. But I ain't. I'm fine, thank you very much.' I sounded a proper twonk.

He picked up his bag and slung it over his shoulder. 'It's easier to be angry than afraid, I get that. But …'

I held my palm in front of his face. 'Don't you dare start your educated psycho babble on me.'

He stopped.

I moved my hand and rubbed my palm on my thigh. The silence and the way he pursed his lips and stared at the floor, told me loud and clear I'd stepped over a line.

'Whatever, Atty.' He looked up, straight into my eyes. 'Whatever. I'm not going to argue with you.'

I hated reasonable people. They got right into my orifices.

It's very hard not to touch the driver when riding on the back of a bike. I sat as far back as I could, my legs spread wide, and my hands on my knees.

Stuart sighed. 'Hold on, Atty.'

'I'm okay.'

He let go of the handlebars. 'Just hold on. I've already scraped you up off the floor once. I don't want to have to do it again.'

He was such a nob. I grabbed his tee shirt but stayed well back on the seat. 'Happy?'

He drove off without a word.

We left the bike in an old stable block at the top of a hill overlooking Craffid. I'd never been to a city before and my stomach bounced around in excitement. I forgot I wasn't supposed to be talking to Stuart and asked him if he knew where to go for the train station.

'Yes,' he said. 'But we can go to the shops first. Then maybe a hotel. We both need to freshen up.' He looked at his watch. 'We might be better off getting a train in the morning. The station is a proper doss house at night so best avoid it if we can.' He didn't sound sulky, simply cold and detached. And he avoided my eye. Fair enough. Better to keep a professional relationship anyway. All that frolicking good fun at the beach had been nonsense.

I set off ahead of him. 'Okay, your call.' He could take this one, the next, if important, would be mine.

When we walked around the shopping centres it soon became apparent who had all the money. The cities, or rather those places that received overseas dignitaries, boasted fully funded teams of specialist security officers rather than the useless rabble of wannabes that made up the Law at home. No wonder they didn't allow the likes of us to move in. Our money might be good enough, but once we spent it they wanted us to sod off home to our hovels. It almost made me keep Stuart's money in my pocket. Almost.

I picked various items of clothing off a rail in a small select store. The girl behind the counter glowed bleach-clean pretty and showed off the same blonde, sun-kissed hair as Stuart. He smiled at her and she cutesy smiled back.

I waved the clothes in front of her face. 'Can I try these on, love?'

'Course.' She indicated a curtain in the corner and fiddled with something on a shelf under the till.

Stuart hovered nearby, his hands in his pockets. 'I'll wait here.'

Yeah. Course he would, being male and therefore so, so predictable. I refused to look at either of them. She was likely skin shallow and brain dense. Good luck to him.

In the changing rooms I took the first good look at my face. My eye, although beginning to open, had no white to it. The pupil was pin-tiny, the usually ice-blue iris had a dark bottle-blue glassy look to it and the rest glowed a vivid red. My upper lip was so swollen it blocked my left nostril and I couldn't close my mouth over my teeth without wincing. Where Stuart had pulled the muck out of my cheek, a blue-purple bruise surrounded a thick black line. What part of my clothes didn't have blood stains, had sand or dust or some other muck stuck to it. I looked like a walking, or rather a hobbling, bomb victim. I held the new clothes up against me, still on their hangers. Yep, they'd do.

'That was quick.' Stuart looked up from the magazine article that bleach-features was showing him.

'Yep. No point in hanging around.' I tried a pointed smile. Sheesh it hurt. 'I'm not one for tarting myself up. How much?' I shoved all the clothes onto the counter.

The girl slapped the magazine closed and took the money with a pout to put a trout to shame.

I smiled more easily. 'Thanks. You've been too, too kind.'

Stuart half-waved to her from the doorway. 'Thank you.'

We stopped in another shop further along the street where Stuart bought some new gear and then we went to a chemist. He filled a basket full of various lotions and potions. I looked at the aisle upon aisle of beauty products. Painted girls with fluffy hair and talons that could pluck your eyes out studied the shelves. I wouldn't have known where to start. Perhaps they taught such things in school alongside geography.

'Do you need anything else?' Stuart said.

'Na.' I tried to pull a face, still hurt. 'It's for girly girls, isn't it? Not for the likes of me.'

He went to the desk to pay. I wasn't entirely sure what I wanted him to say, but he could have said something. Even if I argued with him, told him off for being daft and patronising. I might have faked a blush and simpered a little and said, Yeah, right. My beauty is au natural. But no, he just walked away.

CHAPTER THIRTEEN

Stuart carried all the bags and I limped alongside as best I could. The sun hadn't set but started to dip behind the buildings, lengthening the shadows and cooling the streets. People moved quickly, their heads down, keen to get home. Stuart led the way to a hotel which looked all glass and period furniture. A bloke in a fancy tuxedo opened the door and kept his eyes on the ground. Talk about posh.

Not many places put real people on the doors or in their reception areas. At most hotels, people arrived and touched screens to check-in. They stood on scales and were weighed, measured, and given a spinal alignment assessment so they could be allocated beds that matched their exact physical requirements. But this hotel had a woman with blood-red nails and a beehive smiling at us from behind a blue granite desk. She wore an old fashioned tailored suit and high spiky heels.

When Stuart signed his name as J Frank I understood why he'd brought us for the pricier, personal touch. A top-tart receptionist is more easily fooled than a face recognition box. He showed her a fake ID and when she glanced at me he came over all authoritative. 'She's with me. She'll only be here an hour or two.'

Oh nice. Consider me flattered.

'Of course, sir.' The woman's face had such a thick layer of slap pasted over it she had the plastic look of a doll. 'That will be an extra three hundred pounds.'

Holy Moly. For an hour? It had better be good. For that we should expect the full bundle. I stepped forward. 'Any chance of some Hot Blue?'

It looked an effort, but she did manage to address me directly with polite, if tight, efficiency. 'Of course, madam. I'll have it sent up to Mr Frank's room.'

The room turned out to be well smart. It was more like a giant bedsit with two full-size, squichy sofas and a solid oak dining table full of crystal glass and silver trinkets. The Blue arrived almost simultaneously. Stuart thanked and tipped the waiter and then we were alone. 'Sorry about the, uh …'

I folded my arms and waited.

'You know? The um … she's here for an hour stuff.'

I watched him squirm for a little longer then tried to grin, ouch. 'No problem,' I said. 'It was a great idea, well executed. What do I care what she thinks anyway?'

His cheeks puffed out as he sighed in relief.

I wasn't that scary, surely. 'You must have some weird fetish picking up a tart with this face.' I was referring to my bruises but realised too late it might sound like another dig for compliments, so added quick as I could, 'Nobody would have guessed you were still at school either.' I tilted my head and nodded. 'Impressive bit of confidence there.'

He gave a cute little crooked smile. 'You drink up and relax. I'll use the bathroom first. I won't take long and then you can have a long soak in the tub.' He didn't wait for an answer just disappeared with an armload of stuff through a door that matched the walls. Invisible bathrooms, fake IDs, this was his world but one I could easily get used to, even if it meant being branded a professional tart. I lounged back on the bed, supped my drink and turned my phone on. There were several texts off Gavin and a couple off Joe. I opened the first from Joe. *Where are you, Atty?*

Joe had a quick mouth when he got annoyed but he'd never used it with me around, certainly not at me. I'd only ever seen him being calm and methodical, even when having to make decisions under all sorts of pressure. I opened his second message. *I meant every word about you staying away.* Boogah. *But I shouldn't have shouted. I was worried about you. Stuart is missing now too. Stay away from him. And Gemma – it's being sorted, okay?* I turned the phone off and removed the battery. I didn't know where the chip was located so played safe and put the whole lot into the fish tank in the corner of the room.

'What are you doing?' Stuart stood in the bathroom doorway watching me prod the plastic casing with a spoon to make it sink.

The light from the bathroom shone bright behind him and sprinkled through his sticky-uppy hair. I'd seen him at the beach, but indoors, close up, oh boy. One arm hung loose, slightly away from his body in that way guys with beefy torsos have to leave room for their chest. And did he have a chest. And a stomach. A six-packed, toned, lean begging-to-be-touched stomach. The other hand clutched at his right hip holding the teeniest towel in the world, so low it barely covered the necessary. I looked down to his feet and even they were in great shape. Manicured toe nails for God's sake.

'Atty? What are you doing?'

'You must work out a lot.' I looked back at the fish tank. 'I mean, I'm working at killing my phone. Putting it out. Like a shot. Lot.'

He frowned and walked over to the bed. 'But why? I thought you said it was chipped?' For such a big guy he moved so smooth.

'Yeah, 'I said, 'but Joe can trace it. I think he might be looking for me.'

'To forgive you? Or to …' he looked at me. 'To … I don't know. What do the resistance do to their guys if they foul up?'

I didn't know, not exactly. But this was me, not any old guy. Joe wouldn't hurt me but he was tamping angry, of that I'd no doubt. I swallowed and watched the phone sink and nestle alongside a tiny castle with weeds waving around it. At least the silence wasn't total. There were noises from the street and the sound of water running.

Stuart plucked a bottle of pink liquid out of the chemist bag. 'I'm running you a bath and I'll put some of this in. It'll help with the bruises and aches. I use it after a tough match.' He returned to the bathroom and poured some of the liquid under the taps. When he bent over and swished the water, his stomach stayed drum tight. Not an extra ounce anywhere. He turned the taps off and ambled out. 'All yours.' He rooted through the bags of clothes. 'And yes, I work out.'

Pretending not to hear felt safest.

The bubbly bath water hugged and cossetted my aching body. I have never experienced such delicious luxury. When the water wrapped around my neck I almost wept with pleasure. I couldn't help myself from breathily announcing, 'Oh my God. This is sooo good.'

I lay half asleep until the water began to chill and then examined my knee. It had swollen to twice the size it should have been and looked blue and yellow and red … all colours.

Stuart knocked on the door. 'That's enough. You don't want any open wounds to get too soft. And I've ordered food. It'll be here soon and I want to see to your face before it arrives.'

On the back of the bathroom door hung a white towelling robe. I put it on and studied my face. The mirrors were everywhere so I saw the damage from all angles. Pretty messed up. But I'd taken the odd knock before and survived, this would be no different.

'Sit.' Stuart said as soon as I walked back into the bedroom. He'd dressed in a plain, white tee and black shorts, and had lined up various bottles and jars on the table. He stood over the chair with a pack of swabs in his hand and a grin on his face. 'Doctor Stuart at your service, ma'am.'

I sat. 'Is this what you want to be? A doctor?'

'Hell no. I'm going into politics.' That surprised me and it must have shown. He laughed. 'There's more than one way to make that difference, Atty. And I like my face the way it is. I'm not cut out to do it your way.'

He cleaned my face and applied some paper stitches before he looked at my knee. The way he touched me made me think of Fluff and the twig. Those strong, gentle fingers. I tingled and blushed when I thought what they might be able to do. I fidgeted and looked away embarrassed.

'Sorry,' said Stuart. 'But it needs to be done. We don't want it getting infected.'

I made a show of wincing. 'It's just a bit sore that's all.'

He winked. 'I understand.'

I freaking hoped not.

The food arrived and we ate sitting opposite each other at the table. The lights were low and looking at Stuart set me tingling. I needed to get a grip, we were on the most important job of my life, everybody was chasing our tails, and to top it off he was an easty, which put him on a different planet to me altogether. I gave myself a stern word and put my business head on.

'So, Stuart. What's the plan?'

'We go to bed.'

Oh shivering foofles.

He smiled at the look on my face. 'Get some rest.'

'Yeah, course.'

'And stop worrying. I'm a gentleman. You were safe in the hut, you'll be safe here.'

'Of course. I know that.' I almost added, but will you? As a joke of course, but it felt too dangerous.

He gave me one of his sparkly-eyed looks and winked. 'Not that I wouldn't want to.'

'Um.'

He grinned and raised his eyebrows.

'Way too complicated to go there,' I said aiming for woman of the world-esque sophistication. And I got bossy. 'We have kids to rescue, peace to make, mysteries to solve …' I waved my fork around. 'Speaking of which. If your old man is so rich, why do you think he sold Gemma?'

Well, I know how to kill the mood and that's a fact. Stuart's eyes lost their twinkle and he sat back in his chair.

'The reason he has money, Atty, is that he makes it any which way he can. Nobody gets where he has by being nice.'

'Your mum has money too though, right?'

'Not that I'm aware of. She works as a human rights lawyer. A lot of it is voluntary.'

'Ah.'

'What's that mean? Ah?'

'I'm guessing that's why I was asked to look out for you. You know, she might have defended somebody high up in the resistance.'

Stuart shook his head. 'Nope. She only works for other professionals. Lawyers, politicians, those people who are locked up for whistleblowing and whatever.'

'So.' I said. 'You don't think there are any resistance members smart enough to have a professional career?'

'That's not what I said.'

'But if there was a professional resistance member, your mum wouldn't help them … she'd leave them to rot, yeah?'

'I didn't say that either.'

'Didn't have to.'

He sighed. 'The resistance have specialised people to represent them. We all need to work to our strengths.'

Yeah right, that would be it. But I let it go. 'When did you last see her?'

Stuart took a drink and paused as if considering whether to answer or not. 'Couple of weeks. Or so.'

'I haven't seen my dad for two years.' I said it before I thought it. Weird.

'Woah,' said Stuart. 'What happened?'

He wasn't the first to ask but it was tough to talk about. I didn't think anybody would ever get it. Not Gav, not Fran, not Joe, no one. But Stuart was going through the same sort of thing, even if on a much smaller scale so I talked. 'Over breakfast one day Dad told me he might be late back after work as he had a meeting to go to. I went to my friend's house, came home, and cooked the dinner …' I pushed the last of my food around with my knife, my appetite gone.

Stuart placed his cutlery together in a central line down his plate. 'These are strange times. You must never give up hope.'

'Come back when your mum's been gone two years and tell me that again.'

He wrinkled his nose. 'Fair comment.'

'At least you know your mum's alive.' The words shot across the table far sharper than I intended. 'Sorry. It's not your fault.' I tried to laugh. 'Besides, I'm well over it. It was a long time ago. I'm eighteen in a couple of weeks so I won't be needing him any more.'

Stuart twirled his glass on the snow-white table cloth. 'How do I know she's still alive?' He studied me. 'Do you know she's still alive, Atty?'

I shrugged, 'Pretty sure. Dead people can't request resistance fighters to keep an eye on their kids for them, right?' I snatched at the bottle of Blue and filled his glass, then my own. 'She's alive all right. But first, here's to finding Gemma.' I raised my glass.

'Yeah,' he said, barely above a whisper. 'Gemma.'

CHAPTER FOURTEEN

I woke first and took another long bath. My bones already felt more like my own again. I fancied the swelling on my knee had gone down a little, even if the colours looked more vivid and varied. My mouth looked better too and my eye was fully open but still no white to it. I spent some time trying to disguise the horror and making my hair look good. My new gear made me feel like a proper chic chick. I stretched some muscles, took a few deep breaths and listened to that inner voice. You can do anything when you put your mind to it, Atty. Dad was right. I felt ready to go and rescue some kids. Bring it on.

I crept around the room sorting out the stuff to chuck away. Yesterday's shirt had to go, it stunk something rank. I kicked a shoe and it rolled under the bed. I glanced across to see if the noise had disturbed Stuart and he was lying wide awake watching me. He clearly woke as silently as he slept.

'It's rude to stare.' I said.

He stretched. 'Can't help it.' He swung his legs out of bed and stood upright in one swift movement. 'I'm going to grab a shower then we'll make a move.' I couldn't resist watching him walk to the bathroom door. He turned. 'The kit looks good by the way.' He pushed the door closed and a second later opened it again, a smoky look on his face. 'Verrrrry good.'

I smiled, ridiculously chuffed. I couldn't help but wonder what might happen when all the poop we were in got sorted. I sat in the armchair facing the bathroom door and waited for him to come out. No harm in enjoying the view.

The shower stopped and Stuart whistled as he packed stuff into rustling bags. There was a knock at the bedroom door. I hoped it might be breakfast which is why I opened it with a high degree of melodramatics, like a matador or something, eager to get the food in and the waiter out so I wouldn't miss Stuart walking the room in his towel.

Gavin stood in the corridor.

'Holy shit, Atty.' He stepped in uninvited. 'Who the hell did you rob?' He looked around the ceiling before putting his hand on my hip and kissing me above my ear. 'You look hot, babes.'

I checked the corridor but he was alone. 'What are you doing here?'

'I came to see my girl. Like I said, I'm going to look after you.'

The whistling from the bathroom had stopped.

Gavin sauntered around the room, touching the furniture, mouth open, wowing moronically in appreciation. 'We could get a bundle for this stuff,' he said. 'Take it to that set-up over east.'

'Gavin I don't need you looking after me.' I scrabbled around my head for an excuse to get him out of there. 'I'm on a job.'

'Really?' He sat on the bed, bounced and gave an appreciative nod, like he was some smart-alec hotel inspector. 'Joe asked me to come and keep you company while you lie low.' He opened his arms. 'And here I am.' He chewed his lip and looked around the room again. 'Aha.' He removed the lid of the fish tank, rolled up his sleeve, and dunked his hand to retrieve my phone. His long skinny fingers looked ugly and distorted in the water. 'This won't disable the tracker, Atts. You were out of range for a few days though, where did you go? Joe's been frantic.'

'I was … around.'

'Ah look, the battery has killed the fish,' he scowled as he shook the drops off his hands. 'Made the water stink too.'

The fish floated on top of the water, bug-eyed and slimy. Of course Joe must have known I'd been seeing Gavin. Joe knew everything, especially about me. He'd made it his job to know what I was doing, when, and with whom since the day my dad had walked. Other kids got away with all sorts but not me. Joe would have looked at Gavin on paper and deemed him suitable. Gavin didn't do drugs, kept under the Law radar, and had a solid record of helping out the resistance as and when required. What wasn't to like? The fact that he lacked ambition, slept around and relied on his lean good looks to get favours, slipped past Joe completely. In fact, two of those were admirable qualities if you were a geezer in charge of the resistance.

'Atty?' Gavin lay on the bed. 'Come here.'

Oh God. 'No. You have to leave, Gavin. You can't stay here.'

He sat up. 'Why?'

Still no noise from the bathroom.

'Let's go for a walk,' I said, trying to sound calm.

'Why? Not gone shy on me all of a sudden, have you?'

I squawked a laugh. 'I need some air, that's all.'

'You do look a bit peeky-eyed now you mention it. All the better reason to have a lie down.'

'No.'

'I guess you scammed that soft guy Stuart for a few quids. Do you reckon you can afford a couple more nights here? We'd have a right laugh.' He ran his hands across the bed. 'Especially in this.'

My skin crawled. I thought about Stuart sitting and listening in the bathroom and my hairline heated up a sweat. 'Well.' I slapped my thighs. 'I'm going to take a stroll, coming?'

'I bet he tried it on with you though, didn't he?' Gavin looked delighted, excited even. 'Eh? Them sort reckon all the girls on the west are easy. I bet you gave him a good smack …' He stopped and looked away.

And then I remembered the last time I saw him. 'Yeah, you know how I can give a good smack.' I recalled the gawp on his face as he watched me getting thrown out of the pub.

He had the decency to look embarrassed. 'It all happened so quickly, Atts. I tried to stop them, honest, but before I knew what was happening you were gone. And I didn't know where and … I dunno. It all got a bit messy.'

'Yeah, tell me about it. I bet you never told Joe you watched me getting battered did you? See this.' I pointed at my face. 'Look what they did to me and you stood there and let them. And you've got the fannicking cheek to prance in here stroking the bed and suggesting we have a laugh.' I was panting so took a deep breath, trying to calm myself down and take control. 'I need you to leave.'

'But Joe asked me to come and get you, take you to a safe house. You know what he's like. He'll go mad if I go home without you.'

'Tough.'

We stared at each other. Me knowing I couldn't force him out. It's only that mad, red-rage that gives me the adrenaline boost to do a number like I did on Carl.

Gavin reached for my hand. 'But I'm worried about you. The other night? At your place? It meant everything to me. It's only ever been you I want, Atts.'

Jeeesh. I wanted to leap and put my hand over his mouth or sing 'La la la' at the top of my voice like a kid ignoring a rollicking - anything to get him to shut the hell up. 'Well it meant zero, zilch, sticky sweet nothing to me.' Then added. 'Not that there was anything to feel anything about, we didn't do anything.' I raised my voice for that last bit, to make sure Stuart heard. 'I don't want you, Gav, never have, now please leave.'

Gav's look changed from one of pathetic weed to sneering cockiness. 'Oh. Now I really do get it.' He looked around, hunting for evidence. 'He's been here hasn't he? You've been playing him.' He stood up. 'You've slept with him.' He hooted. 'You have. You've bedded an easty for info. Or was it just to get a night in a posh hotel?' He looked wide-eyed and wired to the max. 'All those times you've banged on about how all those over-privileged nob-heads are responsible for everything from the price of eggs to your mum getting her head knocked off and here you are shacked up in a hotel with some easty ponce and his wallet.' He stepped forward, getting in my face, his breath spattered tiny specks of cold spit against my forehead. 'You're nothing but a slag. No. More than that. You're a hypocritical slag.'

'I didn't sleep with him.' Thank God.

Gavin didn't hear me, or if he did, he ignored me. But he saw the blush. 'Aye, so you should. Joe is going to go mental. You were told to stay away from him. I take it you forgot you were doing the job for M Gee?' He paced and shook his head, a grim sneer puckering his nostrils. 'I've been so patient with you too.' He put on a whiney voice, 'I just don't feel ready, Gav. Maybe next time. When I'm not so upset over my dad or Fran or the weather or any other flaming excuse!'

'That's what you're so pissed about, isn't it?' I yelled back. 'Your ego taking a knock.' I lowered my voice to a shouty whisper. 'You're mad because I didn't choose you.'

'Are you suggesting I'm jealous? He's an easty.' Like that explained it all. 'His sister is no longer your problem. He isn't your problem. He is irrelevant.' He spoke slowly like I was the idiot. 'Jealous, mmf. Whatever he did to you last night I can do better.'

Oh my frilly days. 'Gavin, shut up.'

He snorted. 'Looks like Atty's got one hell of a crush going on.'

'Don't talk soft.'

'Sure?'

'Nothing happened.' I sat at the table with my head in my hands.

Gavin sat on the bed.

No noise from the bathroom.

Gav didn't raise his head to look at me but spoke with a steely edge. 'Joe's told me to collect you and take you to a place where we can lie low until he calls for us. And that's what I'm going to do.'

'I'm not going anywhere with you.'

His eyes were so dark, almost black. 'You have to, Atty. Joe's orders.'

I shook my head. 'No.'

'You have to let the big guys take over.'

'Still, no.'

He switched tactics. 'You've nothing to prove. Or put right. Joe will let this go as a one-off cock up.'

I folded my arms.

'And we can move on from this too. You and me. Whatever's happened, whatever you've done, we can work through it. We're the same, we get each other. We're players. I understand why you did it.' He waved a hand at the bed. 'We're practical. We do what we have to do to get by. No easty will ever understand that.'

'No, I'm not like you. Not at all.' I spoke louder than necessary, made sure Stuart earwigging in the bathroom, heard good and proper. 'I never play anybody. And I don't need some weedy, lying coward to babysit me.' The lying bit I threw in for Stuart's benefit, I hoped he'd heard. 'Tell Joe I'm going to find Gemma and bring her back to Basley.'

Joe would go nuclear if he went home and said that.

Gavin gave up any sort of tactic and simply dug his heels in. 'I'm not leaving without you.'

Stand off. I searched for my dad's advice. *Prioritise, Atty.* First thing, get Gav out of there, away from Stuart. I stood and took fast, huge strides towards the door. 'Like I said, I need some air.'

The receptionist looked down her nose at me as we made our way through the foyer. At the door I turned back, bumping into Gavin who'd stuck close to my heels. I put my hands flat on the desk. 'I haven't been here all night,' I said, 'I came back this morning because I'd left my favourite knickers behind. So don't go totting up all those three hundred quids, because it won't get paid, okay?'

She widened her eyes, stepped back out of spitting range and looked at Gavin over my shoulder.

'No good looking at him, if I wanted to kick off he wouldn't stop me.' I spun round and looked Gavin in the eye. 'He couldn't.' And I flounced out the door.

Gavin stayed close but said nothing. I didn't know where we were or where to go but when I saw the tops of some trees I headed straight for them. Maybe when I die, in my sleep or otherwise, I'll have twigs in my hair and dirt under my fingernails. But these buildings and people were crowding in and getting on my buds.

The park was massive and the air clean and fresh. I walked as fast as my knee allowed until my breathing evened out and then slowed to a less painful strut.

'Feeling better?' Gavin smirked. 'What was that all about?'

'Don't take the piss out of me, Gavin. I'm not in the mood.'

'You left your favourite knickers?'

'It's complicated. And you wouldn't get it if I told you.'

'Have you eaten? I'll buy you breakfast.' He nodded towards a food stall. Several tatty tables with rickety chairs were scattered across a patch of dirt under the trees. 'A sausage sandwich?'

'No.'

'I'm really sorry I didn't step up in the pub. Genuine.'

'Okay, you're sorry. Now go away.'

He kept pace with me, hands in his pockets. 'I've got a surprise for you.'

'No thanks.'

'You'll like it.'

'Doubt it.'

'I know where your dad is.'

'Course you do.'

He pulled a leaflet out of his hip pocket. 'I was going to wait for a nice romantic moment but it doesn't look like that's about to happen, so here.'

I glanced down. 'A propaganda drop. Yippee.'

'Open it.'

The leaflet had been folded four times, like a fan, to fit into Gavin's tight jeans. The front cover read, **'LONDON. Time to expand'**

I tutted. I'd read similar headings a zillion times. All worded slightly differently but all meaning the same thing. Somebody somewhere was pushing for the starry-eyed notion of reuniting the UK, combining the counties, same Laws, same medical care, same education and so on.

'Go on. Open it.' Gavin said again.

So I did and what I read made my heart stop dead. I put my hand on my chest.

'Are you okay?'

'I don't know.' My heart thumped and raced to catch up. 'Is this real?'

'Yes.'

'You haven't doctored it?'

He looked hurt. 'No. Why would I do that?'

'Where did you get it?'

'I found it.'

The picture, the face, with the second paper crease running across under his nose like a thin white tash, was of my dad. 'Where? Where did you find it?'

'There was a pile of them at a newsstand. Read it.'

Award winning International journalist tells us why London should share the wealth and health with the rest of the country.

'He's a journalist.'

Gav nodded. 'An award winning journalist. He's changed his name to Sal Greg. Lives in Europe somewhere.'

'All this time.'

Gavin frowned. 'You're happy though, yeah?'

I didn't know. Of course Dad being alive had to be a good thing. I'd thought he might be dead or locked up, but never did I think he'd just run off to be a journo. 'He left me.' I said. 'Left me and went off to write stupid leaflets. Left me in West Basley with the cons and the paedos.'

'He left you with Joe.'

I laughed, gobsmacked. 'Are you serious? Joe is a lot of things but nurturing daddy he ain't. I wouldn't leave my cats with him let alone a kid.'

'Hey. I thought you and him were tight. He's always looked after you. He's been good to me too, all of us.'

True, but I didn't want to listen to reason. 'Joe should at least have let me know that Dad was safe, don't you think? He watched me cry at night.'

'Maybe he doesn't know.'

'You never were the smartest, Gavin.' I screwed the leaflet up and threw it at him. It bounced off his chest and he caught it. 'Take it back and show him. Tell him I've seen it and there's no need to look out for me any more. I'm going to go and find Gemma.'

'You're not thinking straight,' said Gavin. 'Why didn't your dad tell you, eh? Maybe Joe wanted to tell you but couldn't. Come home, let him explain himself at least. And forget about this Gemma kid. Let Joe handle it.'

And then a spark of the red flash shot behind my eyes. 'Yeah, you're right.' I said, 'I should just forget about Stacey too. Remember her? The baby your mate Carl sold?' Gavin floundered for something to say. 'Stay away from me, Gavin.'

Gavin had seen that flash behind my eyes often enough to know when to keep his distance. It might scare him, but it scared me even more. The fury is real, heavy, like a brick in my chest, squashing my lungs and sticking in my throat. It makes me want to claw at my own flesh let alone any poor sap who gets in my way. I snatched the leaflet back out of Gavin's hand and shoved it in my back pocket. 'I'm going to find out who wrote this rubbish and kill the bricking lot of them.'

I walked back to the hotel, past madam Poshtits and into the lift. Gavin could take the stairs or wait outside, or drop dead. As if I gave a frack. But as soon as I opened the bedroom door I knew Stuart had gone. All my stuff, including the lotions he'd bought for me, lay in the bin. All he'd left behind was a small bundle of cash next to the fish tank.

CHAPTER FIFTEEN

I found Stuart sitting at a table in a café opposite the train station and slid into the seat opposite. 'Hi.'

His face told me nothing about what he might be thinking. 'Hi.'

'I wondered where you'd got to.' I looked at the empty mug he held in both hands. 'Can I get you another drink?'

'Yeah, why not? Coffee, black.'

I fetched our drinks and two huge cheese rolls. Gavin hovered outside but he might as well have been squatting on the table between us.

'Your friend is still with you.'

'Ignore him,' I said. 'And he's not my friend.'

We ate in silence. I wanted to tell him about my dad and the leaflet, but I worried it might look like I was seeking sympathy or trying to detract or delay the inevitable chat about Gavin and everything he'd said. I blushed. The café heaved with other customers. Some were the suited and booted officey type but an awful lot looked homeless and desperate. One guy, lemondrop-skinny, hovered at the doorway asking everybody who passed if they could spare a fiver. Occasionally a security guy happened by and moved him along. Within seconds he was back. I watched but nobody gave him anything.

'I'll get him a sandwich on the way out,' Stuart said.

'It's your money he's after, not food.'

'It's a waste of time giving him money.'

'You think?'

'He'd only buy more drugs and kill himself.'

'Maybe if you had his life you'd want to spend it in an alternate world too.'

He gave a maybe or maybe not shrug. 'Possibly. Lots of people might be better off dead but it doesn't mean I feel comfortable helping them along.' He looked at me. 'Where would you draw the line, Atty?'

'What line?'

'The line where you give up on people and assume that it's okay to give the likes of him the tools to kill themselves.'

I fidgeted. 'None of us have the right to make that call.'

'That's right. So we get him a sandwich.' He stood and went to the counter.

It was clearly time to meet the serious and assertive Stuart but, what I wanted - no, what I needed, as much as I hated to admit it, was a hug. There were a lot of layers to how I felt - betrayed, gullible, abandoned, but top of the list – lonely.

'Coming?' Stuart had returned to the table and was looking down at me. 'Can't sit here all day.'

Stuart didn't simply hand over the sandwich he shook the guy's hand and asked him how he felt, like he was trying to prove some sort of point – maybe that he wasn't just an over-privileged nob-head. I pretended to fish something out of my pocket. If it was some type of good-citizen test, I didn't want to take it. Guaranteed I'd cock it up.

There aren't any trains running to or from Basley, haven't been for years. The trains only run between major cities like Craffid to London or Birmingham. Consequently, there are few seats available and each one is subject to a bidding war. Sometimes even money isn't enough and people have been known to spill their blood to get their family where they need to go.

The station was huge, an ancient warehouse-type building with a cavernous glass ceiling which grabbed sounds and whirled them around the roof space. The platform vibrated into a single mass of bodies, like a giant rolling maggot, and the noise grew and spread until it buzzed a continuous hum.

I stuck close to Stuart as he pushed his way through the crowd to the touts who stood on boxes along the back wall. He stopped when there were about six bodies between us and the action.

'Aren't you going to go up and ask?' I spoke into his ear. Stuart looked behind, scanning the crowd. 'If you're looking for Gavin,' I said, 'he's outside, watching the door.'

A man with a thin, tired looking wife told us he'd been waiting a week trying to secure a ticket. 'Why don't you walk?' he asked us, 'You're both young and fit.' He looked deflated, like all the hope had been wrung out of him years ago. 'People have been known to die waiting for a seat they can afford.'

Stuart ignored him and turned to me, 'Look, this is too obvious,' he said, 'We need to think of a plan B.'

More like plan F.

When we'd moved out of earshot I hooked my arm through Stuart's, trying to force us back to that closeness we had in the hotel room. 'It must be because they haven't much money. But we've got loads, right? We'll get something. Or why don't we go back and get the bike? My arse can handle a bit of an ache.'

'It's probably been nicked by now. Anyway, can't you think of a better idea than going backwards? You're supposed to be the, what was it again? Oh yes, the *experienced* and *practical* one.'

He was likely right about the bike, but I could do without the stroppiness. 'Listen to me. Gavin has weird ideas about reality, warped, we're not even that close.

Never have been. He's different to me. Practical?' I huffed. 'That's the longest word I've heard him say. He thinks he knows me, but he doesn't.'

'Is that so?' he walked faster.

'Ease up. My knee.'

He stopped, hands in his pockets, looking at the sky.

We were standing amidst a bunch of sweaty foreign students that stunk to hell and back, the noise was doing my head right in, and all the while I kept thinking, 'Dad's alive. Dad's a journalist. Dad's alive. Dad's a journo.' Round and round, over and over. And all Stuart's sulkiness did was piss me off even further. 'Yes.' I spoke into his face. 'That is most definitely so. Why would you believe him over me?'

He didn't speak for ages and when he did it was so quiet I had to lean in to catch the tail end. ' … know, more than anything else is, did you tell him?'

'Tell who what?'

His eyes narrowed. 'You know what I mean. Gavin. Did you tell him where we're going, where Gemma is?'

'No.'

He looked so angry.

'No! Why would I do that? You heard what was said, he came looking for me to take me home.' I scoffed for effect. 'I wouldn't tell him anything.'

'Yeah I heard what you both said when you were in the room, but you took him outside. Though I suppose I should be grateful I didn't have to listen to you having a good old mess about on the bed, huh?'

'Mess about? Is that posh easty talk for a shag?'

A passing kid paused to smirk. I gave him the finger and he laughed before strolling away.

Stuart put a dead-end look on his face. 'Such a lady.'

People nudged past, jostling us sideways and into each other. The skin on Stuart's bare upper arm was hot but dry when it brushed my cheek. I rubbed his scent off me and scowled at anybody who happened to make eye contact. Very few.

'Look,' I said, 'can we do this somewhere else?'

Stuart set off at an almost trot.

I tagged along as best I could. 'Where are we going now? Can you at least slow down?'

He headed back into the café, bypassing lemondrop-guy trying to flog his sandwich, and ordered more tea. The easty answer to everything. I stood alongside him trying not to wince with the pain of my poor knee.

'I think you should go back with Gavin,' he said without taking his eyes off the tea being poured out by a fat woman with damp, yellow patches at her pits. When she looked at me I held up my hand.

'Not for me, ta.'

'Gavin's right,' said Stuart. 'It's dangerous and if you go home at least the resistance might stop chasing me down. I've enough to worry about.'

'The resistance isn't chasing you, it's only, well … it's only Gavin.'

'Sent by Joe.'

'Joe's been lying to me.'

'What?'

'He's been lying to me. For years it would seem.'

He raised his hands to stop me saying any more, paid the woman with a note, waved away the change and carried his mug to the same table we were sat at not half hour earlier.

I sat opposite him, as before. 'I thought you didn't like going backwards.'

'Eh?'

'Nothing.'

'I can't think about your problem with Joe right now,' he said. 'In fact, I can't get mixed up in your life, Atty. In case you haven't noticed I've got enough hassle in my own life to unravel. Maybe when I've found Gemma and you've sorted out what and who you want …'

'But I do know. I want to find Gemma and Stacey. Everything else can wait.'

He looked uncertain, wavering.

I kept up the nagging. 'We can do this … we can get Gemma back, your mum need never know she'd gone anywhere.'

He put his head in his hands and groaned. His knees jigged under the table, heels tapping a rapid beat on the tiles. 'I don't know what to do.'

'I do. If we want tickets we look for the greedy guy.' I deliberately misunderstood him and the look on his face suggested he knew it.

'Everybody is greedy for something, Atty.'

'Okay, the greed-iest. In fact, if we just flash a little of your cash about, chances are a ticket guy will find us.'

'I'm not sure.'

'If I don't find a way to get us tickets I'll leave you alone. I'll go back with Gavin and leave you do it your way. Deal?'

'It's not that I don't want you with me...'

'Good.' I stood up. 'Come on, let's get on with it.'

And so we trawled the stalls outside the station, picking up items and bartering. We never showed too much cash at any one table, but each time Stuart took a wad out, it was from a different pocket. To any individual trader, he might look flush, but not so much to risk getting arrested or a beating for trying to steal off him. We let everybody know we wanted tickets. A tout would find us, I felt certain of it.

When we paused to touch and try on some seriously costly scarves I spotted, for the second time, a bloke in a hood shifting in and out the crowd. As he lit a cigarette I noted he was too old for his clothes, must have been around the late thirties mark and still wearing baggie combats and a tog-hood. When we made eye contact he overcooked the deal by raising his chin before walking away. Talk about amateur. I crouched to re-tie my boots and check for any suspect types lurking nearby. None appeared obvious. Apart from Gavin, of course. I stood and lowered my voice to Stuart. 'I think we've got our man already.'

He swung his head round to gawp in all directions.

'Don't.' I grabbed his arm and checked my tone. 'Try and be a little more subtle, eh?'

'Yeah, course, sorry. Who?'

'The guy in the hood, walking up ahead over there.'

'What makes you think …'

'Trust me, okay? We haven't got time to stop and chat about it.'

We followed the hood and Gavin followed us. Like we'd left the romantic thriller and slipped into an old political farce. As the hood dodged into a dowdy looking back-street pub I considered whether we should stop off for a violin case.

Stuart hesitated. 'The last time one of us went in a pub things didn't turn out too great.'

'I survived.'

'But even so.' He stopped and looked at the boarded windows and patched up door. 'Are you sure about this?'

'No. But that guy in there's either got tickets or a twitch.'

Stuart fidgeted.

'Got any other ideas, Stuart?'

'Suppose not.'

'Then let's do this.' I pushed at the heavy door and stepped inside.

Before my eyes had finished adjusting to the gloom I scanned the bar looking for our mark. He stood alone at the end of the bar, his back to us. But, in fairness, I could hardly mistake him as there were no other customers. The only other person present was the barman who was younger than the typical and only glanced at us, 'You got ID?' before looking back to his phone.

'Not stopping,' I said and headed straight for the hood.

Up close I reassessed his age. Maybe late twenties but weathered and likely lemondropped into early wrinkleville. His cheekbones stood out sharp and pale, probably because his face had caved in where his teeth had either fallen out or been knocked out. There is no such thing as a pretty junkie. 'You know where we can get tickets for a train north?'

He looked at my chest. 'Of course.' He closed his eyes in a slow blink. When he opened them he was looking back at my face. 'How do you want to pay?'

Stuart stepped up to my shoulder. 'Cash.'

One of the hood's eyebrows twitched. 'Friend of yours?'

Stuart nudged me sideways. 'I'm the friend with the means to pay. Cash is the only thing on offer here.'

The eyes drifted down, past my chest to my feet and all the way back up. I fought the urge to squirm as my skin crinkled up with revulsion.

Stuart grabbed at my arm. 'Let's go. He's got nothing for us.'

'How much?' The bloke leaned on the bar in an effort to look casual but the angle of his feet, flat on the floor, suggested he felt anything but.

'Depends.' Stuart paused to swap his backpack from one shoulder to another. 'We need to go today.'

'Tonight is the soonest I can get you out. But it will cost. A couple of hundred each.'

Woah. Bargain. I squeezed Stuart's arm hoping to transmit the importance of not showing any excitement. The last thing we needed to do was hint we would pay more.

Stuart snorted. 'You sure know how to have a laugh.'

Easties might not know much, but I should have known they'd know how to close a deal.

The guy smiled and shrugged. All nonchalant smuggery. 'Then don't go.' He reached into his hip pocket and pulled out his ID. 'If you change your mind. I'll be at the Jermaine Street entrance after ten.'

The ID looked authentic enough. It had a chip and a watermark across his grey face and liver spot eyes. Charlie Davies. Stuart stared at it before turning and walking away grabbing my arm as he passed, encouraging me more than pushing me out of the door.

Outside he asked, 'What do you think?'

'We still haven't got any tickets.'

'I know,' he said, 'but would you recognise a ticket if you saw one?'

Good point. 'I got the man though, yeah?'

'Yeah, Atty.' The roll of his eyes was obvious in his tone. 'You got the man.' But he smiled.

We spent the afternoon hanging out in the park trying not to draw attention to ourselves and staying out in the open where Gavin couldn't move in too close. Stuart lay down and turned his face to the sun.

I couldn't keep it in any more. 'Gavin showed me a leaflet with a picture of my dad on it.' Silence. He made out he cared, understood, but then just lay there like a lump of lard. 'Say something,' I said.

'Well, in what context? What did the leaflet say?'

'It was one of those political pamphlet things. An article about how great the world would be if we all united and got ruled from central London.' I waved my hand. 'You know the sort of thing. The photo of the reporter who wrote it, it was my dad.' Only as I spoke did I realise the photo might simply be wrong, but I kept talking, hoping to make sense of it all in my own head. 'It was definitely him, and he looks older than when I last saw him so it might be right.' I showed him the picture, smoothing out the page where I'd screwed it up.

'Where did Gavin get it from?'

'A newsstand so he said.'

Silence. Then, 'Would he lie about something like that? You know, doctor something to lure you home?'

'Gavin wouldn't have the noggin to think something like that up. And we haven't all got access to fancy digi gear, you know?'

'Who else would make it up?'

'Well that's just it,' I said. 'There's no reason why anybody would.'

'It might be a mistake. You know, photos next to each other on a database somewhere, maybe he looks enough like the writer for the leaflet guy to get it wrong. We've all got our doubles out there.'

I shrugged. 'Anyway, that's what we were talking about, Gavin and me, not about you or Gemma, or where she might or might not be.'

'Ooof.'

I looked at him lying there with his eyes closed, topping up his tan. 'What's that supposed to mean? "Ooof".'

'You're trying to guilt-trip me for thinking everything is about Gemma. Well, I know it isn't, at least not always, but for now, for me, it is. If you can't make finding Gemma top priority too, at least for the moment, then it might be best you go back with Gavin and sort out this business with your dad and whatever it is that's going on between you. Sorry, but that's the way it's got to be.' His eyes were open and looking at me in that way that made me feel like he could read every thought I'd ever had, 'When I get Gemma back, I'll help you figure it out, but not now.' He tried to soften his words by reaching across and running his finger up my arm. A shiver rippled up to my neck. I shook him away. 'I'll come and find you later,' he said. 'When life's back to normal.' The air around us hung heavy and serious. His eyes flicked back and forth across my face and everything went quiet. 'You're a …'

'A what?'

The mood shifted and he lay back and turned his face away. 'Nothing.'

'No, come on. Let's get this atmosphere cleaned up. What am I?'

'A … distraction.'

I thought of Joe, *You're a liability, Atty*. A small twinge of panic niggled at my gut. 'You came to me for help, don't forget. What's changed?'

He shrugged. 'I don't want you to get hurt. Again.'

'Eh? I can look after myself, you know? Nothing's changed. In fact, it's even more important I find Gemma and bring her home. I need to sort this mess out. Prove to Joe and everybody else, including my dad, I can be a good resistance soldier. Make a difference.' Anger and determination put a crack in my voice. Stuart was behaving like I'd served my purpose already. Maybe he thought I wasn't worth the cost of that second ticket after all. Or that I was more vulnerable because I was a girl. I gave Stuart a hard look, determined not to whine. 'Without me you wouldn't have got this far. Or have the promise of a ticket. We had a deal. I'm coming with you.'

The hard look I threw at him bounced off and hit me in the face. He was staring at me deadly serious. 'Okay. But Gemma first then your dad, yeah? That order.'

I nodded. 'Definitely. Gemma it is. Who's Dad? I don't know a dad.'

He didn't smile. Not falling for my cheeriness for a second. 'We'll find him, Atty. I'll help you. Promise. But when we do, make sure you listen to his reasons for going off the way he did, eh? No biting his head off without giving him chance to explain himself.'

'Why do you think I would?' I feigned affront, desperate to switch the mood to something more comfy. 'I'm a reasonable person. I'm not aggressive or mean. I'm fair. That business with Carl was a one off.' I flapped my hand and put my nose in the air.

'Mm.' At last he relaxed, even gave a little smirk. 'You killed the fish.'

'That was an accident. Besides, they were fish.'

'And you didn't half put the frighteners on that Gavin chap.'

'Not hard was it?' I laughed.

'It's not funny.' But he grinned. 'He's still out there.' He sat up, leaned on his elbow and looked somewhere into the distance. 'Behind that tree.'

'Okay, not roll-on-floor hilarious, but it's funny enough. Gavin is a nuisance, nothing more. He's got no money so won't be able to get on the train. Ignore him.'

'Fair enough.' Stuart lay down again but reached for my hand.

'We'll sort it all out, you'll see,' I said. Not sure if I was convincing myself or him.

'Course we will. Course we will.'

I think he might have actually believed it. Unless he was playing me. Either that or the innocence of the rich embedded itself deeper than I'd thought. Always possible, in his easty world: things did have a way of working out for the best. I was more used to things turning bad. And the potential for bad looked immense. But the feel of his hand in mine felt good and, well, maybe we'd get lucky.

CHAPTER SIXTEEN

I woke cold and stiff from lying on the hard ground. The sky had clouded over and the sun hovered just above the roofs of the houses skirting the park. Only a few dog walkers wandered the trails and they kept their heads down, hands deep in their pockets. Stuart slept on and I pondered about how far from home we were about to travel. The familiar tingling sensation as the adrenaline raced the blood to my head set me on a natural high. Surprising I'd slept at all.

'Time we made a move,' said Stuart. 'We should eat something before we go to the station. Those cargo trains take hours.' His waking so quietly was beginning to freak me out. I eased to my feet and tested putting weight on my gippy leg. He frowned. 'You okay?'

'Yep, pretty good. That stuff you put on it worked.'

He shrugged and turned away. 'Hope it doesn't rain.'

Another thing about being on a job and the adrenaline kick and belly flutters and all that other stuff, is it makes me lack patience with stupid comments. 'We're about to go jump a dodgy train ride and you want to make idle chit-chat about the weather?'

'No.' He swung the backpack over his shoulder. 'Let's go eat.'

At dusk a different breed of hawker comes out to line the streets and shout at passers-by. They reach out and grab at peoples' clothes. 'Here, love. Look what I got, suit you it will.'

Stuart remained polite as ever. 'Thank you. Not today.' And he put his arm around the small of my back, his fingers hot through my shirt. He leaned in close. 'Just keep walking.' His breath tickling my cheek.

We went to a proper restaurant and sat at a table in the window.

'Gosh, posh nosh what.' I grinned.

'Yeah, well. It's what we over-privileged nob-heads like to eat.'

'Ouch.' I made a show of flinching. 'Those were Gavin's words not mine.'

'So, you've never thought of the likes of me as being over-privileged or a nob-head?' He stared at me, eyebrows raised.

Not sure if it might have been the dim lights but I couldn't figure out whether he was joking or not. He didn't smile but neither did he look angry. 'Well, I might have said something like that at some point but I didn't know you then. Don't tell me, you've always looked at us westy kids with nothing but respect and admiration.'

'I've been trying not to look at you.'

'Yeah, that would be right.' I fidgeted under his gaze. 'You're staring now all right.'

'Only because you're so damn sexy. It's hard not to.'

I laughed - it came out a bit like a hoot. I mean, what the…? I picked up the menu. Talk about awkward.

'When I look at you,' he said, 'I want to touch you, sniff your hair, breathe you in.'

A cool breeze sucked up the hair on the back of my neck and tugged at it gently. It tickled like drying sand and I fought the urge to swipe at it, brush it off. 'Stop it, Stuart. Be serious.'

'I am. You wanted to clear the air and that's what I'm doing. Get everything out in the open. And I have to confess, my intentions for you are not all to do with project Gemma. I have other plans for you too. When Gemma is safe at home, obviously.'

My head felt bulky and exposed. I lifted the menu right up high in front of my face so he couldn't see me. I'd been called tough and cool and snazzy and kooky … but sexy? Never. I couldn't help smiling. 'Behave yourself.'

I realised my error almost immediately. At some point I was going to have to put the menu down and the longer I left it up, the more awkward it would be, but I wanted the stupid tickle, blush, and smile thing to go away first. So girly and so, so embarrassing. Stuart sat in silence waiting. I lowered the menu a fraction but kept my eyes on the list. And then I peeped. His eyes were twinkly and nerve-twanging cute.

'I mean it,' he said. 'I've been struggling to keep my hands off you since that day you spoke to Crawlsfeld in the park.' I looked at his hands resting loosely on the table. Sheesh, I imagined them tickling their way down my belly. My face burned.

The waiter appeared at the table. 'May I take your order, madam?'

I almost jumped up and kissed him. 'Um, yes please. Just a green salad.' My stomach fizzed. It wasn't like my guts didn't have enough to cope with already - no way would I be able to eat.

Stuart sat back and after a brief scan of the menu ordered a steak with a gluttonous variety of side portions. 'Need to keep my strength up,' he said as the waiter wandered away.

'Yes,' I said adjusting my cutlery and flapping the napkin onto my lap. 'Do you think that Charlie bloke is genuine? And can he get us on the train okay?'

Stuart sighed theatrically. 'I'm trying to tell you I find you irresistible and you want to make idle chit-chat about some dodgy twit in a questionable outfit.'

I straightened the napkin and brushed at my lap. 'It's important we concentrate on the job.'

He took a massive breath and sat up straight, hands flat on table. 'Okay. Can we trust him? Will we make it onto the right train? No idea. We're just going to have to take a chance. Nobody ever got anywhere without taking a few risks in life.'

He needn't have given up quite so easily.

The salad tasted of nothing and I pushed it around my plate.

'I've ordered way too much, said Stuart. 'Here,' he emptied the dish of chips and onion rings onto my plate, 'help me out a little.'

It smelled gorgeous and my mouth watered. I didn't get my thunder thighs and cankles by shying away from food. Besides, I was doing him a favour. He said so.

Stuart paid for the meal and we left the restaurant just after nine. The few people left on the streets were walking with a lot more purpose and it wasn't all down to that threat of rain. Stop and search in Craffid stepped up a pace when it got dark and turned frequent and harsh. If Stuart and I got picked up they might contact the Basley Law and then we'd be in several different flavours of poop.

Jermaine Street was more of a wide grubby alley than a street. Skips, wheelie bins and crates full of empty boxes and assorted junk lined the urine-damp mulch which made up the pathway down the centre. The rats and homeless huddled side by side trying to keep warm and occasionally feeding off each other. We live in the recycling age after all, nothing dead is wasted. The smell of rotting meat and sour veg made my throat close. I'd have to be skeletal hungry to appreciate what went free in the city. I stood as close to Stuart as possible without actually touching him. 'Can you see Charlie?' I asked.

He shook his head. 'I can't see any security either.' He reached and squeezed my hand. 'Always look for the positives.' His palm felt rough and warm and soft and strong and gentle.

I didn't know whether my stomach somersaulted due to the fear of the alley or the sensation of his hand, but every inch of me tingled. Such a rush. 'Look. Down there at the end.'

His fingers slipped between mine in a lovers grasp. 'Stay close, okay?'

No way would I have gone anywhere. My hand fitted into his too, too perfect. We walked down the centre of the alley with me half a step behind watching the rear. It wasn't the time or place to decide to play the wussy girl, but that feeling of being protected sent my brain to mush. I had to get a grip. 'Keep an eye out for trouble,' I said, keeping my voice firm, almost bossy.

'It'll be fine. If anybody tries to have a pop I'll hide behind you and you can give them one of your smacks.'

'Ha de ha.'

A line of people stood silently against a graphitised wall. Obscenities and grotesque demons in fluorescent 3-D hovered over agitated men, worried looking women and silent children. It hadn't occurred to me we wouldn't be alone.

'Bloody hell,' said Stuart. 'This must be the cargo.' He let go of my hand and took his backpack off to hold in front of him, like a shield. 'Best get in line I suppose.'

Talk about anti-climax.

A door opened bang on ten and we were herded through a gate. Two men in standard rail uniforms stood either side taking slips of paper from the people filing past. They had a proper underground racket going on. Brilliant but cheeky. Not to mention dangerous. I forced myself to stay focused but Stuart radiated warmth and smelled gorgeous. I whispered into his ear. 'They've got tickets.'

'I can see that.'

Our turn came and Stuart said, 'We made arrangements with Charlie to collect our tickets on arrival.'

Not strictly true.

The weedy man with the bony nose standing in the queue behind us leaned towards the guard. 'If he has no ticket he should be sent packing. Some of us have waited too long already.'

The guard held a hand up and muttered into a radio pinned to his chest. Word spread along the queue.

'Charlie told us to come straight here,' Stuart said to the guard, 'we had a meeting with him this afternoon.'

The man behind shoved his way in front and snarled into Stuart's face. 'No ticket? No ride. Now on your way.'

The queue piled up and crowded in from behind. I couldn't see a way back through the door, the air stank of pure hatred. I clung to the back of Stuart's shirt. 'We need to get out of here.' Stuart gave a teeny shake of his head and kept his eyes trained on the guard, ignoring the man up in his face. 'Seriously,' I said. 'This is going to turn scary any minute now, we need to get out.'

The crowd morphed into a mob within seconds and shouts from the back encouraged those at the front to 'sort it out.' The guard stooped to listen to somebody answer his radio call and the weedy guy leapt forward like some kind of ninja. He grabbed Stuart by the throat, lifted him off the floor and thrust him into the wall. The ticket collector shouted, a woman screamed, and kids wailed. Other blokes jostled between me and Stuart, shouting and grabbing at each other. A chaotic brawl of arms and bodies flailed in front of me. Stuart hung suspended above everybody else. I willed him to relax but he grasped at the man's hands trying to prise them free. I fought to get closer, yanking people out of my way, desperate to help but there were so many and they all looked so furious and frantic.

Somebody grabbed me from behind and pinned my arms to my side. A voice, calm, barely above a whisper, 'Take it easy.'

My first thought should have been how stupid were we not to recognise a trap when we saw one. Or, now we'd never be able to fetch Gemma. Or, holy shamboozles I'm going to die. But my first and pretty much only thought, as I got dragged kicking and screaming through the throng, was, Oh God, please don't let us lose each other.

Whoever carried me down the corridor had the strength of a rhino. I wriggled, squirmed and ground at his shins with my heels the whole way out of there.

'Ouch, Jesus, keep still, you little bitch.'

I hollered and growled. 'Let me go you…' I forgot any promises to Mum and pulled out all the curses I'd ever heard. He threw me into a room full of crates and boxes and slammed the door. I landed on my knees and my right one screamed a burning lightning strike of agony straight to my brain. I curled into a ball and clenched my teeth. 'Dirty, stinking…' The key clunked rather than clicked and I knew the lock must be a biggie.

When the pain eased to a mere agonising torture I opened my eyes. The door stood old yet solid, made with thick planks of oak. No way could I smash through that. It didn't stop me dragging myself up and trying though. I wasn't so much angry as poop-expelling scared. I needed to get back to Stuart. With him, the whole trip would be exciting, like a slick adventure, but without him I felt terrified. For the missing kids, for Stuart and for me.

CHAPTER SEVENTEEN

I hammered and yelled at the door until my fists were grazed and my knee glowed red-hot, like it might burst into flames any second. I collapsed into the dust to get my breath back and the blood rushed to my head when I heard some geezer laugh; none of what just happened was any way funny. I put my ear to the door and tried to listen for more voices, hoping for a clue as to why I'd been locked up and what the hell they'd done with Stuart. But the noise down the corridor had eased off to nothing more than the odd shout in the distance.

Other than what seeped under the door, the only light came from a long strip window up near the ceiling on one wall. I figured the room must be somewhere in the station - a back storeroom or an old office. I pushed some crates and balanced a couple of boxes to climb up and get my bearings. I rubbed the grime from the glass with the chump of my fist and peered through at hoards of people on the platform way below me. I recognised some of the tense, sallow faces from the line outside. They milled around before being picked out, seemingly at random, and ushered into a train that looked like it should be carrying fuel; round, bulbous trucks with red warning triangles splattered across their bellies, hooked one after the other.

No sign of Stuart.

All those people were paying to 'escape', risking their lives, when they'd all likely end up scraping a living in a place like Shanks estate. City people fantasised about this ridiculous image of country living being all farmers markets and leaving the back doors open. The reality is very different. In the villages, and towns like Basley, people are robbed by people they know and probably trusted, rather than faceless city strangers. I stood and watched until the hatches on the trucks were lowered and the train pulled away. If Stuart was on it, I'd lost him. The few people remaining on the platform were pushed and shoved out of a side door back onto the street. I hoped the weedy toad who grabbed Stuart's throat was among the rejects.

Everything went still.

There seemed little point in balancing on top of the crates just watching the rats wake up so I climbed down and began to root through the boxes in the hope of finding something to jimmy the door open with. But they all contained bundles of pamphlets. I opened a batch and held one up to the light, maybe it had my dad in it. The key clunked and the door swung open so I shoved the leaflet in my back pocket alongside the one Gavin gave me.

Charlie stood in the doorway and looked at the floor by my feet, his grey face shining tacky in the light from the passage. 'Come on.' He stood to the side to let me pass and indicated down the corridor. 'Off you go.'

My muscles tightened ready to fight or fly. 'Where's Stuart?'

'He's waiting on board.'

'I'm not going anywhere without him.'

He didn't answer but gestured for me to get a move on.

Charlie ushered me down dim passages to a platform and into a train carriage like a wooden crate, reminding me of an ancient cattle truck. It stank a bit like one too. Inside were mountains of clear bags full of clothing. I climbed on top. 'Where's Stuart? I told you I wasn't going without him.' The sliding door clattered across and slices of light from between the wooden slats striped the bags. It sent my eyes funny. 'Stuart?'

'Over here.'

I crawled through, throwing bags behind me to clear the way. I found him lying in a dip, his nose a mulch of red and black flesh. 'Oh my God. What did they do to you?'

'Hey, you should see the other guy.'

'Shut up, Stuart. That was so lame.'

'Yeah, I guess.' His sss came out as shh.

'What the hell have they done to you?' To my shame I started to cry. I have no idea how it happened, the tears came from nowhere, no warning, nothing. 'I'm sorry.'

'Hey. It's okay. I'm okay.'

He eased himself onto his elbow and pulled me into him. I buried my face into his neck and sobbed. All that grot leaving trails on his collar bone, talk about humiliating. I tried to wipe it away with my hand, then used the neck of his tee shirt.

'What are you sorry for? It's not your fault. Are you all right?' He pulled his head back to get a look at me. 'They didn't hurt you did they?' His chin brushed my forehead and it felt rough but gentle, like a cat's lick.

I shook my head and gave a gloopy sniff. 'No.' I wished for a tissue, I didn't want him to see me all snotty. 'They just locked me in a room and then brought me here.' I whined like a three year old. Stuart flinched as he adjusted position to get a better hold of me. 'Oh God,' I said and rubbed at the damp stain on his shoulder. 'I'm so sorry.'

'Nope, don't be. You stay right where you are.' He snuggled me close and put his mouth in my hair and breathed deep. 'So worth it,' he whispered.

We stayed laying quiet until the carriage squealed into action and picked up a steady, if slow, creep out of Craffid. The crying had given me a headache and I felt stupid and weak. Crying was nothing but a total waste of time and energy. I wanted to make up for it and look after

Stuart the way he'd looked after me, but I had nothing to offer. Stuart's bag had been lost in the scuffle and he'd been forced to hand over all his money. 'Basley Law have put out a call on us,' said Stuart. 'Charlie and his friends took advantage, upped the price and robbed the lot.'

I pulled out the bundle of cash I'd kept hidden down the back of my jeans and counted it out. 'Three hundred and fifty.' It struck me as precious little out of the five grand we'd set out with.

'It should do us,' said Stuart. 'Once we're there we won't need very much.'

'How are we going to know when to get off?'

Stuart hooked me back into his arms and spooned me close, his breath hot on my neck. 'They're going to sling us off when we get there. It's going to be fine, try and sleep.'

I didn't sleep. I lay and tried to imprint the feeling of being held so close and safe deep into my memory. Even as he slept he gave me the occasional squeeze and I hoped to remember how warm and safe it felt, to be held and wanted like that, forever.

The morning light crept through the slats into the truck and the dark mounds of bags took a more solid shape. We rattled and jolted along at a snail's pace. Perhaps my plan to make a leap for it might still be worth serious consideration. I turned over to take a peek at Stuart sleeping.

He gripped me tighter and gave me a crooked smile with his eyes still shut. 'Where do you think you're sneaking off to?'

'Ooph.' I winced at the sight of his face. 'That looks sore.' I pulled away and sat up.

'Yeah, it is a bit.'

'What about the rest of you? Do you hurt anywhere else? Are you up to making a leap for it?'

He opened his eyes. 'I want to stay here, with you.' He held his arms open.

'Um. Gemma?'

'Yeah suppose. You're right.' He sighed, eased himself to a sitting position and tested his limbs. Nodded with an upside down smile. 'It's all good. Don't want to jump though. They said they'd let us off when the time is right.'

'Why should we believe them all of a sudden? After they let those rabids loose on you?'

'Because they've taken a mountain of money and could have let them rabids, as you call them, kill us both. Have you ever seen anything like that before? Unbelievable.' He touched his swollen nose and then thought better of it. 'They're chancers and scumbags but not inhuman.'

I pulled a face. 'Charncers and scarmbargs, eh?'

He tried to smile but it must have hurt too much. 'And they put us in first class.' He raised a finger. 'Always look for the positives. And wherever we get off, it's closer to where we want to be than we were, and it's away from any tails such as Gavin. Now come here.' As Stuart reached for my hand the train jerked to a stop. Somebody shouted from the front and then the scrunch of footsteps on gravel stopped outside our crate. 'Too late,' said Stuart struggling to his feet. 'Sounds like this could be where we get out.'

The doors slid open and the head and shoulders of the friendliest guard in the world poked over the ledge. 'Out you get.'

The jolly guard would normally have irritated me rotten in the way all incessantly cheerful people tended to do. But after Charlie and his mangy mates I felt like hugging him, just because. He grinned and held out his hand to help me off the carriage. I shook my head and he simply moved on to help Stuart. 'Are you two going to be okay out here?' He spoke like everything was completely normal and helping beaten-to-a-pulp stowaways off cattle trucks happened every day. 'You're miles from anywhere by here,' he said with a chirpy chuckle.

Stuart looked around at the fields and hills of nothing. 'We're in north Wales though, right?'

'Oh yeah, that's where they said to drop you, so that's where you're at.'

'Thanks, mate.' Stuart held out his hand.

The guard shook it. 'You're welcome. Take it easy.'

We were back in the holiday movie.

We slid on our backsides down the embankment and waited for the train to clatter away into the distance, the guard waving from a window like the fat controller. Then there was nothing. No sounds: just a hazy heat thick with gnats. I swatted and batted at them with my palms flat. 'Tsk. Why do they like me so much?'

'Good taste?' Stuart got to his feet and studied the sky. 'I can smell the sea.'

'There's nice. But can you remember the address?' The file had been in his bag.

'Sapton Manor, Shepton. Shepton is by the sea.'

Poor thing, all those s's. 'Pardon?'

'Sapton Manor, Shepton. And Shepton…' he turned to look and saw my smirk. 'Ooo. You can be cruel, Atty. So, so cruel.'

'Sho Sho cruel.'

He rolled his eyes and flinched. 'Ouch, that hurt.' He wandered down to a stream and knelt at its edge. 'What do you reckon? Safe to drink?'

'Unlikely, but it'll do to wash your face.'

I bathed his face with the cool water. He looked into my eyes the whole time pulling the occasional flinch and giving me the odd smile. 'I can't wait to get you somewhere comfy, Atty. And that's no lie.'

Oooph. Judging by the weird sensations, like goosebumpy neck and the warmth spreading down my belly, neither could I.

CHAPTER EIGHTEEN

The sun blasted the tops of our heads, racking up my headache to a level that would knock a donkey out. To hell with the remembering being hugged thing, I wished I'd got some decent sleep in instead. The air felt hot and sticky in my lungs, like being in a tent at midday. We meandered along country lanes overgrown with cow parsley and hemlock. Stuart loosened his jeans so they hung low below his bruised hip. He swiped at the hedges with his belt. 'Shall we pick some?'

'What for?'

'It's poisonous.'

'I doubt we'll get chance to grind it into anybody's tea.'

'You never know. I've heard it's pretty easy to do. Put a few leaves in their salad maybe.'

'Now who's been watching too many movies?'

'It's an idea.'

'True. Hello Mr Crawlsfeld, fancy a salad? Well, I happen to have a few leaves in my pocket.'

Stuart shrugged. 'Can't see the harm in being prepared. Just in case the opportunity presents itself.'

We bypassed a few villages by cutting through the fields. We must have looked like we were traipsing home from battle. My eye had fully opened and Stuart examined it. 'It looks like a marble in a puddle of tomato juice.'

I rooted about for a matching compliment to throw back. That smile of his affected my brain and the ideas were slow in coming. 'Your nose,' I tilted my head in mock studious concentration. 'It looks like a donkey's dongle.'

'A donkey's, eh?' He raised his eyebrows. 'Odd how donkeys and dongles are on your mind.'

I slapped his arm. 'Stop it.'

He curled his shoulder away and laughed. 'What sort of come-back is that?' He put on a girly voice. 'Stop it, Stuey.'

'Huh. From the guy who wants to defend us by feeding the enemy salad.'

'Ah but, Atty. A crappy plan is better than no plan, right?' He turned away and went quiet for several seconds. 'A donkey. Sheesh.' He looked at me sideways, a dirty smirk on his face. 'I do hope I don't disappoint.'

Yet another moment for me to deal with and another chance for me to lay down some ground rules, tell him where to get off. But I didn't want to. I pointed towards the horizon. 'Look. I can see the sea.'

'So it is.' He held my hand, fingers loosely entwined, his thumb stroking my palm.

We walked in a silence I'd thought was comfortable but Stuart had clearly been thinking too much. 'Who's M Gee?' he asked.

'Joe's boss.' Keep it simple, felt safest.

'Ever met her?'

'No.'

He pulled a face I couldn't read. Talking of M Gee and Joe led me back to thinking about my dad. I fished the leaflets out of my back pocket. The two were very different but both interesting in their own way. The one from the station was thicker and more official looking than Gav's; it had shiny paper and glossy images. I let go of Stuart's hand to open it up. 'I found boxes of these in the room at the station. Looks like a questionnaire thing.'

Stuart snorted. 'Same old thing but different words I suspect. They're all either for or against unification. Which one is it this time?'

'It's trying to gain support to regionalise more laws.' I read a line off the cover. **'Each county should have the**

right to execute activists without having to wait for international permission …'

'Bin it. It'll never happen.'

I stopped reading aloud until I got to the bit about Basley. 'They've got West Basley as an example, look.' I tried to show him but he waved it away so I kept reading it out. '**Basley has so many cons an entire region of the county has been taken over …**'

'Atty stop.' Stuart took the leaflet out of my hands. 'I just told you, it will never happen. Trust me. My mum works on this kind of stuff all the time.'

'Well that's all right then. She doesn't help people like me though, remember? Who on the west is important, professional and flicking fancy enough to get her attention, eh?' I was up in Stuart's face, the pamphlet in my fist.

'It won't happen,' he said, calm enough to make me want to slap him. 'And some people on the west aren't all Hot Blue and cuddles, you know. For every extreme idea on the east, there's a matching one on the west.' He took the pamphlet out of my hand and ripped it up. 'The two will balance themselves out and the rest of us will find a way down the middle.'

'Just like that.'

'No. People like my mother, your dad, Joe, M Gee …' he squeezed my hand, 'you and me. Us. We'll help make it happen.'

'How?'

'There'll be a way.' He turned and set off again at a meandering stroll. 'I've been thinking. Maybe you were right and Joe knows my mother. Something about the name M Gee rings a bell. Perhaps she's the connection. Maybe it's all connected, Joe, your dad, my mum …' he shrugged. 'Like you said, it would explain why you were asked to watch me and Gemma.'

'Yeah,' I said. 'It's an idea. Not so sure where my dad fits in. I'm beginning to think he might just be a complete tool and buggered off to live somewhere happy-ever-after and write stupid leaflets in the sunshine.'

He put on a judge's lofty voice and mused at the sky. 'Has that idea just popped into your head or have you considered all the facts and come to a calculated conclusion?'

'I am not calculating.'

He laughed and began staggering about the lane holding his face. 'Ouchy. Don't make me laugh … it hurts.'

Somehow, I'd made a twonk of myself. 'What's so funny?' I said. 'Either one of us could be right or we could both be totally wrong.'

'Of course.' He coughed and reached for my hand. 'You're right.' His face twitched and his eyes shone. 'I think the sun's got to me. But remember what you agreed? Back in the park? You have to give your dad a fair hearing, okay?'

'Humpnf.' What else could I say?

Shepton was quaint and touristy-pretty. The hotels along the seafront were painted in pastels with striped canopies flapping above glass fronted doors. But there wasn't going to be anything so upmarket for us. With only three hundred and fifty quid we were forced to book into a small back-street bed and breakfast with a sticky welcome mat and a beer-bottle green reception. I stood inside the door near a hand-drawn sign, FOYER, and wrinkled my nose. 'Hums a bit.'

'Yes. What is that?' Stuart sniffed. 'Smells like curried mackerel.'

Rich people ate the weirdest stuff.

A big woman in a flowered dress puffed through the door at the back of the passage. It swung back and forth on its hinge, wafting a new scent of grease and boiled cloths into the hall. 'What can I do for you?' She hesitated when she saw the state of my face and scowled at the back of Stuart's head as he tried to read the faded-out price list. 'Are you alright my lovey?' She reached for my arm.

'Fine thanks.' I smiled my sweetest and girliest.

Stuart turned around and after a brief glance at his face she withdrew her arm like I'd tried to take a bite out of it. 'Oh my goodness,' she said and put her hand on her cushiony chest. 'What on earth has happened to the pair of you?'

Stuart smiled. 'Rugby match.'

'Oh thank heavens. I thought you might have brought some bother with you.' She waddled past us to get behind the desk in the way people walked wardrobes across a bouncy carpet. She looked like a mega flowery weeble. Stuart blinked and gave her a tight smile as she raised her arm to lift the hatch. I, too, held my breath. Curried mackerel smells like fat women's pits.

'Just the one night please,' said Stuart. 'The best double you have.' He glanced at me, his eyes were hard yet excited and oh so dirty. My face flushed and my snoofle tingled in anticipation.

We stood inside the bedroom door and looked at the grubby duvet. 'Do you think it's supposed to be that colour?' I asked.

'Greeny-grey and brown blotches with patches of yellow?'

I lifted a corner. 'And the rest. There's some pink under here.'

'It's not ideal, granted.'

I shrugged. 'Pah, crotch rot. It'll be okay in the dark.'

'Is that your way of breaking it gently?'

'What?'

'That you don't like it with the light on?'

That stupid grin wouldn't get off my face. I hid it by heading for the window. 'Not a sea view, but could be worse.'

Stuart laughed. 'Let's freshen up and go see if we can find the manor house. Get our bearings before dinner and then we can plan our next move.'

Such a tease. But it would be so much sweeter when we knew the kids were safe. Then we could give each other our full attention, so to speak. 'Of course,' I said. 'We can ask the landlady where it is. She looks like she's been here forever.'

'Good thinking. You ask. I'll wait outside in the fresh air.'

A northern mile is about twice as long as a southern mile, I swear it. Three miles the woman had said, but even with my dodgy knee, and Stuart with his black and blue hip, we should have covered it in less than two hours. But it took three and the sky had darkened by the time we got there. We'd clambered across fields and streams, through woods and waste tips. A true nightmare of a walk. We were both grumpy as hell by the time we crept over a ridge to spy at the manor nestled in amongst some trees. The wall surrounding the grounds must have been almost as tall as the manor itself and was topped with rolls of razor wire, sparkling in the dying sunlight; lethal but, from where we lay, pretty, like fairy lights.

I only spotted the one entrance. 'Big gates.'

'Big cameras.' Stuart sounded defeated already. 'I wonder if they've got ears.'

On top of the pillars, either side of the gates, were huge black balls the size of car tyres. They looked like typical housing for high-tech security surveillance systems.

'We're never going to get in there.' I said. 'Not without an invite.' All we could see of the manor itself were a couple of white turrets poking above the walls.

Stuart nodded towards the sun dipping behind a steep rugged hill. 'We need to get to higher ground, so we can see over the wall and in through the windows.'

'What good will that do?'

'I might see Gemma. She's close. I can feel it.' He scurried backwards until he dropped behind a ridge and was hidden from the cameras. He started towards the hill.

I called after him. 'Shall I watch the gates?'

'Don't be so bloody lazy.'

I scrambled to follow him. 'I'm not being bloody lazy.

I've got a bad knee.'

'Yeah, yeah. I'll race you to the top.'

Hah. Nobody ever beat me on the wall at the gym. 'You're on.'

What most kids don't realise is that the winning is in the selection of the route. Pick a bad one and you've lost before you start. And Stuart picked a bad one.

I waited at the top for him to catch up.

'You cheated,' he said. 'You took the steps.'

'Now, now. Don't be a sore loser.' I wrinkled my nose. 'So not attractive.' He came and sat close so our thighs and arms touched and sent little mini shock waves to my toes. He put his face inches from mine and looked at my lips. I sucked them between my teeth.

He looked into my eyes and made a small breathy sound – like half pain, half frustration. 'I'll make you pay for that later.'

No way would I look away first. Not until he'd kissed me.

He rubbed at his hip. 'How's your knee?'

'It's fine!'

He laughed. 'Only asked.'

He knew what he was doing to me and I wanted to slap him for it.

We looked over to the Manor. The wall stretched around the entire circumference. Only two ways of getting in - a small door embedded at the back, and the massive gates with the mega cameras at the front. A huge white mansion with towers like a palace stood bang centre of the greenest lawns I'd ever seen. The walls reflected the sunlight and almost shone, giving it the effect of a fairy-tale castle. Had it been pink I'd have sworn we'd slipped into La La land. The grounds spread wide and well organised with neat borders of colourful flowers and small clumps of bushes and trees. They all looked expertly cared for. 'Are you sure this is it?' I said. 'I can't see any ponies or go-karts or any of that other stuff from the brochure.'

'No,' he said. 'Ain't that a surprise?'

'What do you suppose it is? Looks pretty quiet. And so … clean. Definitely not a school.'

Stuart wiped his upper lip. 'All the blinds are drawn.'

I'd learned to recognise the lip-swipe as habit, something he did without thinking when he concentrated or got nervous. I shrugged. 'So? The blinds are drawn. Not sure what that might mean.'

'No. Nor me.'

We waited for something to happen. There were no people in the grounds, no deliveries, no gardeners – there must be gardeners sometimes – no movement of any kind. I'd heard people crave peace and quiet but any long spells of silence made me nervous. Sinister things happen in the quiet - bad things never shout. But I was tired and hungry and fed up so my instincts weren't to be trusted. I saw no reason to stress Stuart out more than he already was. 'Doesn't look too bad.'

He sighed. 'No. Doesn't feel good though. But there's nothing to see, come on. Let's go back to the digs. It's going to take us hours to find our way. Perhaps there's an easier route.'

Perhaps, but it didn't feel like we'd found it. My knee throbbed and burned something awful by the time we hobbled back into Shepton. I needed a bath and something to eat. The long walk after a sleepless night on the train made me exhausted and snappy. 'There'd better be some hot water.' Stuart stepped into a chemist and spent a small fortune on toothbrushes and replacing the lotions that we'd lost in the backpack. I wasn't just knackered out but unreasonable and difficult. 'You binned a load of that stuff in the hotel.'

'I couldn't carry it all and if I had, it would have been in my bag.'

Logic held no weight with such a moody bitch as me. 'It's still a waste of money.'

'You don't want any then?'

'I didn't say that.'

When we got to our room, Stuart made me sit in the chair by the window. 'I'm going to scrub the tub out and run you a bath.'

I felt like he wanted to make me feel bad and it worked. 'It's my turn to do it for you.'

'You just sit there,' he said, waving a finger in a mock rollocking, 'and do as you're told.' And then he bent down and kissed the top of my head. I turned my face towards him but he'd moved away and into the bathroom.

I felt cold with disappointment and, for some reason, guilty to the point of being angry at everything. Confused I suppose.

The water wrapped me up, bone-warming hot, and Stuart's potions soothed every bit as well as they had the first time. When I closed my eyes and shut out the grime of the grubby little bathroom, it felt like I was being cuddled and cared for like a precious child. Only one thing spoilt it and that was thinking of Stuart sitting in the shabby bedroom waiting for his chance to soothe his wounds. That hip looked horrible.

'Sorry I took so long,' I said climbing under the multi-coloured duvet wrapped in a bath towel. 'It just felt soooo gooood.'

'No problem. I won't be long. Keep the bed warm.'

Like I needed asking.

Next thing, Stuart was leaning over me and shaking my shoulder. 'Atty. I've got us something to eat.' I sat up and gripped the damp towel to my chest. 'You might want to get dressed first.' He gestured towards the small coffee table in the window. He'd laid out a selection of take-away meals. 'I wasn't sure what you liked so I got a little of everything. I like it all so you take first pick and I'll have what's left.' The only light came from the blue-marbled moon high in the sky beyond the bay window. He saw me looking at it. 'Stunning, isn't it? I swear we're getting closer to it all the time.' I sat on the edge of the bed and again, for no reason, that lump came to my throat. Stuart looked from me to the table and back again. 'I know it's not much, but if we leave the lights off, eat by the light of the moon…' He went to touch my shoulder, changed his mind and ran his hand through his hair instead. He wiped his mouth. 'I'm sorry. I should have kept some money separate. Or asked for more.'

'No.' I said. 'It's lovely.' I smiled at him and at the table. 'It's better than lovely. It's perfect. I'm sorry I'm such a bitch at times.'

He reached for me then and hugged me. Not a sexy hug but a friendly matey-type hug. 'Don't you dare ever apologise for being you, Atty.'

I pulled away. If he'd held me any longer I'd have sobbed for sure. 'I'll just go and get dressed.' Diving towards the bathroom to change wasn't only about being shy, but about getting the timing right. I didn't want Stuart to witness me hauling two-days-unwashed knickers over my damp thunder thighs with nothing but a towel for cover. The potential for a less than flattering first impression was way too high.

He bent down to rifle through a bag at his feet. 'I got you these too. I'm not being, you know, it's just I thought you might like a fresh pair.' He held out a pair of socks wrapped in a tight little bundle. 'I hope they fit.'

'I'm sure they will. I'm pretty much standard average. Thank you.' In the bathroom I opened the socks and found a new cute pair of panties tucked up inside. They fitted perfectly. The last box got a strong, bold tick.

The food tasted delicious. 'That's better. I was starving,' I said and leaned back holding my over-stretched belly. 'Thanks again.'

Stuart gave me that look. That twinkly-eyed, can't-wait-to-get-you-into-bed look. My toes tingled and I rubbed the back of my neck - those new hairs tickled like crazy. Now it looked like it might actually happen, I began to fret about all that girly stuff that usually bored me senseless.

Fran used to talk openly about such things all the time, whereas I found it too embarrassing. I liked to pretend I had no desire or need to de-fuzz and/or scent various nooks and crannies. Well, I hadn't done any of that stuff recently and neither was I going to get the chance to now. Surely he wouldn't appreciate me using that cheap plastic razor he'd left by the sink in the bathroom. Not for the regions I needed it for. And my teeth – I'd need to scrub them again after the curry. I should never have eaten the curry.

'You okay?' Stuart filled my glass from a bottle of Blue he'd got free with the take-away. He looked so relaxed.

'Yeah, sure. I'm great.' Happy, chirpy, care-free me.

'Good.'

'I've been thinking how we can get into the Manor,' I lied.

'And?' He slouched in his chair, one hand holding his glass the other rubbing his flat, hard stomach. His tee shirt lifted slightly to show me the soft line of hair leading down the centre of his belly – he tugged at it absently.

My snoofle shot a lightening signal straight to my toes. 'Um. I've been thinking we'll have to go in through the gate because that razor stuff on top of the wall looks a bitch to get past.'

'Through the gate. Right.'

'Pretend we're delivering something. Confidence will get us in.'

'Confidence. Right.' He smiled, taking the piss.

'So,' I said looking him dead in the eye. 'You fancy your chances leaping the wall? Pole vaulting one of your specialities too, is it?'

'Nope.' He shook his head with an upside down smile. 'The gate sounds like a great plan.'

I scowled and stood up. 'I'm going to clean my teeth.'

'Okay.'

I stopped at the door and turned. 'Only because I got some of that meat stuck in them. At the back.' Just shut the hell up, Atty.

In the bathroom I studied my flat hair – it doesn't spike without the gel; my blood-red eye – it did look like a marble; my slightly bent nose – still sore; and the gash down my cheek - guaranteed to scar. Even with all that taken into consideration I didn't get my problem. It's not like I didn't want this. I began to seriously doubt my sanity. I mean, really. Everybody was doing it. It's time I caught up and got in on the action, found out what all the fuss was about.

'Atty?' Stuart knocked on the door.

Oh be-God. 'Coming. I won't be a minute.' I cleaned my teeth, tousled my hair and took a deep breath. Now or never.

Stuart was standing to the side of the window. 'Come and see.' He motioned for me to walk around the table and chairs so that I stayed out of sight of anybody looking in from the street.

I crept around and stood next to him. 'Look, down there, second tree past the red gate.'

My eyes took some adjusting to the dim light, but somebody was standing under the tree. 'Who's that?'

'Gavin.'

I stood gobsmacked. 'How the hell did he get there?'

Stuart frowned and shook his head. 'I can't think.' His mouth shut into a tight line. 'I can't think about him at all right now. We need rest. Leave him there and we'll speak to him in the morning.' He shut the blinds. Without that big moon the room went a thick blue-black.

'I didn't tell him, I swear.'

'Okay.'

'I didn't!'

'It doesn't matter if you did or not. He's here now and we'll just have to deal with it. But not right now.'

'Stuart, I swear to you. I didn't.'

'Okay.' There was a lengthy pause and the air felt electrified for all the wrong reasons. 'I believe you,' he said, but his voice was sharp, tense. 'We'll talk about it more in the morning.'

The logistics of getting into bed were a nightmare. I learned new stuff every day. I liked learning. Right then, I learned that an ex-boyfriend spying outside the hotel room does not create the ideal atmosphere for a first night of passion. Especially when current potential passion-maker thinks ex is there under girl's request.

I used the bathroom again. Damn neurotic nerves. I washed out my old knickers. If nothing was going to happen I wanted to be at least semi-prepared in case it happened the following day. Stuart would feel guilty about doubting me, for sure. He'd be itching to make it up to me after he discovered I'd told him nothing but the truth. About Gavin anyway. Damn Gavin, he must have jumped the same train as us. Must stop saying damn, it was a Joe-word and so not BBC. The temptation to race out and knock Gavin's teeth out was only outweighed by my wanting to cuddle into Stuart. With any luck, Gavin would have to sleep on the street, serve him bang to rights. We'd sort him out in the morning, on Get Gemma Day – the day everything might change. Anything could happen, we might be captured or even shot. No, surely not. Maybe. And there was I stressing over my stupid knickers. I nudged Stuart's freshly washed boxers along the towel rail to make room and changed my mind as it all looked a little too presumptuous, leaning towards desperate. And erotic. Then I faced the problem of putting his boxers back exactly as I found them. The horror that he might think I'd picked them up to touch them set me in a right tizz. Argh, Atty, get a grip!

In the end I climbed into bed in my tee shirt and new panties, and faced away from the centre of the bed towards the window. Stuart stumbled and cursed his way around the bottom of the bed, patting it to find where I lay. 'Argh, oops, toe, ouch.' The mattress dipped and he settled in. The duvet stretched to cover us both, leaving a gap of cool air tickling the full length of my back sending hairs, which I didn't even know I had, to a static attention. The silence which followed made it difficult to breathe, especially through my bent and sore nose. 'Stuart?'

'What?'

'I'm sorry if I snore.'

'Is that what you're worried about?'

'No.'

'I've got much bigger things on my mind.'

'Yeah, I know. But what I care about most, right now, is you believe me. I did not tell Gavin where we were going.'

He moved closer and his breath tickled my spine. 'I know. I do believe you. I'm just frustrated, that's all. And scared. If those guards at the station told Gavin, then they might have told Basley Law.'

'I'm not sure the Law want us enough to chase us. It was only a DVD.'

'And a break in. And stealing a file from an Approved agent. You might want to add money extortion to the list too if they've persuaded my dad to talk.' Silence. 'On reflection,' he said. 'I think I'd prefer it if it had been you who told Gavin.'

I stayed quiet. That was a heap of charges he'd reeled off.

'I'd forgive you if it was, Atty. I'd forgive you anything.' He shifted in the bed, closer. 'Oh God, Atty. I'm frightened of getting this wrong.' His fingers touched my waist and my toes curled. He snuggled his forehead into the curve of my neck. 'I've only just found you. If anything happened to you I'd never forgive myself.'

I turned onto my back. 'Nothing is going to go wrong.' I paused to marvel how calm my voice sounded. I tried it again. 'Nobody is going to get hurt.' Woah. I sounded well in control. 'If the Law knew where we were and wanted us enough to chase us, they'd have us locked up by now. It's not their style to hang about under trees. That's left to the morons like Gavin.'

Stuart's fingers found the bottom of my tee shirt and touched the naked skin of my stomach. Thank God I was lying on my back. I breathed in anyway. It's a habit, one I'd been trying to kick so I released gently but tried to keep my looser flesh as tight as possible. His warm breath tickled behind my ear and then a teeny barely-there kiss.

His fingers stroked in larger circles, tickling my ribcage and down to my pantie line. 'Is Gavin hanging around outside putting you off?'

Decision time. If I said, 'no' it would mean, 'yes, I want you.' And did I want to confirm the 'all westy girls are easy girls' line? If I said 'yes' it would mean, 'no, not tonight.' But we might not get another chance anytime soon. I wanted him to keep touching so, so bad, but the whole conversation seemed so, I don't know, contractual. It crossed my mind all polite easty boys might like express permission first. In writing maybe. Perhaps he didn't really want to, just felt obliged to try. Maybe he wanted a get-out clause, I offered him one. 'Well, he is a bit.'

'I understand.'

'Not a lot. Just a bit.'

'It's okay. Honestly. When we've got Gemma and Stacey back I'm going to take you to the best hotel money can buy and we will have the best food and the best wine.' He kissed my neck, tugged my tee shirt down over my belly, and cuddled in like a puppy. 'The first time should be the best night ever.'

'Are you going straight to sleep?'

'I'm way too tired to think strategic stuff. We can plan our next move in the morning. I'm knackered.'

CHAPTER NINETEEN

I must have slept pretty good given all that my brain had to deal with because I woke clear headed and keen to get going. But Stuart lay silently beside me with his hand on my thigh. His fingers felt hot and dry and no way did I want him to take them away. So I lingered long enough for the sun to rise and brighten the room. The blinds didn't quite reach the windowsill and the stripe of light through the gap shone like a torch into my eyes. I eased out from under the hand, got up, found some money in Stuart's pocket, and crept out to buy us breakfast.

At home, the key to avoiding random street checks, was to look as rich as possible. I walked with a deliberate purpose, jiggled the coins in my pocket and held my head high and confident.

Shepton didn't appear to have an underclass like Basley. It was much smaller and everybody moved very slow and laidback. The local equivalent to our Reds dressed casually and chatted to passers-by like they were all old mates. Perhaps they were. Despite my strut, I must have stuck out like a lemondropper at a tea party - a walking disaster; never had much, never will; written off without a hope. That's what was lacking in Basley – hope. The Law had us believe every county had its problems but Shepton seemed to be doing okay. There were enough window boxes and pretty paint jobs to suggest there was wealth to waste.

I found a small café which did some great cheese rolls and even let me take away drinks – I ordered a big, black coffee for Stuart and a rich Hot Blue for me. 'This is a very pretty area,' I said to the middle-aged woman behind the counter. 'Is there much opportunity for work?'

I might as well have asked if she served puppy's brains in a sandwich. Her face changed from amiable to guarded within a fraction and I swear the air chilled.

'Most places are family owned,' she said. 'Passed down from generation to generation.'

'I don't just mean the cafés and B & Bs, what about other places? Factories of some kind?'

'No.' She turned away.

Charming. And she hadn't even seen my papers. For all she knew I might have been a local.

Gavin had followed several meters behind and waited in the doorway of a bakery over the road. Now I didn't have Stuart to distract me, things began to make sense. The guards would never have told Gavin anything unless he'd handed over a truck load of money. Gavin never had money. The only way he'd know we were in Shepton, was if he'd put a trace on us.

I pulled the leaflet out of my back pocket, ran my fingers down the centre crease, and found a small bump halfway down, disguised by the fold. I rubbed at it until the paper rippled and the upper layer flaked away. A tiny circular tracker, the size of a miniature watch battery, stuck to my finger like a contact lens.

The woman behind the counter placed a brown paper bag containing our breakfast on the counter, 'There you go. Have a nice day.' Nice words but her tone was decidedly dismissive.

'Do you have a back door?'

She pointed down a passage. 'Past the toilets and through the yard.'

Stuart woke as I slammed the bedroom door. 'Woah. Morning.'

'That cheating, squirming worm!'

'Uh? Who?'

'Gavin!' I paced back and forth across the room at the bottom of the bed. 'He put a tracker on us.'

Stuart looked confused and fumbled with the duvet to sit up. 'How?'

'I'm going to kill him,' I said.

'Really?'

'Yes. Really. I'm going to rip his arms off and stuff them up his backside.'

'Oh. Nice.' He swung his legs out of the bed and yawned. 'I need the bathroom.'

I'd noticed.

Stuart drank his coffee and said nothing until I'd ranted myself out. He nodded and looked at the carpet. 'He's a naughty boy,' he said.

'Naughty? He's a sneaky, conniving, cheating git.' I slumped in my seat and scowled at the breakfast. Not saying what I really thought, using full floral swear words, made me feel miserable. 'A proper git.'

'Yeah, I get it. So anyway, where was the tracker and where is it now?'

'It was buried in that stupid leaflet he gave me. I stuck it on some old biddy where I bought the breakfast. He's probably at bingo or something now. But he won't be fooled for long — we need to finish up and get out of here.'

He nodded. 'So it was on you, not us.' I shot him a look. He raised his hands in surrender. 'Just getting the facts sorted. At least now we know how he got here and that the guards aren't gossiping. That's a good thing. Positives.' He did his signature finger waggle thing before turning serious. 'I think we should wait here, let Gavin come and talk to us. We've seen where the kids are being held, now's the time to tell Joe where we are. Joe can contact my mum and they'll figure out how to get the kids out of the Manor.'

I weighed the idea up. Knowing where the kids were didn't quite have the same heroic zim as taking them home ourselves. My fantasy ran away with itself again and I pictured myself smiling, holding Gemma's hand, walking along the pavement to greet Joe. 'You don't think we can get them out by ourselves?'

'I think the safest way, for the kids and us, would be to let the experts take over.' He held my hand and fiddled with my fingers. 'I'll make sure Joe knows it was thanks to you we found them.'

'I don't need you to tell him anything but the truth.'

'Of course not.'

'But feel free to point out all the good bits. The riding the bike, the …' I tried to think which moment had been entirely mine.

'Naturally,' Stuart said. He smiled. 'Trust me. Joe will think you're ripe for chief commandant or whatever the group call their top man. Or woman.'

There was a knock on the door. 'Mm,' I said. 'Sooner than I expected.' I opened the door.

'Very funny, Atty.' Gavin strutted into the room and stood all macho-esque in front of the window. 'These things cost money, don't you know?' He waved a small box, about the size of a ring case. 'You're lucky I got it back.'

'Or what?' I demanded. 'What would you have done?'

'Huh. You don't want to know.'

I scoffed and folded my arms. Like he, the bonzo of Basley, had the nerve to try and scare me. 'Where did you get that from anyway? Not Joe, surely.'

'I bought it.'

'Yeah right.'

'I did. It's mine.'

Stuart came and stood alongside me, not touching, but close enough to leave no doubt whose corner he was in. 'It doesn't matter where or why or whatever. The point is, Gavin. We need you to get in touch with Joe and tell him where we are. We've found Gemma. We need Joe to contact my mother and they can arrange for Gemma, and maybe the others too, to be taken home.'

'Well, duh uh,' said Gavin all sarky, 'if I could get to speak to Joe I would have already. Nobody can get in or out of the west and all communications are cut, it's under lockdown.'

I dropped to a sit on the bed. 'Please tell me you're lying.'

'Straight. Something to do with the riots. Joe's locked in and we're locked out. But Gemma and Stacey are okay where they are. They're in some big house playing with ponies and go-karts.' He looked around the room at the grubbiness and sniffed. 'Don't know what we're going to do though.'

'We?' If he thought he was about to snuggle up between me and Stuart he could think again. 'Where did you sleep last night?'

He grinned and gave me a need-you-ask look.

I snatched at the duvet and made a show of tidying the bed. 'Well you can sod off back there again tonight.'

'Why, don't you want me getting in the way? Moved on to the next step have we?' he spoke all sarky and whiny.

I swung round but he was looking at Stuart, and not in a happy way. The flaming cheek of him. 'It's none of your business.'

'Guys,' said Stuart, 'can we cut the squabbling. I'm trying to think.'

Squabbling was what it was, childish and petty. I tried to raise the tone. 'We need to find out if time is an issue. If the kids are safe we might as well leave them there until the lockdown is lifted.'

'They're good, I told you, they've got ponies and go-karts to play with.'

'No Gavin. They haven't. There are no ponies, no go-karts, no anything. Who knows what the hell is going on in that place?' Stuart paced the room. 'We can't risk waiting for help. If they're being mistreated we'll have to get them out ourselves. There's no saying how long the lockdown will last.'

'Okay, if that's all true, then I'll help you. So long as I don't have to deal with the creep with the gold tooth.'

'What do you know about him? And how did you get here? Train? They're pricey tickets.'

'I came on my bike.'

This was getting more confusing by the minute. 'You haven't got a bike,' I said.

Gavin grinned like a loon. 'I have now. You'll love it. It's a sport with a thousand cc and it's got …'

'Gavin.' Stuart stepped up to Gavin's face, his palms facing the floor, shoulders tight. 'Shut up. We get it, you've got a bike. Now all we want to know is — what do you know about Crawlsfeld? The bloke with the gold tooth.'

Gavin glanced at me and turned all coy and daft. 'Well. It's complicated.'

'Just tell us, Gavin.' Stuart used his bulk to lean into Gavin, making him squirm and back away.

'Okay. Straight. He caught me nicking a car over east, let me off if I could introduce him to anybody wanting to give their kid up for adoption. Paid me too.'

I couldn't believe his ability to be so blasé. 'You earned money by introducing Crawlsfeld to Carl.'

Gavin stepped towards me. 'You don't get what it was like for Carl. He's not a bad bloke. Just some young lad working all the hours he's awake in some crummy, mindless job. They paid him in kiddy vouchers mainly. He had nothing for himself. Or Fran. She wasn't happy, Atts, honest she wasn't. I didn't think she'd do what she did, but it was no life for any of them. Including Stacey. Especially Stacey.'

'Nice speech,' said Stuart. 'But why did Crawlsfeld want them? Did you ask him?'

I sneered. 'Or did you just ask, how much?' Things had been tough for Fran, but that was because Carl let them down. He should have stepped up. 'If the job didn't pay enough, Carl should have got a better one.'

Gavin snorted. 'Yep. Just like that. Because that's what it's like, isn't it, Atty? A guy needs money to feed his girl and kid and, if his job don't pay, all he has to do is go out and get another one.' He spat the last three words like he wanted them to stab me through the eyeball. I studied the pattern on the manky carpet. Everything stank. And I didn't know how to put it right.

Stuart spoke quietly into the silence. 'And Gemma? Do you know why Crawlsfeld picked Gemma?'

'My girl over east. She knew your mum was away and, well, your dad ain't the best, is he?'

'Did she earn enough for a bike too?'

'She's got enough money of her own.'

I laughed. 'You kept her money too, huh? Wow. You the man, Gav. You the man.'

'I've said I'll help get them back.'

'Yes. You did. But what do you think you can do to help us?'

'I can find out what's going on in the Manor.'
'How?'
'Well I'll ask Mary.'
'Who's Mary?'
'She put me up last night. I'll ask, she'll tell me. How hard can it be?'
If only all our lives could be as simple as Gavin's.

CHAPTER TWENTY

Gavin's bike shone blinding silver in the sun, like something from a movie about old-town America. The sort of machine kids from either side of the river might kill for. Stuart walked around it and whistled. 'Beautiful.'

Gavin almost rubbed himself with pleasure. 'Isn't she?'

Suddenly they were the best of friends with all that macho rivalry tucked neatly out of the way while they bonded over a few bits of metal. Though, to be fair, a granny could see the appeal. It was a stunning machine. I wanted to touch the tank and run my fingers along the smooth black seat. I put my hands in my pockets out of harm's way. 'You won't be able to keep it out of trouble for five minutes at home,' I said. 'Some cons will nick it, or a Red will confiscate it. Guaranteed.'

'Maybe I won't go back to Basley. Stay out, touring the open road.'

'Don't be such a doughnut. How will you survive?'

'I've managed okay so far.'

'It's only been hours. Hardly enough time to get hungry. And what about your family? They're going to worry about you if you just vanish. Specially in the middle of a lockdown.' The image of a bunch of forget-me-nots flashed in front of my eyes.

'Okay, let's keep focused on today,' said Stuart, 'We need to find this Mary.' His eyes still had that glint of anger about them, but it softened when he spoke to me. 'Joe will handle the stuff at home, try not to worry.'

Gavin kicked up the stand and pushed his bike along the gutter. 'Yeah. Joe will be fine.' All the emphasis on Joe. He wasn't so blasé about his family as he'd like us all to think. His mum and kid brothers were back there too.

I opened my mouth to say something reassuring but Stuart shook his head so I left it. After all, I didn't know his family would be okay. Or even if Joe would be okay come to that. None of us knew anything.

Mary was a stupid name, it didn't fit the person at all. Mary's are old, plump and bubbly, not six foot tall and string skinny. This Mary had blonde fluffy hair, boobs busting out of a plastic tube-like thing, her legs orange and endless - a typical Gav-looking girl. She studied me from neck to toe. Despite all the paint on her face she looked sour-mouthed and hostile. 'Who's she?'

'These are my friends,' said Gavin. 'Is it all right if they ask a few questions?'

'They can ask. Not going to promise I'll answer.' She folded her arms and gave Gav the glare. 'You left without saying goodbye.'

'I'm here now, aren't I? How could I stay away?'

She pulled away from his outreached hand. I managed not to smile. She clearly wasn't as dumb as she looked and I felt a twang of respect.

We were standing in the street outside a small antique shop. The owner, her boss and possibly her father, fiddled with pieces of paper at the counter, his eyes never leaving us for a second.

Stuart stepped forward. 'Perhaps we can take you for a coffee. Or lunch.'

'What do you want?'

'We're doing a project on old buildings and their uses. There's a big Manor house a couple of miles up the road. We just want to know what it's used for? What goes on inside it?' He shrugged. 'Boring stuff like that.'

No way would she believe that one.

'What's it worth?' she said, quick like she'd dealt with such things a million times before.

Gavin looked shocked. 'Eh?'

Mary ignored him and I almost laughed aloud.

Stuart took off his watch. 'This is all I have left but it's worth a few quid.'

Mary looked but didn't reach out. 'I like the bike.'

'No way.' Gavin shook his head. 'Not a hope. I've only just got it.'

Mary shrugged and looked at her own watch.

Stuart spoke to Gavin, 'You can get another bike.'

Gavin shuffled his feet and stroked the handlebar. 'No way. Jeez. I'll never get the chance to have anything like this again.'

Stuart stepped closer and spoke quietly into Gavin's face. 'There are lots of bikes. I have one sister.'

Mary and I watched as Gav and Stuart had a minor stand-off. There might be lots of bikes in Stuart's world, but odds were this would be the only one Gavin ever got a hold of.

'I'm not giving up my bike.'

Any other time I might have relaxed and enjoyed the fun of seeing Gavin squirm but the last thing we needed right then was a public scrap in the street. 'Listen, Gav,' I said, 'you can't take it home anyway, how would you explain where it came from? And you will have to go home. You know as well as I do that no other county will allow you to get a job or anything. You can't live off fresh air. If you have to lose the bike, it might as well be now, for a good reason.' I didn't want to say much more, not in front of Mary who stood watching with a slimy smile on her perfectly made-up face.

'But I could sell it.' He stroked the seat.

'Gav please.' I leaned in and whispered. 'Think what Joe will say if he finds out how you got it.'

'Aw, sheesh.' He pushed it towards Mary. 'We want to know everything there is to know about that place. Everything.'

Mary turned and nodded at the man behind the counter and he came out followed by two steroid-bulked guys who must have been hiding under a table or something. I glanced at Stuart who watched Gavin hand over the bike. Gavin put his hands into his pockets, slouched his shoulders, glum as a week old plum. I patted his shoulder. Like I cared. Stuart turned his attention back to Mary and I began plotting where to light the flame on the shop-front if she failed to keep her side of the deal.

'It's a research centre,' she said. 'A chemical laboratory developing drugs for kids. Something to do with keeping the population down – chemical sterilisations or whatever.' She shrugged. 'Some foreigners have commissioned it. Brings a lot of money into the town. That's all I can tell you.' She turned and stepped through the door. Her dad closed it firmly behind her and Gavin, Stuart and I were left standing on the street like an unwanted delivery of muppets.

'How many words was that?' Gavin waved his arms about. 'A bike like that baby for what? A dozen words?' He pointed through the window towards the man who had returned to the counter like nothing had happened. 'Are we going to let them get away with that?'

Stuart spoke icy cold. 'Yes. We don't need any trouble and I already told you, I'll get you another bike.' And to me, 'We need to get the kids out of there. Today.' He walked away.

Gavin looked like he might cry. 'Atty?'

'I guess if it's all Mary knows, it's all Mary knows.' I followed Stuart.

'But,' Gavin danced alongside me, 'but we could take them, come on. What's happened to you? You never used to be so … so obedient.'

'I'm picking my battles.'

Gavin sneered. 'You're being a wuss.' He faked a wussy voice, 'It'll work out, Atty.' Then he played it whiny, 'Okay Stuey wooey, I'll just roll over and do everything your way.'

'Shut the a-hole up, Gavin,' I said, 'it's running away with itself and talking crap again.' And to think I almost felt sorry for him having to give up the bike.

'If it was your bike I bet you wouldn't walk away so easily.'

I stopped. 'And if it was one of your kid brothers in there, getting drugged up to stop them breeding, would you walk away with the bike?'

If Gav loved anybody it was his brothers. He looked everywhere but my eyes. 'We don't know whether Mary is even telling the truth.' But the fight had gone clean out of him. He turned quiet and sulky. 'I should have just kept riding and left you to it. Gone up to Scotland or somewhere.'

'It's not too late to keep walking. Go.' I strode away to catch up with Stuart knowing Gavin would follow. He had nowhere to go, nobody to run to, and, without the bike, no way of getting there.

It only took two hours to hike to the Manor. And this time, we all climbed the easy route up the hill, one after the other. We sat side by side, me in the middle, looking over into the grounds. The blinds were still drawn and nothing moved anywhere. It looked like a painting.

'So,' said Stuart. 'Ponies and go-karts, eh?'

Gavin ignored him. 'What do we do now?'

Stuart adjusted his position. 'We have patience. Something has to happen sometime. And then we watch and learn.'

Brilliant. More waiting.

After what felt like several awkward hours, but might have been only five minutes, a truck with 'International Security Specialists' written across its flank, pulled up at the Manor entrance. A man got out, keyed a number into the pad, and the gates swung open.

'That looked easy,' said Gavin.

Such a dork. 'Yeah,' I said. 'He used a code, Gavin.'

'We can get a code.'

'How?'

'We'll stop him down the road and ask him.'

'What - you think he'll just spit it out? Or have you got another bike we can bribe him with? Stashed in your pocket perhaps?'

He glanced at his lap and waggled his eyebrows. 'I'm just delighted to see you again, Atty.' He laughed. 'We can persuade him to hand it over. A little not-so-gentle encouragement should do it.'

'You mean batter him.'

'You got a better idea?'

Stuart sighed. 'Guys, you're going to have to cut out this senseless squabbling. If we're going to do this we have to try and work together.'

It felt like a slap in the eye. 'What? There are three of us now?'

'He says he wants to help. We need all the help we can get.'

'But, you agreed he's not on our team. What happened to it being just us? We can't trust him. It's all his fault.'

Gavin put his hand on my arm and tilted his head in mock sincerity. 'You can trust me, Atty. I promise.'

I rounded on him. 'Don't you dare touch me.' I gave him my most evil eye. 'Ever again.'

'Look,' said Stuart. 'I'm not asking you to kiss and make up. Just to put your differences to one side while we get Gemma out of there.'

Stuart and his all dancing, duck-plucking sensible, understanding, reasoning. He made me feel stupid and juvenile. 'Fine,' I said. 'But it would be much better if we just stowed away in the back of the truck. Then, if there is somebody monitoring the camera, they will see a familiar face punching the keys.'

Stuart nodded. 'Excellent suggestion.'

I felt ridiculously chuffed despite a sneaky suspicion he might be being more than a teeny bit patronising.

Gavin looked from me to Stuart and back again, confused and gormless. 'So when we batter him, we mustn't batter his face.'

Brains of a banana might be the best description.

Stuart continued in the assumed role of guvnor. 'We need to get a means of following the truck when it comes out.' He pointed at Gavin. 'You can steal us a car.'

'What now? Where from?'

'That's up to you. You're either in our team or not. Get us a car and wait for us down there. Park up behind the clump of trees.'

Gavin pouted, bit like trout face, but twisted onto his knees and put one leg over the edge of the cliff. And then he looked at Stuart. 'You won't go anywhere and just, well, leave me here, will you?'

If only his estate mates could have seen him. Talk about pitiful. I shook my head and sighed in sympathy. 'Wow, Gav. Did you see that?' I looked up at the cloudless sky. 'That bad-ass meadow-fracking image you took all those years to establish? It just rocketed straight out the atmosphere.'

CHAPTER TWENTY-ONE

Gavin's head disappeared over the edge of the cliff. Stuart put his arm around me. 'You shouldn't tease him like that.' He nudged my head with his forehead. 'Naughty.'

'He asked for it. You should see him strutting his stuff at home. He thinks he's the donkey's plums.'

'You appear more than a little obsessed with donkeys and certain parts of their anatomy.'

'And you appear pretty obsessed with pointing it out.'

He gave me a squeeze. 'I like the reference.'

I laughed but it sounded false. I coughed, left a couple of beats then asked, 'Are you feeling okay about all this?'

He swallowed. 'As much as I could be, I suppose.' He still looked angry but smiled at me. 'Yeah. Better when we get Gemma back, which we will. But yeah, I'm okay. You?'

'Of course.' I clenched my fists and held them up to my chin. 'Experienced, remember? I'll be fine.'

'Great stuff.' He winked. 'You can go in first.' Before I could reply he said, 'So what do you reckon? Do you think Gavin will make a run for it or come back with some wheels?'

'Oh he'll be back. He only wanted to run away so he could keep the bike. And even if there was no lockdown, Joe would go mental if he ran home without me.'

Stuart kept his arm hooked around my neck. 'He must think a lot of you. Joe.'

'Yeah. He's been good to me.'

'Will he be okay? I don't mean now, the lockdown, I mean after all this is done? Will he take you back?'

I swivelled to look at him straight on. 'What? It's not like … that. He's old enough to be my father. He's my dad's best mate, that's why he looks out for me.'

'I know. But back into his confidence I mean.'

'He'll be okay.' I thought about it. Given what I'd learned about Dad, I had as good a reason to be mad at Joe as he had to be mad at me. Well, almost. Maybe. Anyway, whatever, Joe might be a buffoon mobster but he loved me even if he might be bad at showing it. It would take something seriously rotten for him to write me out of his life. Thinking harder, it wouldn't happen. 'He'll come round,' I said. 'Why?'

'I just don't want any of this mess to cause you any long-term grief.' He looked at me and rolled his eyes before gazing back down into the valley. 'You know I like you.' A long pause. 'A lot. I don't like to think of you being lonely.'

'I'm used to being on my own. I like it.'

We sat and watched the gates while we waited for Gavin. After an hour or so the delivery van left and headed back towards Shepton. Stuart groaned. 'Gavin's not very quick, is he?'

'Maybe he's got caught.'

He tutted. 'Wouldn't that be just what we needed?'

'Perhaps we should have stolen something ourselves,' I said. Judging by his panic after nicking the DVD I doubted Stuart had ever nicked anything else, certainly not a car.

He turned away, squinting into the sunshine. 'Mm.'

But we didn't have to wait much longer before a jeep came crashing down the lane, bouncing off the hedgerows. I groaned. 'What's the betting?'

'So long as he's on his own, who cares?'

Gavin created an untidy doughnut around a mash of brambles before skidding to a hand-brake halt behind the trees. We watched to make sure nobody had followed him before we clambered down the cliff.

'Nice one. Thank you,' said Stuart as he slipped into the passenger seat. I climbed into the back. Stuart no longer appeared impatient or fed up at having to hang around waiting. Quite the opposite. His ability to maintain super politeness whatever the occasion, with whoever was around, even Gavin for sanity's sake, was beginning to get right up my rear. He slapped Gavin on the shoulder like they were best buddies. 'Let's go find that truck. It left about twenty minutes ago, heading towards Shepton.'

The jeep bunny-hopped out of the field, my head nearly bouncing off my shoulders.

'Is it supposed to be doing this?' I said, my voice shuddering with the rattling.

'I'm still getting used to the clutch.'

'We'll hardly keep a low profile going through town bucking like a kangaroo on acid.'

'Do you want to drive?'

Stuart put on a sing-song voice. 'You're doing it again. Arguing like two-year-olds.'

I glared at him. 'A girl can go off somebody, you know.' As soon as the words were out I wanted to snatch them back. Gavin grinned at me through the rear-view mirror. I smacked the back of his head. 'Watch the road.'

Most shops along Shepton seafront were reserved for seasidey stuff, such as sticks of rock and bikinis. So when we saw the van parked half way along, we guessed the driver had likely gone in the one general store. Despite, or maybe because of all the CCTV, the place heaved with people and a lot of them were security. I didn't fancy testing their tolerance.

'We need to keep going,' I said. 'Don't stop.' The Shepton Law might have appeared all warm and cuddly but I suspected the town was only so welcoming because they had a good hold on the petty stuff. Like jeep-nicking.

Basley Law took the hard-line approach so the town was a wreck and I assumed places with a soft, ineffective Law would be equally shambolic. It looked like Shepton Law had the balance pretty much perfect. It seemed to make for a happy home. Of course a dodgy science lab offering ample jobs, possibly even community-boosting hush-money, might also have had something to do with it.

Gavin cruised past the store. 'We'll ambush him along the lane, half way up the hill, where it's quiet. That way, if he gets uppity we can give him a slap.'

'The less violence the better,' said Stuart. 'All I want you to do is distract him while Atty and I climb in the back of the truck. Hopefully he'll take us all the way into the Manor.'

'How am I going to get in?' Gavin gave me the filthiest look in the rear-view mirror.

I liked being picked because I liked Gavin's ego getting bashed, but I wasn't sure about going into the Manor without any sort of plan. Not that I admitted it. Quite the opposite. 'No probs,' I said, grinning like a monkey.

'We need you to wait outside with the jeep,' Stuart said to Gavin. 'Ready to get us away. That small gate at the back of the grounds looks the best bet. Wait for us there.'

My stomach flip-flopped and my voice sounded weak, even to me. 'What if we get caught?'

'We won't.' This must be macho, tough-man Stuart. He was so full of surprises I'd run out of boxes to tick.

Before we headed off up the hill, we stopped at the B&B to steal the duvet cover.

'It'll be doing the next guests a favour,' said Stuart.

'Stained, is it?' Gavin raised his eyebrows at me.

Stuart sent him a big-man scowl. 'I'll be slapping your bloody head in a minute. Now just drive and stop being a bloody …' He tailed off, screwing his mouth up in frustration.

I laughed so hard I worried hysteria might set in. Joe was after me to dish out the rollicking of a lifetime, the Law were chasing me down for all sorts of reasons, creepy Crawly was doing … something - God knows what - and I was about to try and sneak into a place teeming with International Security Specialists. All with an easty who couldn't bring himself to be even a little bit rude to Gavin. I had to be insane. The way the boys frowned and glanced at each other confirmed it.

'I think she's finally lost it.'

'You could be right.'

I gathered myself and coughed. 'I'm fine.'

Half way up the hill out of Shepton, we found a viewing point where tourists could sit and look out over the ocean. We sat on a bench and watched the main road out of town. A red van appeared first. It drove out of sight as the road swerved behind a hill and I counted twenty-seven seconds before it reappeared further along at an untidy copse. Then it vanished for another fifty-three seconds before passing the viewing station. The second vehicle out was a blue car. Twenty-eight seconds and it reappeared.

'Here comes the truck,' said Gavin. 'He's much slower than the cars.'

'You need to wait for the blue car to pass … fifty seconds.' I counted. Sixty … seventy …

Stuart wiped his top lip. 'In about another twenty seconds he'll be here.'

'… eighty. The blue car must have turned off. 'Do it now,' I said.

All the arguing stopped and we looked at each other, wide-eyed terrified. I felt so wired like I could fly, win battles single-handed, feed the world, take command of the universe. This would be the stupidest but most fantastic thing any of us were ever likely to do.

Gavin drove the jeep to the middle of the road, cut the engine and climbed out to lift the bonnet. Stuart and I ducked into the hedge behind brambles and nettles. Logic told me it should hurt but I didn't feel a thing. My nerves were stretched so taught they felt guaranteed to snap.

The truck arrived, trundled to a halt and the driver stepped out. 'What's up, mate?'

There flashed a moment when I almost didn't do it, a moment where I wanted to turn and run. It wasn't my sister in there. And what would I do with Fran's baby when I got her? I couldn't look after her and I didn't want to give her back to Carl. And what about planning? We hadn't planned anything. It was all happening too fast. But then Stuart's arm stiffened beside me and when he stepped up I did too. As we reached the back of the truck he scooped his hands together to give me a leg up.

'Don't be daft,' I whispered. 'I beat you to the top of the cliff, remember?' I entwined my fingers for a step. 'Get in.' He shook his head, mouth open, a look that yelled, Do me a favour. He put one hand on the back of the truck and leapt in as quiet as a cat. I clattered after him and we lay snucked up against the front section, behind the driver's cab, under the duvet cover. 'Holy frosties, what are we doing?' I whispered.

'Shhh.'

'I really need to pee.'

He put his finger over my lips. I wanted to bite it. Definitely insane. There were a few shouts and then a clear, 'Cheers mate,' and the driver restarted the engine. The truck meandered into a slow rolling rattle along the narrow lanes, jerking through its gears. I wanted to jump out. We hadn't thought it through at all.

My voice shook when I asked, 'Are you sure about this?' I really, really wanted to make a run for it. 'Stuart?' The truck stopped at the gates. Now or never. The driver keyed in the number and the truck inched forward, over a bump and through the gates. Too late. Shit, shit, shit. Perhaps shit was an acceptable part of BBC speak. When they were really, really nervous. Besides, I'm pretty sure any pledge to my mum would be null and void if I died. I wondered if seventeen was too young for a heart attack. Stuart's mouth nestled against my forehead, his nose in my hair, his breathing rapid and hot. The truck stopped but the engine kept running. Steps crunched in gravel.

'Did you get me my sausage sandwich?'

'Yep. Ten quid.'

'Park up around the back and I'll meet you out front. We can eat in the sunshine.'

A short, rocky trundle and the engine stopped, the cab door opened, slammed, a few footsteps, and then silence.

Stuart moved his hand. I squeaked.

'He's gone,' said Stuart.

'I know but … eee.'

'They're at lunch. Come on.' He peeled back the duvet.

We leapt out of the van and crouched behind the wheel to scan for any movement in the Manor house. Behind us the grass opened out flat and clean. I felt enormous. Huge. Nobody could fail to see us.

The back of the Manor had fewer windows than the front and appeared to be a lot less grand. The walls were a dirty grey and old-fashioned air conditioning units, drainpipes and rusty brackets from satellite dishes made it look ugly and derelict. Only one door, but several sash windows, all with blinds drawn, one of them open. When

Stuart ran, doubled over like in an old war movie, I followed, but I didn't like the sneaking about. An idiot on crack would know we didn't belong there the way we were behaving. 'We need to stand up,' I said. 'Act normal, confident, look like we have a right to be here.'

Stuart put his ear to the open window before peeping through the slats. 'All clear, you go first.'

Great.

We were in a bathroom, very convenient. As soon as I saw the loo my bladder almost popped. 'I've got to go.'

'Okay.' He put his ear to the door. I jigged. 'Go on then. I won't look.'

'No I know, but …' He stood with his back to me. It was a natural function; everybody did it, better than peeing my pants. I tried to be quiet, aimed at the side of the pan, and prayed I didn't fart.

Stuart did that whispery-shouty thing. 'Finished?'

I flushed. Pipes rattled and hummed. It sounded like the ships were coming in. Stuart glared. 'I can't stop it now,' I said.

He beckoned me over to the door. 'You go out first.'

'Thanks.'

'You're better at this stuff than me. Experienced remember?'

I had said that but it seemed a very long time ago. 'Only in Basley.'

'We can't stay locked in here.'

He was right. We'd got so far. All we needed to do was find Gemma and get the hell out. If it looked an okay kind of place, I might even leave the others there until Joe could sort it out. The drugs mightn't even work. I opened the door and stepped out into the corridor. I strolled down the passage like I was bored of living there, but we met no one. I pumped myself up, determined to get the adrenaline flowing. My voice came over all lofty arrogant. 'Let's take the stairs.' Bring it on, Mr Crawly Crawlsfeld. Hell, nobody would be daft enough to challenge me. Get in. Easy. Yowza yay.

Stuart gripped my arm. 'Somebody's coming.'

Hey, it would all work out. 'Relax and look chilled.'

Trotting down the stairs towards us were two women dressed in suits with groomed hair and pasted faces. 'Good afternoon,' I said, in the poshest and deepest BBC ever.

'Good afternoon,' they tweeted back. They tip-tapped on and we rounded the bend onto the next flight.

'Bloody hell,' said Stuart. 'What a rush. I see why you do it now.'

'It's just my job, Stuart, just my job.' Very, and without a doubt, certifiably bonkers.

There were three floors and we went right to the top. We pushed through into the corridor but, unlike the one downstairs, it had carpets, soft lights and the general ambience of a hotel.

'Let's listen at a few doors,' said Stuart. 'Gemma never stops talking, if she's in any of these rooms, we'll hear her.' I took the left, he took the right.

Stuart moved faster than me. 'Hey, Atty. Look here.' A door to an office had been left open. 'Shall we take a quick look? We might find something.'

'Like what?'

'I don't know. A list of patients. Like in a hospital.'

I stepped in and shuffled a few bits of paper on top of a desk. They all had the pony and go-kart pics and Sapton Manor in fancy lettering spread across the header.

Stuart scuttled in after me. 'Quick hide, somebody's coming.' Before I could stop him he dunked down behind a leather sofa onto his hands and knees.

'Oh, hello,' said a short round man with comb-over hair.

I couldn't keep my eyes from staring at his huge bulbous nose. It bulged all knobbly and was covered in the spidery threads of the typical alcoholic.

'Are you looking for me?' he said.

I smiled. 'I've been told you might know which room little Gemma is in.'

He frowned. 'Gemma?'

'It's her birthday, seventh I think it is.'

He squinted and looked at me more closely.

'Ah,' I tried to look apologetic. 'I've confused you, I'm so dreadfully sorry. I must have wandered into the wrong room. Mr Crawlsfeld, I'm supposed to speak to.'

His face relaxed and he smiled. 'Not just the wrong room I'm afraid, wrong floor.' He reached out his arm to guide me into the corridor. 'Floor below, room 15.'

'Ah, thank you so very much. So sorry to have inconvenienced you.'

'No problem.' And he shut the door.

CHAPTER TWENTY-TWO

I stood in the corridor and looked at the door for several moments before a woman's voice said, 'Are you lost?'

'No, no. I'm fine thank you.' I walked to the end of the corridor, back into the stair tower and panicked. Shit, shit, SHIT.

'Are you sure you're okay?' The stupid cow had followed me.

'Fire.'

'What?'

'We need to empty the rooms. There's a fire.'

'May I see your pass?' She wore her pic pinned to her breast in a plastic wallet.

I slapped my hand to my chest. 'Oh dash it. Wherever might that have gone? I must have left it in the office.'

'Really.' She stared hard. 'I'll come back with you, help you look.' She glanced at a camera high up on the wall.

'Oh please do. Four eyes are always so much better than two, don't you find?'

She adjusted her pink framed glasses on the bridge of her nose.

'Um, I didn't mean. I meant …' I gestured at my face then hers, '…you've got two and I've got two, that makes …' Oh shititty shit.

'Four. Yes, I know.' She stepped aside. 'After you.'

In the corridor I kept my eyes on the carpet and patted my chest and pocket in an it-was-here-a-minute-ago fashion, but inside everything disintegrated into panic mode – blood cascading, thoughts collapsing to mush, sweat pumping out of every follicle, the full shamboozle.

The woman overtook me and rapped sharply on the squidgy-nosed alcoholic's door. It opened. 'Hi,' she said.

'Your guest appears to have lost her pass. Did she leave it in here?'

I looked at the ceiling and screwed up my mouth in what I hoped was a hapless but lovable little-girl-lost look. 'Doh. Dropped it somewhere.'

'She's here to see Crawlsfeld,' Alcoholic-nose said to the woman. Then he turned to me. 'I'll give him a ring, tell him to come and get you. Might be best. Though he hasn't been about much lately.' He headed back in the room to his desk and picked up the phone. As he pushed in a number he said, 'What was your name again?'

The woman crossed her arms and tilted her head, school ma'am style. 'And apparently,' she said, 'there might be a fire.'

I laughed. 'No. Flyer. As in leaflet. I read a flyer saying the rooms needed emptying. Didn't you get it?'

'Strangely enough, no.'

I tilted my head in a bemused fashion. 'Oh dear.' There was no sight nor sound of Stuart.

Alcoholic replaced the phone. 'I'm not getting an answer, didn't think so. He's been a little selective with his company since he got back from that Basley place.'

I thanked the last flying duck for that but tried out my disappointed isn't-that-a-dreadful-nuisance look.

He checked his watch. 'Maybe he's on lunch. I could do with a bite myself.' He ran his thumbs around his waistband. 'I'll walk you down.' He picked a set of keys up off the desk and bounced them in his hand. 'Thank you, Sharon. I'll take it from here.'

We all three stepped into the corridor and the office door was locked, the keys placed securely in Alcoholic's hip pocket. Sharon wandered away.

'Thanks for your help, Sharon.' I called after her.

My tone didn't get lost on Alcoholic. 'Yes,' he said. 'She can be a little officious at times. Only started last week, she's still a bit keen.'

'It's no problem. I think I might take a walk in the grounds while I wait for Mr Crawlsfeld to finish his lunch. It's such a beautiful day.'

'Good idea. I'll walk you to the door and security can issue you with a new pass.'

'That won't be necessary, I can find my own way.'

'It's no bother.'

'I'd rather not put you to any more trouble.'

'It'll be my pleasure.'

'Thank you.'

Polite people are a proper pain in my rack.

I had three flights of stairs to come up with a plan. I needed to get the keys and then lose the helpful leech. Anything would be worth a go. Aim at the weak spot, Atty. 'Is there anywhere we can get a drink?'

He raised his eyebrows as he opened the door at the top of the stairs. 'A drink?'

'Yeah, you know.' I sniffed and glanced around. 'To take the edge off.'

'Sapton Manor is a dry zone. That should have been explained to you at your induction.'

'Yes it was, of course.' I tilted my head and gave him a sideways look. 'But, is it really?' Then I treated him to a slow wink.

He licked his lips and swallowed. 'Yes. Really.'

We passed the first floor. The cameras winked at me from every corner. I would have to run for it. Batter the office door down to get Stuart out. Find Gemma, get past security, climb the wall. A line of sweat ran down the back of my neck. We'd never make it.

'Of course,' said Alcoholic. 'I keep a little something aside for special occasions.' He smirked at me and my guts hurled towards my throat. Uh oh, he actually fancied his chances.

I supressed a heave and came over all simpering call-girl. 'There are ways of making every moment special.' I wiggled my eyebrows. Oh the cheese.

'I'm sure there is.' He looked at my chest, then my lips.

We reached the ground floor. I'd met enough old fools to recognise a lonely old wino, desperate for a bit of attention. After all, West Basley is full of them. All I needed to do was share a little snifter, it's not like I didn't fancy a drop to settle my nerves in any case, then, with a little flattery and ego stroking, I would sweet-talk him into taking me back to his office and figure the rest out from there.

He hooked my arm through his elbow and led me down a narrow, empty corridor. I didn't expect him to flaunt me or our illegal drink in public, but I'd have preferred somewhere closer to some people. He led me away from the offices and down into the silent cool air of a little-used corridor lined with tatty doors. The only sound was his panting and my heart racing like a greyhound on speed.

Alcoholic dropped my arm to put his weight to a door. He grunted and shoved with both hands and a knee. 'Sticks sometimes,' he said. 'Nearly there now.' Behind the door wormed a tiny passage. The pink of bare plaster walls and a grey concrete floor gave the impression it had only just been built. The chill of the air on my face felt like I might be about to enter a fridge. 'Where is this?' I asked.

'It's okay. Nearly there.' He smacked his lips. 'You'll love what I've got for you.'

I put my hand on the door jamb. It looked pretty isolated and away from any cameras.

'Come,' he said and gripped my arm. 'It's okay. I'll look after you.'

Yeah, course he would. My instincts yelled loud and clear and they weren't happy.

'Come on, have a drink with me. It's down here, not far.' He looked away while he searched his pockets for something.

I considered doing it right then - left punch to his right temple, right knee in the nuts, followed by a right fist up and under his ribcage while I fished the keys from his pocket with my left. I glanced behind me. The corridor might be empty but cameras sat high near the ceiling. There were a lot of stairs and corridors between me and Stuart, no time to cover them all. I stepped through the door. 'Lead on. I'm very thirsty.'

'Good girl.'

His footsteps slapped noisily as we headed down the passage and my stomach started to rotate. He might be older, but so was Joe. He might look flabby under that suit, but so did many a muscleman. People were often different to how they looked on first glance. I considered dropping back a step so I could catch him from behind - a fist just behind his ear followed by a jab to his kidney.

He opened a door to our right and twisted at the waist to push me into a walk-in cupboard - all in one fast and easy motion. Not only was he quicker than he looked but his fingers were more solid, bonier, stronger.

'We've not got long,' he said yanking at his belt. 'I'm not as stupid as you think. Do as I say and I might help you get out of here alive.'

There were wide shelves on three of the walls leaving precious little floor space. Boxes protruded at various heights and I stumbled and skidded on plastic bags strewn across the floor. I'd left it too late. I was trapped, squashed against shelves which left me no room to move. My arms were pinned between boxes and bags and all sorts of general junk.

Alcoholic dropped his trousers to his ankles. His shirt hung long, creased and greasy, the hem almost skimming his pale, knobbly knees and shiny nylon socks. His left hand groped for my belt, he leaned in, the open pores on his face glistened with oily sweat and he panted hot whisky breath so strong I tasted it. I turned away and closed my mouth. 'Don't be shy, we need to hurry, the cameras …' He pressed me against a shelf and it dug into my spine. I worked my arms in front of me so they were between us. There was no room to swing so I had little option other than to grab. I groped at his left hand and found his thumb, yanked and twisted it so hard my wrist cricked. His right hand tried to prise my fingers open. I pulled harder, gritting my teeth and looking him dead in the eye. He roared and pulled his head back but I read his mind and ducked so when he butted, my forehead connected with the fat veiny nose. His blood, warm and sticky, splattered across both of our faces. He grunted and we both grimaced.

I so nearly let go of his thumb to wipe his blood away, but he was strong and I already felt my grip weakening. 'Shh,' I said. 'Somebody might hear. You wouldn't want to get caught with your pants down, would you?'

'I don't know who you are,' he said, 'but that was a big mistake.'

I had sod all left to lose, so twisted and tugged in a last ditch attempt to tear his thumb clean off.

He changed tack and stepped away, tripping over his trousers and letting go of my wrist as he tried to save himself from falling. I dropped his thumb and he slumped to the floor leaving me the space to swing my leg and catch him square between the legs with my boot.

He mewed like a kitten. Curled up like one too.

I swiped at my mouth with the back of my hand. 'You miserable, filthy, disgusting, old soak.' I plucked the keys from his trouser pocket and left, shutting the door behind me. I wiped my face clean with the hem of my tee shirt and walked as quickly as I dared for the stairs. I ran up, passing two blokes on the way with a cheerful, 'Got to keep fit, lads.' All the while I itched to scrub my hands, my neck, my hair. And to clean my teeth, get the taste of that smell out of my gums and off the back of my tongue. I breezed through the doors at the third floor and a quick scan told me it was all clear. I fought the instinct to run. Every muscle tensed taught and every millimetre of my skin tingled filthy and stinking to the point I wanted to claw at it and tear it away from my bones.

A door opened and Crawlsfeld stepped through, looking down at a sheet of paper in his hand. I lunged through the nearest door closing it behind me as quickly but quietly as I could, all the while praying the room would be empty. I put my forehead against the door, held my breath and listened. My heart was giving it proper welly, I couldn't hear booger all else. I paused to allow my eyes to get used to the dim light before turning around. The room was a cupboard and almost identical to the one I'd just escaped from, with the same limited floor-space and wide shelving. Phew. The shelves were long drawers fronted with shiny steel, stripy in the sun that filtered through a slatted blind covering the tiny window. Perhaps I'd give myself a minute, take a breather, and give Crawlsfeld, and whoever else was outside, some time to get well away. Like France or somewhere.

I forced my breathing under control and scrubbed my face with my sleeve in a vain attempt to get rid of the fat man stink. Things were not going well. I pulled open the nearest drawer hoping to find clues to something, heaven knows what. But I figured the more trouble I got into, the more evidence I'd need to convince Joe I'd stepped over the line for good reason.

The drawer housed sheets but not very tidily. They were shoved in scruffy and crinkled. I rooted through, not sure what I hoped to find but enjoying the sensation of cool linen against my hot fingers. My hand hit something and I grabbed at it instinctively, brushing the sheets aside. It took seconds to register what I'd touched and when it did I nearly yelled out loud. All those tattered nerves of mine snapped simultaneously and I scrambled backwards to the far wall. In the drawer, staring up at me, was Mary.

CHAPTER TWENTY-THREE

Dead people's eyes aren't glassy and vacant like in the movies. At least dead Mary's eyes weren't. They were alive and staring at me - they even spoke to me, *'Think you're going to get out of here? Think again.'*

I closed my eyes. *'Don't panic, Atty.'* For the first time I wanted to yell back at Dad's stupid voice. Don't panic? Jesus. Try being me. Don't panic, my foofle. Panicking was about all I had left. I wasn't cut out for this. Born to be an activist, my backside.

I stretched out my leg and nudged the drawer closed with my foot. There must be at least twenty drawers. If they all had a body in them … No, that body must be fresh today or there'd be a stink. And flies. Big bluebottles were supposed to nest in bodies. I breathed in through my nose; the warm scent of office-block leather with an undercurrent of blueloo - nothing like the distinct, ripe whiff of Fran swinging from the bannister. And Mary's cheeks were still soft. Dead things went hard after a while - I'd seen road-kill, frogs and stuff. I swallowed and closed my eyes. Calm.

The simplest thing to do to keep my sanity was pretend I hadn't seen the body at all. At least I hoped there was a body attached to her head, I wasn't going to check. And she might have dropped dead from natural causes for all I knew. Fell off the back of a bike. Ha. Oh no, the hysteria was back.

I crawled to the door and listened. My back felt vulnerable and tender, my neck in particular, tingled cold with terror. I had a word with myself. Mary didn't frighten me when she was alive, so she certainly shouldn't now she lay dead in a drawer – get over it, move on. I peeked out to check the corridor was clear and, to hell with looking calm, shot out the door and ran for Stuart, praying he was still where I'd left him.

The fat alcoholic's door swung open easily. I whisper shouted, 'Stuart!'

He popped up from behind the sofa, a piece of paper in his hand. 'I got it.'

'We need to get the feck out of here.'

He stepped up to me. 'What's happened? You're bleeding.'

I swiped at my face and brushed at my t shirt. 'It's not mine.'

'What? Then what …'

'Never mind. What's that?' I reached for the sheet of paper. Not that I gave a crap.

'They're in the east tower.'

'We can't stop. We have to get out of here. Mary's dead.'

'Who?' He put his hand up. 'Doesn't matter. We need to get Gemma.'

'Jesus, Stuart. If we don't go now we're dead too. Seriously.'

'I'm not going without Gemma. This way.' And he ran out the door, down the corridor and veered off down a passage. I followed, pausing only to pick up a mop conveniently left against a door jamb. I'd have preferred an AK-47 but beggars and choosers, etcetera. Stuart burst through a door into another stairwell, narrower this time, more like an old fire escape. I searched the ceiling, found the camera, and battered it with the mop.

'What are you doing?' Stuart squeaked in horror. 'They're going to know we're up to something.'

'Oh for shitting shits sake, Stuart. How deep in it do we have to get before you wake up?'

But destroying the camera would be pretty pointless. The next one would pick us up and then the next. There was no escaping them. I looked out of the window and watched guards running towards the boundaries. And they carried guns. I didn't know what sort, but big, BIG guns. I looked at my mop head. 'We are so dead.'

The door opened and a man in a sharp suit stepped through. 'Good afternoon.' He held out his hand and Stuart shook it. 'Delighted to meet you. My name's Commander Jenkins. I'm head representative of International Security Specialists. Welcome to Sapton Manor.'

People stepped out of their offices and took a good look as, flanked by guards, we were taken to the ground floor and locked in a room with a barred window.

'Now what?' said Stuart.

'I can't believe you shook that guy's hand.'

'It's habit.'

'A freaking stupid one.'

'And what about your habit of smashing people's faces in? I've only known you a few days and that's two already. Not counting ours.'

'You're blaming me for our black eyes now, are you? I said we should get out of that station but, hell no. Stuart knew best.' I stomped around looking for something to prise the bars off the window with. In one corner stood a desk, two hard chairs and a broken mirror; in another an old filing cabinet lay on its side with a lonely looking print of a flower propped up against it. 'We're so dead.'

'Yeah. So you said already.'

'Well nothing's changed, has it? In fact things have just got a whole lot worse. Commander of International Security?'

'Nobody is to blame here, Atty. We need a clear head if we're going to think of a way out of here, so just cool it.'

'I am cool.' God alive. "Cool" was on a par with "oops." 'I mean I'm okay.'

Stuart shook his head and looked out the window. When he turned to face me his hands rested loosely on his hips, the sun shone from behind him, and he stood in a ring of light, like some sort of solar idol. Then he spoke and spoilt it. 'Do you think we might be about to get arrested or something?'

I gaped at him, there were no words to express how I felt. None.

He looked sulky, like a kid on the naughty step. 'I don't think they're going to let us go.'

I walked in a circle, hands on my head. 'How the hell did I end up here with you?'

'Stop getting grotty with me, Atty.'

If he'd fronted it out instead of hiding behind the sofa we wouldn't be in the mess we were in. There was little point in being a beefy academic if common sense didn't feature – anywhere. I looked him in the eye and kept my voice calm. 'Okay, I'll just shut up while you catch up and state the bleeding obvious then.'

'That's not what I meant and you know it.'

I raised my eyebrows.

'I'm just thinking aloud,' he said. 'You know, bouncing ideas around.'

'Oh, ideas. I'd love to hear them. But if all they amount to is, "I think we might be in a spot of bother", then you can keep them to yourself.'

'Well you could try too. Instead of griping at me, think of a way to get us out of here. Getting stroppy and argumentative is getting us nowhere.'

'Oh, I know,' I said, wide-eyed like an idea had popped into my head, 'let's feed them salad.'

He sighed and turned back to the window. 'You're impossible.'

Seconds of silence turned into minutes. Oh Jeesh. I had a sulker on my hands. 'All right, all right, I'm sorry. Can we do the bouncing idea thing?'

'You don't sound very sorry.'

God alive. 'I'm really, truly, honestly, begging you sorry.'

'We can't keep arguing with each other. We're all we've got, remember?'

Breathe Atty, breathe. 'What ideas have you got, Stuart? Let's hear them. And be quick. I reckon we've got minutes to dream something up else we're going to end up with our heads in a drawer full of linen.'

'Uh?'

'Forget it.'

'I wonder what the bloody hell they're going to do with us.'

'Kill us. They're going to Bloody, bloody, BLOODY kill us. Do you get it now?'

Stuart actually looked hurt. My knees wobbled, I dropped to a crouch in the corner and put my head in my hands. It was little wonder Joe had tried to get me home. He thought he'd sent me on a nice cushy and cosy job to watch a couple of soft easty kids. No way would he have sent me anywhere near the ISS and dodgy research centres. All those years he'd kept me bubble-wrapped and safe and then, within a few short days, the bottom had fallen clean out of my comfy little box.

'It's all Gavin's fault,' I said. 'If he hadn't pointed his skanky finger at Stacey none of this would have happened. Fran wouldn't have killed herself and I'd have been around to keep an eye on Gemma.'

'Gemma is my little sister and my responsibility.' Stuart paused, leaning against the wall as if stood waiting for a lift, hands in his pockets. 'But neither of us could have stopped Crawlsfeld taking Gemma. He had Dad's permission, remember?'

Perhaps having a dad go walkabout was better than having a crap one at home after all.

'And,' he continued, 'it would have been somebody else's baby if not Fran's.'

I snorted and swallowed some self-disgust. 'You're a better person than me. I came here for my sake, not theirs. Chasing promotion, wanting to escape Basley, impress my dad. Selfish.'

Stuart looked to be pondering on the weather, not how to save our necks. 'That's not true, Atty. You sorted that Carl bloke out good and proper. Not many people would have gone in like that. I certainly didn't want to.' He looked at me. 'That guy whose blood you got down your shirt, what did he do to you?'

'Nothing. He tried and failed.' I rubbed the palm of my hand down my thigh, scrubbed at the corner of my mouth with the cleanest corner of my T-shirt. 'I need a shower.'

He looked back out of the window. 'I bet a place like this is crawling with paedos.'

'Stuart, I'm nearly eighteen.'

'Everything is relative. Come and look at this.' I got to my feet and joined him at the window. An army of men in black overalls, flak jackets and caps darted about the grounds directing what looked to be a mass evacuation. We watched as high-heeled women and thick-waisted men in suits climbed into various modes of transport and left through the gates.

'It looks like they're expecting the end of the world,' said Stuart.

There was something about bunches of nervous looking grown men in bullet-proof vests that scared the bejeesus out of me. Stuart held my hand. 'We'll be okay.' But it didn't look good.

CHAPTER TWENTY-FOUR

'We can't just sit here and wait for something to happen,' I said after we'd been locked up for what felt like hours. 'We need to be pro-active.'

'Have you seen the size of the guns out there?'

Good point, but patience and I weren't becoming any better friends. 'There has to be somebody outside the door. If not I'm going to knock it down.' I went over and hammered on it. 'Oi! Open up!'

'What the bloody hell are you doing?' Stuart stood staring at me like I'd lost it. He might have been right. Probably right.

I hammered again. 'Oi! I need the bathroom!'

'You haven't long been.'

For an educated guy he wasn't half thick. I gawped at him. 'Are we wanting the same thing here?'

'I just don't think we should make them angry. At least without formulating some sort of plan. What are you going to do when you get out?'

'We'll wing it. All our plans have gone to hell so far. We must be on plan Q by now.' I kicked at the door. 'Oi!'

It opened and I stepped back out of the way in case they came in fighting, but, crouched over the prone body of a guard, with a finger on his lips, was Joe. 'Shhhh.'

Joe and I have never been the cuddly types, but I leapt up and hugged his mega block head until my arms locked. 'Oh my God. Is it good to see you? What are you doing here?'

'Rescuing your lily-white arse.' He prised my legs from around his waist and lowered me to the floor. 'I told Gavin to bring you home. Where is he?'

'Um.' I'd forgotten about him. 'He's our getaway man.'

Joe gave me a look that confirmed how daft an idea that was. 'Please tell me you're yanking my chain.'

'He's waiting by the back gate,' said Stuart.

'I doubt that,' said Joe. 'Have you seen it out there? And have you heard from your mum?'

'No. How? Why?'

'She's been looking for you.'

'Where? When? Why?' Stuart looked wide-eyed and bamboozled.

'This is nice - this little catch up thing - but that guy's waking up.' I nodded towards the guard rolling onto his hands and knees just outside the door. 'Shouldn't we be making a run for it?'

Joe grabbed the guard's hair and slammed his head into the wall. 'Sorted. Come on.'

We walked down the passage and up the stairs, Joe in the middle, gripping us by our elbows. Somehow he'd managed to acquire a security pass. 'Can you get us one of those?' I asked.

'Bit late for that now, don't you think? Shut up and try and look frightened.'

It wasn't too hard to achieve. 'There's a dead girl in a drawer with sheets.'

'What girl?' Joe frowned. 'No. Don't answer that. Just keep quiet.'

What was it about people not wanting to know about bodies everywhere? The corridors were silent. Only a few people bustled past carrying files and bags, and their jackets over their arms, all keen to get away before some type of massive turd hit the fan. Though I doubt they were as keen to escape as me.

Only one bloke challenged us. 'What's going on?'

'Putting them with the others,' said Joe. 'Jenkins' orders.' He led us to the second floor and right at the end of the corridor was a blank door which I would have guessed led to yet another faffing cupboard. He knocked. A tubby woman with grey curly hair opened it within seconds.

She scanned me and Stuart before muttering at Joe. 'It's looking worse than ever out there.'

Joe nudged us into a huge room with enormous windows on two walls. It contained several sofas, three unmade beds, a cot, and lots of clothes and clutter across the floor. Very homely.

'STUEY!' Gemma raced towards Stuart and jumped to cling around his neck, her legs dangling, her Perfect Princess wedding-gown riding up to show fluorescent green leg warmers. If they were indulging her fashion sense she hadn't suffered too much.

'Woah, Gem Gem. How're you doing?' Stuart swung her around and closed his eyes as he hugged the life out of her.

'Owerr. Put me dowwn.'

'You look amazing.' He put her back on her feet. 'Let's have a look at you.' He held her hand. Gemma twirled like a ballet dancer and performed a little bow. Stuart grinned. 'Stunning, as always.'

The girl from the park was sitting on a chair at the window bouncing Fran's baby on her lap. 'Hi,' I said. 'You okay?' She nodded but gave me the cold teenage stare before continuing to watch Stuart and Gemma's display of happy, reunited families. 'And Stacey? Is she okay?' I asked.

She looked at me, huge eyes, tearful yet sparking with defiant anger. 'Sure.' She stood and handed the baby to me and walked away through a door into another room. Naturally, Stacey yelled.

'Shh, shh.' I patted and jigged her.

Gemma came over and shouted up. 'Oi, baby Frannie. What's the matter with you now?' Baby Frannie stopped crying.

'She's called Stacey,' I said.

'Well we didn't know that so we called her baby Frannie. Fran was her mummy's name,' Gemma said full of importance. 'She cries a lot.'

Great.

Joe spoke to the woman who had opened the door. I didn't recognise her but by the way Joe leaned in close, pointing his finger like he might be uttering instructions, I'd throw a good guess she worked with him, and not Jenkins.

'Who's that lady?' I asked Gemma.

'Matron. She came this morning to look after us.'

When Joe walked towards me he looked more than serious, he looked scared. And he never got scared. My belly flipped. If Joe was scared then we all had good reason to be bricking it.

My voice sounded different as if it belonged to some soppy sap. 'Is everything going to be okay?'

'I hope so. Just stay here. I'll come back for you.' He looked at Stuart. 'Look after her for me.'

Stuart nodded and held my hand. 'Yes, Sir.' I'd normally have laughed but seeing Joe like that turned me too numb-bummed-terrified to do anything much at all.

Matron looked around the room. 'Where's Chelsea gone?'

There was only one person Chelsea could be. 'She went in there,' I said, nodding towards the door.

'The bathroom,' said Gemma.

Stacey wriggled but I didn't want to let go of Stuart's hand. I tried to jiggle her back up onto my hip with the one arm.

'Here,' said Stuart. 'I'll take her.' He let go of me and plucked Stacey away. She snuggled into his shoulder like she'd known him forever.

Matron frowned. 'I have to go with Joe. I need you to keep your eye on Chelsea, she's been through a rough time.' Matron and Joe left without another word or looking back.

'What the hell have we done?' I said. 'We should have stayed away.' I should have listened to those instincts. That split, fraction of a second in the hedge, I should have said "no" – insisted that I'd changed my mind and convinced Stuart it was a dumb idea. 'We should have stayed out the way,' I said, 'All we've done is given them two more kids to rescue.'

Stuart wrapped his free arm around me. 'Bloody big bloke Joe, isn't he?'

'He's scared.' My hands were shaking. 'I've never seen him scared before.'

'He looked okay to me.'

'If ever a black man goes that pale, that's the time to start panicking.' I tried to lean into his cuddle, sharing the space with Stacey.

'At least he hasn't locked the bloody door. I was getting sick of being locked in.' He squeezed me tight and put his mouth in my hair. 'Bloody, bloody.'

'Not now, Stuart.'

'Okay.'

Stuart had been right about Gemma. She didn't shut up. She didn't just prattle to us and Stacey but to Mr Table and Mrs Bed and Mr and Mrs Cup. I desperately wanted to wash my hands and face, maybe even grab a shower. 'Does Chelsea spend a lot of time in the bathroom?'

'Yes she does.' Gemma spoke so posh it was as if she'd been trained by royalty. She might have been an interrogator for the BBC in a previous life. On and on. 'Why hasn't anybody come to take her home? Where's her mummy and daddy? Has she got a big brother like me? Why is your hair a funny colour? Do you always dress like that?'

'Chelsea will come with us,' I said.

Chelsea's uncle must have sold her. Maybe I'd seen him from time to time walking the streets of Basley. Pretending to be normal.

Gemma wandered away and I watched Stuart sit Stacey on the rug and feed her a pot of something he'd found in a hamper. 'You read Chelsea's file, right? Do you know her uncle?' I asked. 'He's supposed to be looking after her since her parents died.'

'No. She lives further west than me. Near the river.'

'I wonder how much he got for her. Can you remember?'

'I didn't read it very closely.' He shrugged. 'Maybe he believed in the whole ponies and go-kart stuff.' He stopped and looked at the bathroom door before back to me. 'Do you think they've started already? And, you know, given them something?'

'They all look okay.'

Gemma made her way back to us and kept up her chattering. 'Mr Crawlsfeld comes to see Chelsea sometimes and they go in there for some special time.' She looked at me and spoke very seriously. 'And there's a bath. She likes to lie in the bath for ages and ages.'

Stuart swiped at his lip and leaned forward. 'Gemma. Did Mr Crawlsfeld do anything special with you?'

She shook her head and screwed her mouth up. 'No. He said when I got to be a little bit older he'd take me too. But I have to wait my turn.'

'Did he give you any funny sweets or drink that you've never tasted before?'

Gemma sighed and flopped her arms around. 'No. I just told you. He only likes Chelsea. I'm too little.' She looked at the floor and went the stillest and quietest I'd ever seen her.

'What, Gem?' said Stuart. 'What? You seem sad.'

'I didn't want special time anyway. Chelsea always cries all the time.' Gemma's eyes were big and heavy when she looked up at Stuart. 'I don't have to go anywhere with him when I'm bigger, do I?'

'No. Definitely not.' Stuart gave her a tight hug before standing to pace the floor. If I thought I'd seen angry Stuart before, it wasn't a patch on this one. I followed and put my hand on his arm. He shrugged me off. 'She's twelve!'

Gemma stared at him, her fingers fiddling with the bow at her waist.

'You're frightening Gemma,' I said.

'Twelve!' He looked at the ceiling and took some deep breaths before turning on me. His eyes went such a pale grey I stepped back. Never mind Gemma, he was putting the jeeblies up me.

I held my hands up. 'She'll be okay now. Joe will make sure of it.'

He strutted about looking so furious I feared his head might explode. 'If they've already started …'

Gemma crept over and held his hand. 'Are you okay, Stuey?'

He picked her up and squeezed her so tight she screwed her face up. 'Yep,' he said. 'We're all going to be okay. Don't you worry.' He put her down and crouched to speak to her. 'Why don't you go and play with Stacey for me. Make her giggle.'

'Okay.' Gemma trotted back to where Stacey lay playing on the rug.

When Stuart looked out of the window I went up behind him, wrapped my arms around his waist and leaned into his back. He felt warm and solid and smelt of grown-up man and soap.

'It can't keep happening, Atty.'

'I know.'

He turned and gave me a squeeze. 'Things will be very different when I get in office. There'll be no Early Release Programme for a start. People like Crawlsfeld will be locked up for good.'

'I know.'

We stood there just holding each other. I closed my eyes to pretend we were somewhere else, safe. 'I'm sorry about before. I didn't mean to get so shitty.'

'Pah. Forget about it.' He rubbed his hand up my back and tickled my arm with his fingers, sending a tingle deep into my stomach. 'I'm going to make sure places like this are shut down and the buildings used to benefit the community,' he said.

'Good idea.'

His body relaxed and melded into mine. Then he shifted position and a gap opened between us. 'I wonder what's going on outside. What do you suppose Joe is up to?'

I pulled him in close again. 'He knows what he's doing. If anybody can put a stop to all this mess, it's him.'

Stuart bent to snuggle my neck. 'You will still want me when this is over, won't you? When I can give you my full attention?'

Oh God, would I ever. I leaned my head against him. A few days ago, the idea of having an easty boyfriend would have been so ridiculous I'd have laughed myself stupid. But things had changed. Everything had changed. When we got out, if we got out, maybe we could be together. 'Lots of guys have girlfriends from over east.' I said.

'Like Gavin.'

'Yeah, like Gavin.' I said. Not the best idea mentioning him. 'He's not the only one though, lots do but I don't know of any that last. East – West, different worlds.'

'We'll be the exception.'

I breathed his scent and savoured the moment. If we got separated I wanted to be able to remember every touch, smell and sensation. And I tried, really tried, to believe that we might be different. 'What about your mum? She's going to hate me after all this.'

'Nah. She'll understand. She'll soon see how you and I are made for each other. How we both want the same things. We're not so different.'

'Don't you reckon?'

'Of course not. We're just fighting from a different angle, that's all. But we're on the same side, for definite.' He kissed my forehead. I lifted my face and his fingers brushed my cheek, crept around the back of my neck, lifted my hair and sent mucky sensations to my toes. He looked at my lips and it felt like the sun crept under my skin, warming me up from the inside out. Then the fireworks went off. 'Bloody hell.' He leapt away from me. 'What was that?'

'Probably nothing.'

'You think?' Stuart snapped. He picked Stacey up off the mat. 'It's okay.' He grasped Gemma's hand. 'There's no need to panic.'

He looked pretty panic-struck to me. What with all that fast breathing and glancing about. 'I know.' I said. 'And I'm not.'

'Let's get out of here.'

'No! We have to wait for Joe.' I'd already caused him enough grief. 'And we're supposed to be keeping an eye on Chelsea.'

Stuart handed me Stacey and knocked on the bathroom door. 'Hey, Chelsea. Are you all right in there? We need to leave. Now.'

'Stuart. I really think we should wait for Joe to get back.'

He knocked harder. 'Chelsea.'

When Chelsea opened the door Gemma reacted first. 'Don't cry. We're going home. Stuart's here.'

Chelsea sniffed and shook her head. 'I've got soap in my eyes.'

Her eyes were red and swollen. She looked at me and I felt her sadness deep in my throat. I swallowed. 'It's okay,' I said. 'Everything will…'

'My parents are dead. And I'll tell you why my uncle signed me over. Because I asked him to. I thought I was going to a place where there'd be loads of other kids, and parties, and it was all going to be a laugh and stuff.'

I looked to Stuart. We should never have talked about her like that, Crawlsfeld and his special times and, oh God, her being sold. 'I'm sorry,' I said.

She tried to smile at Gemma. 'Silly me, eh?'

'Listen, Chelsea,' I said. 'Joe can fix anything, honest. He'll talk to your uncle and sort all this mess out.'

She snorted. 'I can't go back there.'

'Of course you can. Once your uncle finds out …'

'He can't find out. Nobody can. They'll never let me forget it.'

The 'they' must be the girls in the park. I looked to Stuart for help.

He stood to one side, watching. 'Crawlsfeld will be punished, Chelsea,' he said. 'I promise.' He looked so genuine I believed him myself. He cleared his throat and stepped towards her. 'Are you okay to make a run for it? It's just that we really should be getting out of here.'

'Sure.' Her voice cracked and she bent over to fiddle with her shoe. She put her hand up to her face, let her hair fall forward, and did everything she could to hide her misery. But it filled the room, stunning even Gemma into silence.

Stuart broke the moment first. 'Listen, Chelsea. I'm so sorry. For everything. I can't begin to understand what you must have gone through.'

I willed him to stop the sympathetic floundering. Everybody couldn't help but cry when they were given sympathy. Chelsea stood up and looked out the window while Stuart gazed around the floor with his hands in his pockets. She caught my eye. I wanted to tell her that I got it, and I'd do all I could to put it right, I knew people, Joe, M Gee, and together we'd sort it. I wanted to be firm and strong and let her know we were all on her side and to hell with her uncle - she had us. But I turned away and said nothing. Crap.

Matron burst in and popped the discomfort bubble. She headed straight for Stacey and scooped her up. 'Come quick. We need to leave - now.' Stuart snatched Gemma's hand and reached for mine but I grasped Chelsea's. She, more than anybody, needed somebody to show they cared.

'Come on,' I said. 'Let's get out of here.' She nodded and sucked on her lips to stop more tears. 'You will be okay,' I said. 'I promise.'

Matron led the way along the corridor to the stairs. 'Joe is at the bottom,' she said. For an old fat woman she moved pretty fast.

I wish she'd warned us. The shock of finding Joe sitting propped against the wall knocked the air out of me. I dropped to my knees. 'Jesus, Joe. What happened?' His hand gripped his side and his face twisted in pain.

Matron took Gemma's hand and told Stuart to help me. 'We need to get him out to the truck.'

I saw and felt my hands grabbing Joe's arm but it was like I'd been drinking. My arms moved independently. I had no control over what they were doing or what they'd do next.

Chelsea stood trembling and crying. 'Oh please no. Oh please no.'

'Shut up,' I said. 'If you're not going to help just go with Matron.' My new caring touchy feely side needed to be nurtured to maturity at a less stressful time.

Stuart knelt the other side of Joe and we met each other's eyes. 'Don't worry,' he said. 'We can do this. We're going to get out of here and we're going to be together.'

Right then, with Joe's blood on my hands and people running around outside the door wanting to kill us, I decided we'd, not only get out, but we would get that posh hotel and we would, indeed, be the exception. I almost snarled at him. 'We bloody well will and all.'

Between us we managed to get Joe to his feet. I never knew the human body could lose so much blood and still live. It spread everywhere. My jeans stuck to my knees and my feet skidded on the tiles as I struggled to take Joe's weight.

'Sorry about this,' he whispered.

'Lean this way,' said Stuart then looked at me. 'You okay?'

By Christ he weighed the same as a small mountain. 'Yep. Let's go.'

Matron raced ahead across the gravel towards a truck. But we couldn't keep up. There were more mini explosions from the other side of the grounds. When I heard gunshots I put my head down and put all my strength into getting the hell out of there. Joe's feet lost their way and we dragged him through the gravel, his knees and toes bouncing behind us.

Matron left Stacey with Gemma in the back of the truck and climbed in the cab. She revved the engine and it screamed as she slammed the truck into reverse and came straight towards us. She stopped, thank God, and got out to help us heave Joe into the back.

Gemma sobbed and called out for Stuart. Stacey screamed such a high piercing yell of terror it went right through my brain and out the other side. 'Can't you do something with that screeching kid?' I yelled.

I would not be taking her home with me, best friend's baby or not.

'It's okay, Gem, stay there,' said Stuart. He touched my shoulder. 'I'll be right back.'

'Where the freaking hell are you going?'

'Chelsea!' He ran back towards the manor.

The very last ounce of sympathy I might have mustered vanished. There was nothing wrong with her legs. She should have been right behind us. Stuart was a much, much better person than me. All I wanted to do was run like the gallops.

But then I spotted Crawlsfeld - with a gun, a big gun, and he had his arm around Chelsea's neck, trying to drag her back inside.

Joe groaned, Gemma and Stacey screamed, and Matron yelled, 'Get in, we need to go!'

'One minute!' I yelled back. 'Wait, one minute!' I ran to help Stuart, my every thought stood out clear and vivid, like in loud, red, ballooned letters in my head. Well weird.

Crawlsfeld pointed the gun at Stuart. I shouted to Chelsea, 'Drop!' She didn't take any notice but squirmed and fought like she'd gone wild. Crawlsfeld glanced at me. Stuart grabbed his chance and dived to rugby tackle his legs. When the gun fired my ears jangled and everything else went silent. The shot hit the gravel and sent stones flying into my legs. I danced way too late to avoid them and shit they hurt, like getting pebble-dashed with nails.

When I looked again, Stuart held the gun.

Crawlsfeld laughed. 'Don't be an idiot.' He let go of Chelsea's neck and dragged her back towards the Manor by her arm. She stopped crying and dug her heels in.

I ran harder and dived into the tangle of arms and legs. I tried to help prise Crawlsfeld's fingers off Chelsea's elbow and kicked out at his plums, screaming into his face the whole while. 'Let go of her you miserable, dirty, paedo, stinking …' In short - I lost it. Stuart lifted the gun by the wrong end, the deadly end, and crashed the fattest part sideways into Crawlsfeld's head, just above his left ear. As creepy Crawley hit the deck, deader than a sausage, Stuart dropped the gun as if it had exploded. I wiped some splattered drops of blood off my face and, like a total loontune, Chelsea laughed.

I swear the world stopped. The guns, the kids screaming, Chelsea laughing, all of it. The only sound was a thrump, thrump, thrump in my ears. I sat in the gravel leaning back on my hands, grit digging into my palms. I scuttled backwards away from Crawlsfeld and his staring eye. His left hand twitched and a foot jerked, just the once, and I saw his white ankle above a blue nylon sock. The thrump slowed and faded away. And so did the hate in Crawlsfeld's eye.

Something flicked a switch and the world fired back up. Matron reversed the truck towards us. 'One last chance you guys. I'm getting the hell out of here - right now.'

Stuart pulled me up off the ground. 'Come on, let's go.' My legs wouldn't work and I couldn't drag my eyes off the bloody crack in Crawlsfeld's head. Stuart leant and yelled into my ear. 'Atty, come ON!'

In the truck, I sat with Joe's head in my lap. His eyes flickered and he made scratchy noises in his throat as if he was about to choke. He had to be okay. I refused to think he wouldn't be. I needed him. If he died it would be my fault. He told me to lie low. He told me he would sort it. If I'd only done as I was freaking well told. My voice shook. It sounded like somebody else speaking from somewhere above or behind me. 'Joe?' the voice said. 'Everything is going to get sorted.' I looked at Stuart. He sat with Stacey and Gemma, cuddling them, muttering nonsense, trying to stop them from crying. I wanted him to look at me and tell me I was right, but he didn't. He stared out at the trees flashing by and ignored me. Chelsea sat silent, looking at her hands on her knees as she knelt in the corner by herself.

We only travelled for a couple of minutes before Matron pulled into a field. Joe cried out as we bumped over the rough ground. I'd never been a believer but by God I prayed to anybody who'd listen, 'Please let him be okay.'

People arrived to help us out the back but Matron said, 'No. Leave Joe there and I'll take him straight to the hospital. He's in a bad way.' Hands plucked Stacey and Gemma from Stuart and carried them off to join a crowd of other kids. It looked like our kids were a few of many.

Stuart looked at me. 'What have I done?'

'You saved Chelsea… us.'

'I've ruined everything.'

'What? No. It…'

He shook his head, jumped out of the truck and walked away.

Matron stopped me from running after him. 'He can wait. You need to be with Joe.'

'But…'

'No buts. Joe's looked after you all this time, now it's your turn to give something back.'

I looked at Joe, pale and still. I climbed back in the truck. I didn't know what I'd have said anyway.

'Don't worry,' Matron said. 'If that boy loves you, he'll wait for you.'

CHAPTER TWENTY-FIVE

Matron drove to a hospital tucked behind some woods half way up a mountain. When we stopped and I climbed out of the truck, it felt like stepping into a rain-cloud. The mist permeated my skin and dampened my bones. Somebody wandered over my grave and the shiver wouldn't ease up: it even set my teeth chattering. Once we were inside, they came and took Joe away from me, wheeling him on a trolley that rolled with a genteel whoosh down a long white corridor.

Matron looked me up and down. 'Look at the state of you.'

Bits of Alcoholic's nose intermingled with Crawlsfeld's scalp, smudged by a whole lot of blood, tie-dyed my t-shirt. 'None of its mine.'

'Well that, at least, is something.' She pointed to a chair in a line of three against the wall. 'Sit there and warm up a little. I'll try and find somebody to help us out.'

But, oddly, I didn't feel cold despite all the evidence to the contrary. My head hummed and the fuff fuff of my top teeth against my lower lip sounded loud in the silence. I struggled to control my shakes and figure out exactly what had just happened. The more I thought about it, the more confused I became. Perhaps I really had gone insane.

'Atty?' I looked up at a nurse not much older than me. I didn't want to speak in case I still sounded weird so simply nodded, gormless and gungy. She smiled and handed me a square parcel. 'If you come with me I'll show you where you can get cleaned up.'

The shower ran hot enough to scald. I stood and leaned my forehead against the tiles so the water hit hard on the back of my neck. Perhaps the brain can only take so much crap at any one time, too much and it shuts down or stalls. Mine still seemed to be struggling on Fran. *I've always wished I could be more like you, do you know that?* Her body hanging so still. Then I saw Stuart's face smiling and his lips heading towards mine, his fingers in the hair at the back of my neck. Joe bleeding, *Sorry about this.*

My knee throbbed. It swelled so large it felt like it might pop like a water balloon. I used a nailbrush on my hands to get the stench of the fat alcoholic off me. His stink coated my skin and I scrubbed all over again and again. By the time I climbed out of the shower, my skin glowed red and squeaky clean.

The square packet off the nurse contained matching white underwear and a blue nurse's uniform, a set - trousers and smock, like pyjamas. I put them on and left my new, trendy but mangled, gear crammed into the small, white dustbin in the corner. I needed to get out of there. All the white was giving me a throbbing headache and my stomach queased. I felt dizzy and travel sick.

Matron was waiting for me in the corridor. She was dressed in the same blue outfit so we looked like odd-ball twins in an asylum for the strange. Or jail.

We sat together in silence until the doctors came out of the operating theatre scratching their heads, unable to figure out why Joe hadn't died. 'It's incredible. He's been hit by a single bullet, straight through his side, but it missed his vital organs and he should make a full recovery.'

'It's quite some miracle,' said yet another kid not much older than me. He, like the others, must have been through the schools – rich privileged nob-heads saving Joe's life.

'Thank you,' I said.

He smiled and put his hand on my shoulder. 'You're very welcome. It's my pleasure. He's asking for you by the way.' And that's when I cried. And did I ever make up for the dry period. I slobbered violently with snot everywhere.

Matron sighed. 'It's the come-down, love. Anybody can fight, but the mark of a true soldier is how they cope after the event.' She sniffed. 'You'll get used to it.'

'No way.' Now it had been set free, my self-pity knew no bounds. I snivelled and whined. 'I'm not doing anything like this again. I'm going to get a job in a shop or something.'

'From what I hear, you show great promise.'

'Huh. Yeah right.'

She laughed. 'Joe's been saying for years he'll be handing the Basley reins over to you.' She touched my leg. 'When the time is right.'

'Hell no. He's not stupid enough to trust me again.'

'Now you're just feeling sorry for yourself.' She took her hand away, tucked it in her lap and tutted. 'Pull yourself together.'

I sat and watched Joe sleep. Another quiet snoozer. He breathed slow and even; his strapped-up chest barely moved. Overnight I nodded off but only for minutes at a time, my head falling forward, jerking me awake.

When Joe woke he gazed at the ceiling before sensing me sitting to his right. He looked and grinned. 'Hey, Atty bam bam. Thanks for saving my shiny black backside.'

God I loved him so much. Nobody else would ever put as much effort into making me feel better about myself. I wanted to let the tears have their head again, tell him how sorry I was, and swear I'd never cack up so catastrophically again. But his eyes weren't grinning. His eyes were wet and sad. If I cried it would upset him and, despite his pain, he was putting in the work to make things normal so the least I could do was play along.

I grinned back. 'No problem. Anytime you need me – I'm there.'

'I know that.' He gave me a serious look that read everything going on in my head, right to the back of my brain. Probably even those things I couldn't make sense of myself.

I rolled my eyes and turned away. 'Stop doing that.'

'Things will get better, Atty. There'll be other jobs. Other chances.'

I looked at the ceiling, tapped my heels on the shiny floor and tried to think about something neutral. But there wasn't anything. My eyes stung and my throat closed up. I so did not want to blub all over him. 'Sure there will.' I forced myself to look at him and smile. 'I know that.'

He nodded and flinched.

'You okay? Shall I call someone?'

'No. I'm bound to be a bit sore.' He looked at me sideways. 'Though, it's just a scratch, of course.'

Another middle-aged lamer but I forced out a laugh. 'Course it is.'

'Hey. Your face don't look so pretty.'

'Thanks.'

'You're welcome.'

The child-nurse came in. 'Ah, awake already? Fabulous.' She faffed around with his chart and drip, and scribbled something on an old-fashioned tablet which she then placed in her pocket.

Joe pulled a face behind her back and mouthed 'How verrry farrbulous.'

She turned and caught him at it, slapped his hand. 'Don't take the piss out of me. Else I won't be putting any gin in your drip.'

'Okay, bossy knickers. No need to get physical. How soon can I go home?'

She looked at me. 'Is he always so impatient?'

Nurses and their happy chatty conversations about nothing at all - people like her chirruped away all the time to pass the hours and lighten the mood. I don't know how they do it, day after day.

By the time the nurse left the room, Joe had brightened to the point of being almost chirpy. 'Did that boy of yours get home okay?

'Stuart? I don't know where he is. I left him in a field near the Manor.'

'Gavin.'

Oh sheesh. I'd forgotten about him. Again. 'Um. I'm guessing so.'

Joe second-glanced me.

'Well,' I said, deliberately reading him wrong. 'I wanted to be here with you, when you woke up. He could be anywhere.'

'I hope you haven't got attached to that easty lad.'

'Why not? He's on the same side as us. We're fighting the same battles.'

'Don't kid yourself. Different planets.' He lay and looked at the ceiling.

The silence thickened the air. I hated it. 'What is this place anyway? Is it secure?'

'Yeah. Activists come here from all over the country. Lucky for me it's right where I needed it, uh?' He smiled but he kept the strange look in his eye. 'I'm going to have to be straight with you, Atty. The kids on the west will stop trusting you if you hang out with an easty.'

He could talk. 'That nurse you've just made old-man's eyes at. She isn't exactly from good westy stock, is she?'

'I'm not saying we shouldn't get along, work for the same cause, we can even share the same dreams.'

'So what are you saying?'

'We're just different, that's all.'

'That's no answer and you know it.'

'If you want to be a lead player, you need to keep a certain distance. Respect the boundaries and stop trying to break in some easty lad.'

'I do. I mean I'm not. He's not a horse.'

'So you're going to move east, are you? Start painting your nails?'

'Don't be daft. I'm just gathering a little easty support is all.' No way did I want to talk about Stuart with Joe. Not then. Not ever. For a few days I'd been elsewhere and somebody different. Everything had been flipped inside out and I didn't know what I wanted or where I wanted to be any more. Being a part of the resistance might not be as important to me as it once was. Certainly not if it meant I couldn't be with Stuart.

'You need to find Gavin,' said Joe.

I opened my mouth.

'I know, I know.' Joe shook his head like he oozed disappointment and bitterness. 'He's messed you about a bit. But deep down he's a good kid.'

'You want me to settle.'

'I want you to be happy. I'm not saying this Stuart doesn't mean what he said, just that the situation, you know, the adrenaline and fear, it does strange things to a kid. Even if he meant all he said at the time, and tomorrow, next week, even next year. Eventually the differences between you would rise to the surface. Like scum on bath water. And then all that teeny love and mush-crush you got going would start to stink.'

'You're wrong,' I said. 'We'd be the exception. And it's not a crush.' I hadn't intended to ask questions which might stress him out or have a fight with him, but since he'd started it, 'And if my happiness is so important to you, why didn't you mention my dad is definitely still alive?'

His head jerked around. 'Who told you that?' He stared wide-eyed, mouth open.

'Oh, didn't you know?' Sarky and angry, not a tear bursting from anywhere. 'I've even seen a photo of him. On a leaflet promoting unity, would you believe?'

Joe leaned back against the mountain of pillows and looked at the ceiling. 'Ah. That.'

'Yes. That.'

'I'd been waiting to check out if it was true before I said anything.' He sounded weary. 'It could be a load of tosh and I didn't want to build your hopes up.'

'I keep telling you, I don't need your protection any more…' I tailed off. If he hadn't turned up at the manor I might have been a little snooked.

A nurse came in. 'I think Joe could do with some rest now. There's somebody here to take you home.'

Joe watched me stand up, his eyes deep and soft. 'Atty I swear to you, if he's alive I'll find him.'

'You should have told me.'

'I know. Sorry.'

Some people might call what we had volatile, all the ups and downs, the fights and the banter. It had worked for a long time, but something had changed and I wasn't sure if I liked it. I stepped up to the bed and leaned over to kiss his cheek. I'd never done that before. His face felt smooth and dry. I wanted to thank him for caring and for forgiving me and for loving me – and tell him how much I loved him back. But we didn't do the emotional stuff and the words wouldn't come. 'I'll see you later.'

'Things will get back to normal soon enough, Atty. You'll see.'

'Yeah, course.' But for the first time I doubted him, we'd changed, I'd changed and maybe things would never return to how they were. Ever.

CHAPTER TWENTY-SIX

Matron led me outside to an old car waiting at the entrance with the engine running. 'You need to get home before people start gossiping.'

'I thought we were under lockdown.'

'It's been lifted. A couple of hours ago.'

'Really? So quick? Is everybody okay?'

'Of course.' She opened the passenger door. 'In you hop. If anybody asks, you were holed up in your carriage for a couple of days, keeping your head down.'

'Like nothing ever happened, uh?'

Her eyes narrowed and she gave me a sarky smile. 'Exactly. You know how to keep your mouth shut, don't you?'

She was a hard-faced bitch. Standing there, dishing out orders. 'Who exactly are you?' I asked.

'It's not important. What is important is you maintain a professional silence,' she said. 'None of us are indispensable.'

I thought about Mary stuffed in the drawer. And Joe, *Sometimes it's better to sacrifice idiots like you.* 'Are you threatening me?'

'I'm being honest.'

And then it hit me. 'Are you M. Gee?'

She tilted her head, just a touch. 'Get in the car. Go home and rest up.'

I thought about trying to suck up a little, or at least undo some of the damage, just in case, to keep my options open. All my tears and stroppiness wasn't the best impression I could have made. But I really didn't feel up to the conversation, not even sure I cared. Going home, seeing the cats, getting back to some sort of normality was what I needed right then. My body ached for my bed. The mountain air had got even colder and this time I felt it, harsh and cutting. It dampened my skin, numbing my fingers and face to freezing. I climbed into the warm car, Matron slammed the door and I waved bye-bye to any hope of a career in the resistance.

The car pulled away. 'Hey, you okay?' The driver spoke soft and friendly. 'Don't worry. She's not as cruel as she'd like to think she is.'

I turned to look out at the coarse hillside, blinking hard, furious at myself. The self-pity and crying had to stop, but I felt so desperately lonely and bone-breaking tired. I laid my head against the headrest and tried to think happy thoughts. I'd talk it through with Stuart; he'd know what to do.

When I woke the sun shone blinding bright into my face. I twisted in my seat and wiped the corners of my mouth. Oh dolloping granny, I'd dribbled and must have been snoring like a drunken old con. I looked at the driver who took his eyes off the road to glance back. 'You okay?' he said.

'Yep. Sorry if I slept loud. I was knacked out.'

'No problem.'

We were rumbling along a country lane, dodging pot holes galore, the overgrown hedges whipped at the car. 'Where are we? Nearly there?'

'Not far off.' He put a pale, bony hand on the gearstick. 'Things aren't quite as you left them, Atty. The ISS went in and cleaned the place up a little. Took out a few of the recently released cons, arrested a couple of others. Nobody you'll miss, I don't think.'

How did he know who I'd miss and who I wouldn't? I studied his profile - familiar but not. 'Do I know you?'

He pulled a face. 'We've met once or twice.' Then he looked at me with bluebottle eyes and grinned. 'Bethany.'

I pointed to his head. 'The tat was false, right? Like one of those kiddy stickers.'

'I wear it when I'm in Red mode.' He winked. 'Helps me get into the role, looking like a dick.'

Sheesh. Another person faking it. 'So who are you? Really?'

'A friend, is all you need to know.'

'Why did you introduce me to Stuart?'

'I fouled up. As we all do from time to time.' He shot me a look. 'You were supposed to go back to Joe and tell him your cover was blown and him get somebody else on the job, but you and Stuart had other ideas. I underestimated the pair of you. I won't make that mistake again.'

'Why didn't you just tell Joe?'

He gave me a don't-go-being-so-daft look. 'When was the last time Joe listened to a Red and his advice?'

My head buzzed. 'Hang on. Are you saying you and Joe don't know each other, yet you're both working for the resistance?'

'But I don't work for the resistance. At least not directly. I've just slipped in for the moment to have a quick word with you before I head back to London.'

I rubbed my eyes. 'Oh Loudy Lord. I have no idea what's going on. Please tell me you're not ISS or something and I'm being shipped back to that manor place.'

He laughed. 'I'm taking you home.'

'The Law are after me.'

'No. Not any more. I've sorted it. They've had much bigger things to fret over lately anyway. Investigations from International officials, for one. The heads of ISS aren't overly impressed with the way the Law have turned

West Basley into an open jail. Not least because cons tend to keep escaping and finding their way to London.'

'Hence turning the cage on.'

'No. That breaks International Rules. There's no way they can get away with doing that. No more live fences for Basley.'

We'd all heard that before. 'So you're not a real Red, you're not ISS, you don't work for Joe. Who the hell are you? And how did you sort it?' I put such sarky emphasis on the last two words my nose ached.

'I'm on your side, Atty. And I'm not the only one.' He slowed the car and took an extra long look at me. 'Your dad is respected by a lot of people and he has lots of people working for him.'

'You work for my dad? Where is he? What's he doing having his photo spread across leaflets? Why doesn't he send for me?' My voice cracked. I coughed. 'Will you take me to him?'

He stopped the car. 'Atty. One day things will be good again. But right now, the safest place for you is in Basley. There are two types of Reds – those who want you there to lure your dad out of hiding, and those who work for your dad. Both want to keep you safe. Double whammy. And that's before you take Joe into consideration.'

So I'd been the privileged one all along. Protected from the east and the west. 'But why can't I go and live with him and he can look after me himself?' And I still managed to sound like a whiny kid.

'It's too dangerous. Besides, Joe needs you at home. To help keep things as normal as possible at ground level, in the community. Word's got around about you giving Carl a pasting. It's not like anybody is going to give you a hard time, is it?' He put the car back into gear and drove on.

There were loads of questions I wanted to ask but when I practiced them in my head they sounded selfish and infantile. But when the car finally stopped I had one more that I needed the answer to. 'If I hadn't gone to the manor, would anybody have bothered to rescue those kids?'

He looked shocked. 'Of course. Your dad is important, but no more important than Stuart's mother. She's a top dog in the lawyer world. She's on a very big case in London at the moment. She thought Stuart and Gemma would be safer in Basley but I can't see her leaving them behind again. Not that any of this could have been helped, by her or you. Just one of those things.' He paused. 'You've got a lot to digest. Take your time, but remember,' he pulled an imaginary zip across his mouth, 'keep it tight.

'Do you think my dad would approve of Stuart?'

He mused for a moment. 'Yeah, I think he probably would.' He leaned over and plucked a bunch of forget-me-nots out of the foot-well behind my seat. 'Give these to your mum, will you?'

CHAPTER TWENTY-SEVEN

By the time I arrived home it was mid-morning. The hot spell had broken but it hadn't rained and the sky stretched high and white. A sniff of cold autumn air made me wrap the smock snug about my neck. I passed by Bastion Square and laid the fresh forget-me-nots on the stone slab. 'I'm okay, Mum. These are off Dad. Can't think why I didn't think of him before. He's got his eye on us. Though I suppose you already knew that.' I turned to leave but changed my mind. 'Oh, by the way, I've met someone. You'd really like him. And dad. I'm going to be happier than ever now.'

The cats ran to meet me and rubbed at my legs. The carriage felt cold and damp so I lit the oven and left its door open to warm the cabin up and chase the chill from my bones. I crawled into bed and slept.

Fluff woke me and I lifted her up to rub my face against her fur. 'What have you been up to, eh?' She purred and padded her paws against my neck. The dishes were still piled in the sink from when I'd cooked dinner for Stuart. Just days ago. I washed them and cleaned up the whole place before showering and changing.

I shaved, plucked, tweaked and gelled. I wore my favourite jacket and folded a fresh pair of knickers in the pocket. I learned from my mistakes. My toothbrush hooked neatly into the back patch on my jeans and I took one last check in the mirror. My eye still shone red, but if he wanted a deep meaningful look, he could look in the other one. Everything else looked more or less okay. As okay as I'd ever get anyway.

I arrived at Stuart's road just as the sun went down. All the lights were on in his house and vans with the Law logo lined the street. Neighbours hovered around at the edge of their lawns chatting and nosing. Reds in white overalls carried boxes and items out to the vans in clear plastic bags. Even Gemma's teddies and dolls were bagged and carted away as possible evidence. I felt sick and watched from the corner, not knowing what to do. I wished I still had my sonic ear.

Matron appeared alongside me. 'Hey. How are you?' She looked me up and down. 'You've put some effort in. Smell nice too.'

'What's going on?'

'The Law have gone in declaring the Under-occupancy Act.'

'Isn't his mum coming home?'

'No. They're moving on.'

'Where to? I need to speak to Stuart.'

She sighed. 'He killed an ISS approved agent, Atty. If the Law found out…' She gave a helpless-looking shrug.

'But he was a scummy paedo. They can't arrest somebody for taking out a paedo. Not even this lot would put up with that.' I gestured at the neighbours. 'Look at them. Poking around.' I'd raised my voice, wanting them to hear.

'Some things are best left in the past.' Matron said. 'The Law will be looking for somebody to blame for the whole sorry mess. And it won't be you and Joe. Somebody has to take it.'

'But he's an easty.'

She laughed. 'Doesn't make him immune to the Law.'

I'd always thought easties had it so easy but it appeared not. Even their kids got sent away to be experimented on. 'Has the manor stopped the programme?'

'Of course.' She spoke so matter of factly, like I'd asked her if she'd remembered to pick a pint of milk up on the way home. Listening to her, nobody would have thought lives, including mine, had been turned upside down. Certainly not bodies stuffed in drawers.

'What about Mary? The girl who helped us, I found her body in a drawer at the manor.'

'If she's dead already she isn't worth rescuing, is she?'

The guy with the bluebottle eyes had been wrong. She was cruel all right.

'And Chelsea?'

'She'll get the help she needs.'

'So all's sorted then.' I swallowed. 'Except Stuart is expecting me to meet him.'

'There is no way he can come back here. It would be professional suicide. He's gone to another county where he can start afresh.'

'You said he'd wait for me.'

'I said if he loved you. Did he tell you he loved you?'

I gritted my teeth and thought back. *I kind of like you.* And, *Will Joe take you back? I don't like to think of you being lonely.*

Matron made a some-you-lose gesture with her hands. 'I'm sure it wasn't an easy choice for him to make. But it is the right one for both of you. Even if you weren't a soldier, he needs a woman who can entertain, host dinner parties, and discuss global politics and such nonsense.'

'I can do that.'

'Yeah sure. But can you do it without all that colourful language Joe dragged you up with?'

'I can speak BBC-speak. I don't ever swear.'

She shook her head. 'You're fantasising. You know it. Nobody's fooled by all that frolicking frog nonsense.'

'You're saying I'm not good enough.'

'I'm saying we all need to use the talents and knowledge we have. You're born to be a resistance soldier not a pretty trinket on some politician's arm.'

'Stuart doesn't want a trinket. He wants me.'

'Sometimes a guy puts what he needs first. Like Gavin. He needs you.'

'Great. Gavin likes the easties but needs me, huh?'

'You're twisting my words.'

No I wasn't. 'What about Gemma and Stacey?' I said. 'Where are they?'

'They've gone with Stuart. They'll travel with his mother from now on. She'll take good care of them both. You aren't really in the best position, are you? To take care of a baby. I know you mean well but…'

The tears spilled down my face. So much for trying to look good. I swiped at them. 'So I'm the only one left behind. Everybody else is moving on, having this nice new life somewhere pretty and exciting. I've no doubt it's where the stupid sun shines all day long and birds sing over rainbows and shit.'

'You're sounding sorry for yourself again. Wallowing.' She rooted around in a canvas bag hanging from her shoulder. 'Here.' She thrust a bunch of keys at me. 'Joe needs you to look after the caff until he gets back.'

'Will they let him back?'

'Of course. He's the one who keeps the west rational. Without him there'd have been even more bodies to deal with. In the meantime, you've got the opportunity to impress. Put the west back in order, keep the people calm until Joe returns and who knows where you could go from there.'

I wanted to stamp my foot and scream at her. She just didn't get it. But neither did I. I didn't want to go anywhere, not without Stuart. He'd said so much stuff.

Touched my neck, wanted to kiss me. He'd meant it. *We're going to get out of this and we're going to be together.*

I watched Matron walk away. After a few steps she hesitated. Her voice quietened, became softer, and her eyes kinder. 'You belong here, Atty. This is your home. Here with Joe.'

I hated being patronised. 'How would you know where I belong or where I don't? You don't know me.'

'Of course I do. I used to be like you. And, who knows, one day, you'll be like me.'

'I doubt that.' No chance. She looked well worn out and haggard. And by then, things will have changed. Her assumption that we'd still be fighting the same battles pissed me off. Just because her generation had cacked all over everything, didn't mean we couldn't make it better. And to think all I'd wanted to do was impress her.

'Your adult papers should be finalised by now. Use them wisely.' She raised her hand in a half wave. 'Stay safe, Atty.'

I loitered until the last of the vans pulled away before wandering up to look through the windows of Stuart's house. Everything had gone, even the tiles off the floor and the taps out of the kitchen. Blinds shivered and curtains twitched as the neighbours watched me stride away, head high.

My knee throbbed too sore to run so I walked home, pausing outside the station. The butcher's van threw out a rapid rock beat while a guy on a saxophone played swing on its roof. The sounds mish-mashed together into a tune that set the kids on the slab bouncing. It looked like they were in an old rock and rackit movie. Tarts Table reeked of enough blind lust and ignorant youth to make me want to vomit.

Gavin jumped off the platform and stood three feet away, shuffling his feet. 'Hey, Atts. How're you doing?'

'When did you get back?'

'Yesterday. I waited like you said but some guy turned up and told me to come home. Gave me a lift to the door. Is Joe still mad at me?'

'How about asking if he's okay first? Or if those kids are okay? Or if Stuart is okay?'

He curled his top lip and sneered. 'Well you're okay. Why wouldn't they be?'

A girl, dressed in a micro mini and pink bra, tottered to the edge of the platform. 'Gavvy?'

Gavin scowled and called up to her. 'I'm busy.'

I put my hands in my jacket pockets and looked at the sky. Even if I never saw Stuart again my days of hanging out at the station were done with. The get-togethers might be a good start but we needed to do more than dance and get rat-faced together to make a proper difference. The girl tip-tapped away towards the slab.

'Atty? They are okay, aren't they?'

'Yes, Gavin. They're okay. But we all need to stop playing games with each other. That girl. Do you like her?'

He shrugged. 'She's an easty,' he said. 'She's not like us.' He stepped towards me.

I gave him a look that said, don't even think about it. 'Yes she is.' I said. 'She's exactly like us.'

'Eh?' He looked at me like I was the prize dimwit.

'Forget it. Enjoy your night, Gavin.' I walked on towards home.

He called after me. 'You're going soft, Atty. You've lost the plot.'

Yeah, whatever.

CHAPTER TWENTY-EIGHT

Joe burst through the caff door ten days later like he'd never been away. 'Hey, Atts fats. What's been happening?'

'Not much.'

'Get that kettle on.' He pulled out a chair and sat down. 'I need lots of TLC.'

He didn't look too sick to me. 'How's the war wounds?'

He drew in his breath and patted his chest. 'Doc reckons I should drink lots of brandy and eat curry five times a week.'

'Sounds like hell.' I poured him a mug of tea and joined him at the table in the window. It was hard to believe how much had changed since we'd sat in the exact same spot just a couple of weeks before. If he mentioned my dad being proud I had every intention of poking him in the eye.

'No visits from our friends in the Law?'

'Nope. The odd Red has come in for a bacon roll and it's like nothing ever happened.'

'Most of them probably don't know anything did. You know what gorms they are. They wouldn't sense a bad atmosphere in a riot.' He slurped his tea and smacked his chops together. 'Good stuff.'

'No it's not.'

He winked. 'Things back to normal then? What damage did the lockdown leave?'

I twirled my mug. 'A fair few lemondroppers have disappeared. Rumour has it the Law dished out some free stuff that might have killed a few off. I've got a list of those who need burying.'

'Blessed release for some of them, I've no doubt.'

Stuart's words about drawing a line made me look at Joe with fresh eyes. 'You think it's okay?'

He sat back in his chair. 'That's not what I said.'

Pretty much. But like Matron said, if they were already gone, waste of time fighting their corner. 'And that bunch of lads,' I said. 'The ones who were robbing the stores – they've been arrested. Things seem calmer than ever.'

'I need to get you a new phone and sonic ear so you can go over the gym and see if you can find out where they're being held.'

'What? You're kidding.'

'Best get straight back on the horse.'

'No way.'

'I can't have you losing those back legs. You did good.'

'I haven't lost any legs.' Gavin thought I'd gone soft, Joe thought I'd lost my nerve. 'There are other ways to change things. Better ways.'

'Oh for eff's sake, Atty. We need to hit them both ways. Maybe one day we'll meet in the middle, until then let Stuart do his thing and you carry on doing yours.'

For days I'd been listening out for advice from the voices in my mind – my dad, Fran – but they'd gone. And despite him sitting there, big and moody, I felt Joe slipping away from me too. 'I can't do it any more,' I said. 'I'm done.'

He looked into his mug. 'Why don't you take that holiday? The one you should have taken after Fran died.'

'I don't need a holiday.' He went on like I was some special kid, needing help. 'Just because we don't agree on everything, doesn't make me in need of a holiday or anything else.'

'That's not what I meant. I simply think a break will do you good.'

Whatever he thought didn't really matter but, even if his reasoning was off, a break couldn't do me any harm.

Besides, I didn't have the fight to argue. 'Okay,' I said. 'But I'm choosing when and where, okay?'

'Okay with me. When you get back we'll talk again. Maybe even find you a proper job. Promise.'

Yeah, we'd lost each other all right. Probably for good too.

I found the beach easily. The first night was cool so I made a fire and watched the flames flash against the blue-black sky. I curled up in the hut and slept sound.

In the morning the sun rose above the sea, turning it pink, white and then blue, and, sitting there wrapped up, arms tight round my legs, watching the ocean, I finally got it. The world was a mess. Nobody trusted anybody, bodies and drugs, agents and soldiers – all would come and go, but this stuff - the sea, the sun, the sky, they'd been here forever and would still be here long after we'd all gone. They were safe. And here, being a part of them, so was I.

I heard him but didn't turn around. He crouched behind me, his mouth at my hair, his hands, those fingers lifted my T-shirt and touched the flesh at my waist, his warm breath on my neck sending tingles to my thighs. 'Is it doing it for you?'

'Do you know what?' I said. 'I think it bloody well might be.'

A barely there kiss on my collar bone set my skin to hyper-sensitive. I turned to face him.

Stuart touched my face before his fingers slid around to tug gently at the hair on the back of my neck.

And then he kissed me.

Acknowledgments

Many thanks to Sam at
www.jefferson-franklin.co.uk
for her encouragement, support
and excellent editing skills.

Massive thanks to Craig at
www.craigpearce.co.uk for
taking time out on his birthday
to design the cover

And to the best writing buddy
ever, K E Coles, aka Kazzy,
author of the marvellous
Mesmeris and Infixion.

Thanks Kaz, you've been a true
pal and inspiration.
Grrrrrrrrrrrr.

And most of all thank *you* for
reading.

Please visit Bob at
www.bobsummer.co.uk

Made in the USA
Charleston, SC
22 July 2014